Have You Read Them All?

STEP ON A CRACK

The most powerful people in the world have gathered for a funeral in New York City. They don't know it's a trap devised by a ruthless mastermind, and it's up to Michael Bennett to save every last hostage.

RUN FOR YOUR LIFE

The Teacher is giving New York a lesson it will never forget, slaughtering the powerful and the arrogant. Michael Bennett discovers a vital pattern, but has only a few hours to save the city.

WORST CASE

Children from wealthy families are being abducted. But the captor isn't demanding money. He's quizzing his hostages on the price others pay for their luxurious lives, and one wrong answer is fatal.

TICK TOCK

New York is in chaos as a rash of horrifying copycat crimes tears through the city. Michael Bennett investigates, but not even he could predict the earth-shattering enormity of this killer's plan.

I, MICHAEL BENNETT

Bennett arrests infamous South American crime lord Manuel Perrine. From jail, Perrine vows to rain terror down upon New York City – and to get revenge on Michael Bennett.

GONE

Perrine is back and deadlier than ever. Bennett must make an impossible decision: stay and protect his family, or hunt down the man who is their biggest threat.

BURN

A group of well-dressed men enter a condemned building. Later, a charred body is found. Michael Bennett is about to enter a secret underground world of terrifying depravity.

ALERT

Two devastating catastrophes hit New York in quick succession, putting everyone on edge. Bennett is given the near impossible task of hunting down the shadowy terror group responsible.

BULLSEYE

As the most powerful men on earth gather for a meeting of the UN, Detective Michael Bennett receives shocking intelligence that there will be an assassination attempt on the US president. But are the Russian government behind the plot?

HAUNTED

Detective Michael Bennett is ready for a vacation after a series of crises push him, and his family, to the brink. But when he gets pulled into a shocking case, Bennett is fighting to protect a town, the law, and the family that he loves.

JAMES
PATTERSON
& JAMES O. BORN
HAUNTED

arrow books

1 3 5 7 9 10 8 6 4 2

Arrow Books
20 Vauxhall Bridge Road
London SW1V 2SA

Arrow Books is part of the Penguin Random House group of companies
whose addresses can be found at global.penguinrandomhouse.com.

Penguin
Random House
UK

Copyright © James Patterson 2017
Excerpt from *NYPD Red 5* © James Patterson 2018
Excerpt from *Murder Games* © James Patterson 2017

James Patterson has asserted his right to be identified
as the author of this Work in accordance with the Copyright,
Designs and Patents Act 1988.

First published by Century in 2017
First published in paperback by Arrow Books in 2018

www.penguin.co.uk

A CIP catalogue record for this book is available from the British Library.

ISBN 9781784753733
ISBN 9781784753740 (export edition)

Printed and bound in Great Britain by Clays Ltd, St Ives plc

MIX
Paper from
responsible sources
FSC
www.fsc.org   FSC® C018179

Penguin Random House is committed to a
sustainable future for our business, our readers
and our planet. This book is made from Forest
Stewardship Council® certified paper.

For Dan Cronin

PART ONE

PART ONE

CHAPTER 1

I LOOKED DOWN the barrel of my Glock 19 service weapon. Lori Armstrong, a tall detective with long blond hair from the Forty-Third precinct, stood across from me. Hector Nunez, a crimes and missing-persons detective, who looked like he should play linebacker for the Jets, was about to knock on the door.

We were three stories up in the dark, musty, hot hallway of an apartment building off Castle Hill Avenue near the I-278 overpass. I could feel the vibration of every semi that rumbled by.

This was an arrest I needed. I desperately wanted something to occupy my mind and satisfy my sense of justice. Some cops found refuge in their homelife. I found that it worked both ways. Right now, I needed to be at work and get some distance so I could be the man I wanted to be at home. I had to get my mind off my son Brian any way I could.

The suspect was a career dope dealer named Laszlo Montez, and I made him for a double homicide in Jackie Robinson Park, near 153rd Street, in sight of Bethany Baptist Church. He'd used a knife on another dealer and the dealer's girlfriend. The dealer had been stabbed from behind, unaware of the threat. His girlfriend had been slashed over and over. It was messy. Senseless. The guy in this apartment was good for it. And his ass was mine.

Hector looked my way. I nodded, and he knocked. Politely at first. No sense in scaring the suspect.

A voice from inside shouted back in Spanish. *"¿Quién es?" Who is it?* Like any good NYPD detective, I had a working knowledge of basic Spanish.

Hector said, "It's me. Open up."

There wasn't even an answer from inside. That meant the game was up.

Hector said in a flat voice, *"Policía: abre la puerta."* Then in English he added, "Now."

My sergeant was in the alley behind the building in case Montez managed to navigate the ancient fire escape.

Hector shouted out, "Don't play, Laz. Open up." He waited five seconds, then kicked the front door. It splintered in half and fell in pieces onto the hard wooden floor. A cat leaped away from the door and over a ratty couch.

I darted in first, my pistol up. Lori came in behind me. I scanned the shitty little apartment quickly. Bedroom, bathroom, nothing.

The window was open, and I muttered "Shit" as I wedged myself onto the fire-escape landing. It was a long way down. Cops with a thing about heights shouldn't climb around on fire escapes. But there was no choice. Montez was already a floor down and jumping onto an adjacent apartment's fire escape. Then he swung down to the second floor. I followed as Lori alerted the sergeant to be ready.

Montez was young and nimble. I was older, and, well, no one ever called me nimble. As soon as he saw me, he did the unexpected. He kicked in a window and dove into an apartment. Immediately I heard screaming. A moment later, I was in the apartment behind him.

A heavy woman wearing some kind of shower cap screamed in Spanish. By the front door, Montez stood with a knife to the throat of a teenage girl with long dark hair. She was shaking like a wet dog in January.

Montez said, "Get back. I'll cut her." He flicked the knife, and a cut opened on the girl's slender neck. A trickle of blood ran down to her white blouse. The girl let out a yelp.

My gun stayed on target. His face in the front sight. He backed to the door. The woman in the corner screamed, and a bead of sweat rolled into my left eye. I started to time my breathing. His head ducked behind the girl's face every few seconds. I felt my finger tighten on the trigger.

Then the door burst open behind him. Lori and Hector had their guns on him as well. Montez turned to face them. This time his voice cracked as he shouted, "Get back or I'll slit her throat."

His back was to me, so I acted. He had threatened a kid. She couldn't have been more than fifteen. I was pissed.

I silently holstered my pistol and stepped forward quickly. I used my left hand to block the knife from the girl's throat, then I put Montez in an arm bar. I misjudged it slightly and

5

felt the knife bite into my hand, slicing my palm as I wrenched him away from the girl.

Lori yanked the girl to safety.

Now it was just this asshole and me. I looked to see where the knife had landed and was shocked to see it was still stuck in my hand. Holy shit.

That was it. I threw a right cross and watched as Montez stumbled back. Then I jerked the four-inch blade from my hand. Before he regained his footing, my right knee connected with Montez's head. He was on the floor, and I fell on top of him. A two-hundred-pound sledgehammer. Then I just started to throw elbows and fists into his face. Blood splattered everywhere. Some his, some mine. I needed this. Therapy. What the hell—I was only human.

Then I heard someone shout, "Mike!" I felt a strong hand on my wrist. My sergeant pulled me away.

I looked down at what I had done. Shocked as anyone. I could've ended this with a single punch. I had lost it.

My sergeant said, "Jesus, Mike. We got him."

I looked past my raw, bloodied hands at the pulp of this punk's face. This wasn't how I operated. I was embarrassed. Ashamed.

My sergeant said, "Stand down, Mike. In fact, after you have that hand taken care of, go home. Stay there. I'll handle this. You've got enough problems to deal with at home."

Unfortunately, Sarge was right.

CHAPTER 2

I FUMBLED WITH the pancake batter because of the stitches in my hand. The Bennett household kitchen wasn't small, but this morning it felt like I was on top of Mary Catherine as we whipped up enough to feed all ten kids. Wait a minute. Nine kids.

Somehow the eight-room apartment on the Upper West Side seemed empty, even with eleven people in it. The quiet was unsettling. It'd been like this for days.

Mary Catherine laid her head on my shoulder as a show of support, but all it did was remind me how bad things could get. Once I had two plates ready for serving, I forced a smile. I burst out of the kitchen and said, "Who's the hungriest?"

Usually this would elicit a battle between kids going after the first of the food. Today I got no response. None. Then Trent and Eddie motioned me over like hipsters trying to be cool in a trendy restaurant.

After I set the plates down, I winked at Chrissy and pinched her nose. I would have given anything to have one of her smiles at the moment. She tried, God help her. She showed her teeth, but it wasn't the usual breathtaking spectacle of a little girl's sincere show of happiness.

I shuffled back into the kitchen to return to work. That was the only way to stay sane for the moment.

Mary Catherine had more plates ready, but I just stood there like I had forgotten my job. Like I had lost my purpose.

I looked at Mary Catherine's blond hair as strands tumbled onto her shoulder. She had told me she learned to focus by helping her mom feed three brothers and two younger sisters. She was made for this. I still remembered our first awkward meeting, when she showed up after corresponding with my late wife, Maeve. She came directly from Dublin and just stared at me as I informed her we had ten kids. Ten. But she never faltered. Even in the face of my grandfather Seamus, who thought I brought her in to replace him. It didn't take long for the lovely young Irish girl to win over my surly grandfather.

That was all in my darkest time. Maeve was in the last days of her fight with cancer, and I was lost. Somehow I had survived.

Now I was trying to figure out how to face dark times again.

CHAPTER 3

THE KIDS MADE their usual assembly line to clean up the breakfast plates, with Juliana and Jane acting as supervisors. Those two had CEO written all over them. I could hardly believe my little girls were such beautiful young women who didn't shy away from responsibility. If you added Mary Catherine to the mix, you could say that women had kept me alive and functioning for many years.

Mary Catherine worked on getting the youngest kids' backpacks and lunches together. It was seamless. And I stood in the corner, almost useless. Mary Catherine looked up and winked at me. How had this lass from Ireland gone from the kids' nanny to my love in a few short years? My heart broke a little bit when I thought about what the family had to deal with now, but this was not the time to give up or abandon my job as a father.

I clapped my hands together and said, "Okay, gang. I'm going to bring the bus around front. Three minutes, and the Bennetts renew their assault on civilization."

That got a smile from Bridget. That was enough for me.

The short ride to the kids' school, Holy Name, was silent at first. Everyone sat like zombies in the twelve-passenger Ford Super Duty van. It had years on it, but not that many miles. I remember the look on the car salesman's face when I proved I could fill the van with just my own kids. It was a stretch financially then. Now it was a necessity. A fact of our daily life.

The kids were seated with the youngest in the back, as always. Poor Chrissy and Shawna would never move up until someone went to college. Just thinking about that and the fact that college was not in Brian's future right now made me want to cry.

Eddie said, "When will Brian come home?"

Ah, my Einstein always knew which question was most important. I took a moment to form my answer and said, "Well, buddy, I just don't know." *Real helpful, Dad.*

Ricky said, "I thought you knew all about that kind of stuff."

"I wish I knew more. What's important is that we put Brian in our prayers and he knows how much he's missed."

Fiona started to sniffle. It was a precursor to crying, and that would cause a ripple effect throughout the van. I'd seen it too many times already. I had to do something fast.

I shouted, "Look!"

All heads turned to the right and looked out on West 96th Street, where I was staring.

Jane said, "What do you see, Dad?"

"I think it's Derek Jeter."

"Where?" came a chorus.

"Right there in front of the Gristedes supermarket." I pointed at a huge man in a blue Brooks Brothers suit with his flab poking out around his belt. "Looks like he's put on a little weight since retirement."

Trent wailed, "Noooooo! That's not Jeter." He followed the Yankees better than he followed any of the classes he was in.

"Are you sure?"

Now there were some giggles as little voices said, "Not Jeter." That turned into a chant. "Not Jeter, not Jeter, not Jeter."

We pulled up to Holy Name, on Amsterdam Avenue. I knew I had survived another morning. For a change we were on time and got to see what it looked like when we weren't racing to beat the final bell and shoo the kids in before the door was locked. Sister Sheilah even waved to me.

As each kid filed out, giving me a quick hug, I felt Brian's absence like a missing limb.

CHAPTER 4

I PARKED THE van in Queens and took advantage of the bus to Rikers Island. I'd been to New York City's main detention facility dozens of times before, but today it felt grim. The narrow bridge from Queens to the island in the East River made me anxious. The island itself is a giant facility where people booked on crimes from misdemeanors to homicides are processed. Today I got off in front of the main building, having used my connections to make things move quickly. There were several buildings in the facility, which could hold as many as fifteen thousand prisoners at any one time. I was told to go to a building near the front of the complex.

This main building housed males in pretrial status. Many of them were poor and couldn't afford bail. Others, like Brian, had been denied bail altogether. Our lawyer had already told me that the district attorney's office would be tough. For them, this was a chance to change the media narrative about the racist judicial system. They were charging him as an adult. My little boy was considered an adult this one wretched time.

My throat was dry as I cut away from the miserable little crowd that got off the bus. They shuffled to the main visiting entrance while I moved to the side, where I was supposed to meet an old friend. Even the bright sunshine couldn't give the jail any kind of pleasant facade.

I nodded when I saw the lieutenant who had already been wildly helpful. "Hey, Vinny. I appreciate the assist."

The pudgy middle-aged bald man said, "No problem, Mike. I'm a dad, too. I know this has got to be tough on you."

I said, "Is he doing okay?"

"I just saw him, and he looked fine. You know this place is no summer camp."

He led me through a side door to a tiny room that contained only two institutional metal chairs. There was no Plexiglas. No phones or surveillance cameras. This wasn't an interview room. It was probably a place where corrections officers could get away from the stress for a few minutes. This guy was really helping me out. A rare perk of being one of New York's finest.

I stood silently in the ten-foot-by-ten-foot room; it had bland two-tone beige walls and no windows. The door opened, and Brian stood there, wearing a simple orange jumpsuit and black flip-flops. He sprang forward and gave me a hug.

The uniformed corrections officer gave me a bob of his head and backed out of the room tactfully.

I held my boy. The young man I had raised. Nursed through the flu. Tutored in math. Taught to love sports. I held my boy, who was now facing up to ten years in the New York State prison system. I held him and started to cry.

Finally we both plopped into the two lonely chairs and just stared at each other. Was this our new normal?

Brian's eyes were bloodshot, and he had a light stubble on his face—like a tiny sparse forest. Christ—he only started shaving a year ago.

I focused and said, "Look, Brian, we're doing all we can. You've talked to the attorney. She's the best. A former ADA."

He just nodded.

I didn't want to get into the *why* of what he did. Status? Money? Who cares? I never made that much as a cop, but we had everything we needed. More than once I wondered if Brian's crime had something to do with the loss of his mother years ago. Maeve's memory still affected me every day, no matter what I was doing. Even after falling in love again. Who knows what it did to the kids, no matter how open we were with each other?

I just couldn't believe it. What had happened to Brian? My son, arrested for selling drugs. Both meth and a new form of ecstasy. It was almost too much to process.

I hadn't lectured or yelled. He knew what a terrible mistake he'd made. He realized what could happen. Now I needed answers. I had to get to the bottom of this and save him. It didn't matter to me if he wanted to be saved or not.

I said, "You've got to help us. Help yourself. I need to know who gave you that shit to sell."

He just stared at me. There was no answer. Barely an acknowledgment.

"And right there near Holy Name. The kids…" I caught

myself. I channeled my inner Joe Friday. *Just the facts, ma'am.* I gave it thirty seconds. Half a minute of dead silence in this tiny room. The chilling sounds of the lockup drifting inside. Cell doors slamming. Men yelling insults back and forth. For the first time in my career, it was depressing to me.

Finally, I calmly said, "Who gave you the drugs?"

Brian's voice cracked as he said, "I'm sorry, Dad. I can't tell you." He was resolute.

My world crashed down around me.

CHAPTER 5

BRIAN AND I were done for the day. There was nothing left to say. He wasn't going to tell me what I needed to know. It could've been stupid stubborn teenage pride. Acting like a tough guy, or, more likely, fear of what would happen if he talked. That was relatively new in the culture cops operated in. The whole "snitches get stitches" attitude had popped up in inner-city neighborhoods and spread through music and TV shows. Now it seemed to be the mantra of anyone under thirty.

When the door opened, I had to snatch one more hug from my son. He wrapped his arms around me as well. Then I watched silently as a corrections officer led him away. He moved like a robot. His feet shuffling and the flip-flops making a sad slapping sound on the concrete floor.

I headed toward the exit, where my friend Vinny was waiting to lead me out. I said, "Is there anything you can do to protect him?"

He smiled and patted me on the shoulder. "We have Brian in what we call the nerd ward. Hackers and financial guys who decided they weren't going to follow the rules. Those sorts of perps. He only comes into contact with the general population if he goes out to exercise once a week or if we have to move people around because of trouble. But I promise, Mike, we're keeping a close eye on him."

This was special treatment because I was a cop. I wasn't going to refuse it.

When he told me Brian was safe for now, I thought I'd break down and cry right in front of him.

What did people without friends working in the jail do? What about people with no access to a decent lawyer? It made me think about cases I had worked and how I would persuade people to cooperate. Now I saw that they often had no other choice.

Then Vinny took my arm, and as we started to walk, he leaned in closer and said, "The rumor is that the DA's office wants to make an example of Brian. Wants to show that they'll go after a white kid as hard as a black kid. And they want to look fair by not showing preference to a cop's son."

I wasn't sure I wanted to hear the truth like that all at once. It felt like a punch in the gut. I slapped the cinder-block wall in frustration. The jolt of pain through my body reminded me that I had stitches in that hand. Blood stained the white bandage.

Vinny draped his arm over my shoulder and subtly headed us toward the exit.

I found myself shuffling, just like Brian. I wondered if it had something to do with this place.

This place I would never look at the same way again.

CHAPTER 6

WHEN I LEFT the jail, I knew exactly what I had to do. By the time I got back to my van in Queens, clouds had drifted in and given the streets a particularly gloomy look. I couldn't go in to the office. I was on leave. Officially for my injury, but unofficially for beating the murder suspect Laszlo Montez. Thank God no one asked too many questions about a guy who put a knife to a teenage girl's throat and murdered two people.

My sergeant told me to just go with it. There might be an investigation later, but for now I was a hero who'd been stabbed by a murder suspect. The city sure didn't care much about heroes' kids.

But I was still a cop. And, much more important, a father.

Like any cop worth his salt, I had informants. The word *snitch* had fallen out of favor in police work over the last few years. But it's hard to find words that rhyme with *informant*. "Snitches get stitches" is catchier than something like "Informants get dormant."

Informants are a fact of police work. People like to point out all the problems with using informants, but few understand the benefits. They can go places cops can't. Cops can't be everywhere at once. Informants help in that effort. They also give insight into how a criminal thinks.

Jodie Foster didn't need Anthony Hopkins's help in *The Silence of the Lambs* because his character was a Boy Scout. He was a psychopath, and he found the break in the case. Informants are vital and horrible at the same time. And cops need them no matter how they feel about them.

I knew people. Some through favors and some through fear. Both seemed to work well. My biggest issue was that whoever gave Brian that shit was somewhere near Holy Name. At least that's where he was operating. I had to be discreet.

My first stop was at a deli—or, more precisely, behind a deli—off La Salle Street. I ditched the van and walked to the alley behind the North Side Deli. After just a few minutes, a skinny white guy with a shaved head and tats up and down both arms stepped out for a smoke.

He didn't notice me until I said, "Hello, Walter." It was satisfying to see him jump. "You could pass for either a skinhead or a chemo patient. You need to eat a little more while you're at work."

The young man turned and said, "No labels, man. I just like short hair now. Besides, some of my beliefs don't go over so well inside."

I didn't have time to waste. I said, "I need information."

"I'm clean. You got nothing on me."

"I don't *need* anything on you. The statute hasn't run out on the guy you stabbed over near Riverside Park."

"That was self-defense. You even said he was just a dope dealer. I already paid that debt. I told you about the West Side gang's gun stash."

"You paid part of your debt. Now I need more. Unless you want the judge to decide what, exactly, is self-defense and what's just a senseless attack."

"But the guy wasn't even hurt bad. A few stitches, a little blood. Who cares?"

I looked down at my bandaged hand and said, "I bet he cares. And I still have his contact info."

Walter looked resigned as his head dipped. He mumbled, "What do you need to know?"

"Who's giving meth and X to local kids to sell?"

"Man, this ain't my neighborhood. It's none of my business."

"Make it your business."

Walter caught my tone and looked up at me. "This means something to you, doesn't it?"

I gave him a silent stare.

He said, "You'll owe me."

I just nodded.

"Big-time."

I said, "Don't push it, Walter, or some of your white supremacist asshole buddies might find out that your real last name is Nussbaum."

I knew he'd do as I said.

CHAPTER 7

I SPREAD THE love for ten blocks in every direction. By midnight I'd be a curse on the tongue of every dealer and informant on the Upper West Side.

I spoke with Lenny Whitehead, a black crack dealer whose daughter I once rescued from a gang he owed money to. Back then he'd offered to kill anyone I wanted him to. I thought it was a joke, but I didn't want to push it.

Manny Garcia, a slick former Latin King, talked to me because I'd helped him when he was fingered for a homicide he didn't commit. I found the real killer, and Manny had been my best friend ever since.

Billy Haskins, a former set designer I put away for selling coke to Broadway actors, talked because he didn't want any trouble. The little Bostonian had no use for New Yorkers other than as drug customers or producers willing to pay union scale.

Everyone was part of the program. I'd have answers soon.

All the social interaction with lowlifes had made me late to pick up the kids. When I pulled the van into the pickup lane, I saw my brood lined up along the fence talking with Sister Sheilah. That was never a good sign.

I rolled to a stop and hopped out, knowing the best defense is a good offense. Whatever Sister Sheilah was asking, I was prepared to answer.

I was shocked when she smiled at me. I wasn't sure exactly what she was doing at first, because I'd seen her smile so rarely. I stammered, "S-sorry I'm a little late."

She said, "Ten minutes is a little late. Forty-five makes me worried you'd forgotten you had kids."

Was that a joke? I was too terrified to ask.

The sister said, "It's no problem, Mr. Bennett. Bridget and I were discussing the fine points of bedazzling and other crafts." She stepped toward me and led me by the arm away from the children as they started to file into the van. In a low voice she said, "We've been so worried about Brian. Anything new?"

"No, Sister. Not yet. There's a long way to go."

"We'll pray for him and for you."

"Thank you, Sister. I need prayers right about now."

Once we were back home, I opened the door to a smell that made me smile. It was one of Mary Catherine's standards. It took me a minute to pinpoint the aroma. Irish pot roast with brown gravy. I caught the look on each kid's face as he or she crossed the threshold. Sometimes it's the little things that can perk you up.

Mary Catherine came out of the kitchen looking like a young housewife from the fifties. A white apron, a smile, and a twinkle in her eyes.

She said, "Dinner in two hours. Two hours of hard labor. Homework first. The chores next. Cleanup last, and in that order." She looked across the room, and for the first time I noticed my grandfather Seamus standing in the corner, looking out at the street below. She said to him, "You're in charge of homework. Make yourself useful if you want to be fed."

I doubted she had ever spoken that way to a priest when she lived in Tipperary or Dublin. But it was hard to think of my grandfather as a priest unless he was wearing his clerical collar. And sometimes even then it was hard to believe. But despite his impish and mischievous nature, he had been a blessing to me since my childhood. And now he was here for my children.

CHAPTER 8

I WATCHED THE miracle of dinner at the Bennett house unfold. Mary Catherine was the author of this blessed event, and I couldn't express how much I appreciated her efforts to keep the kids' lives normal. She awed me. By dinnertime, the kids had their homework done, their chores completed, and the table set.

Once again the crowd was quiet. The empty chair where Brian normally sat didn't help matters.

Seamus, sitting at the far end of the table from me, bowed his head, as he did before each meal. The kids followed his lead. He said in a low, comforting voice, "Lord, thank you for our many blessings. Thank you for our time together. Thank you for allowing us to realize how fleeting it can be. Please bless this family and protect our precious Brian. Amen."

A quiet chorus of "Amen" followed.

Dinner proceeded with the clank of silverware and the occasional comment just to break the silence. Mary Catherine engaged Chrissy. She was our best chance if we wanted to hear a quirky, funny story from the day.

Mary Catherine said, "What did you learn in history today, Chrissy?"

Usually the little girl would light up at a chance to tell a story in front of the whole family. Instead she mumbled, "We talked about the men in Boston who decided we shouldn't be part of England anymore."

Mary Catherine took a moment and managed to gather everyone's attention without saying a word. Then she said, "Listen, everyone. I know we're worried about Brian. You can believe your father is doing everything he can to help him. But sometimes things don't work out the way we expect them to. Not better, not worse—just not like we expect."

Now she was playing to the crowd's full attention.

"My brother Ken wanted to come to America. He's a big, burly lad and a great fan of the Kennedys. All he talked about was coming to Boston. But he got in trouble."

Shawna said, "What kind of trouble?" We were all hooked.

"It was a bar fight, and Ken punched a man who hit his head when he fell on the floor. My brother was charged with assault and later convicted. He didn't have to go to jail, but he had a conviction on his record, and that kept him from doing what he expected to do. That conviction kept him from coming to America. But you know what?"

Chrissy and Bridget both said, "What?"

"Things turned out differently for him. He met a lovely girl. And now he lives right there in Dublin with two beautiful kids. He has a good job and is happier than he could ever think of being. It's different from what he expected, but certainly not worse. Sometimes things happen in life, and we just have to accept them."

I could almost see the kids understanding what she was saying and feeling better. It felt like the pace of eating even picked up. But Seamus was still quiet. None of his usual silly quips or semi-risqué jokes. When I looked at him, I could see why. He was silently crying, trying to hide it from the kids.

CHAPTER 9

THE MANHATTAN NORTH Homicide Squad sat in a clean six-story office building off Broadway near 133rd Street. It was lush by NYPD standards but pretty average by business standards. The building housed borough-wide units such as gang enforcement, intelligence, and even the occasional terrorism task force. The main difference between officers in those units and the homicide detectives was that we usually dressed better than everyone else.

Across the street from the building, the elevated train tracks provided shade for people who got in early and found a parking spot. The regular 1 train rattled the front of the building. I still appreciated walking in the doors that early Tuesday morning.

The sergeant let me come back the day after my stitches came out. Although he was usually terse, he met me in the hallway near the front door that day and spent a long time talking with me to make sure my head was screwed on straight. Once he was satisfied, he told me about a recent homicide. A high school kid. Just fifteen years old. The details were horrendous and included torture and decapitation. The crime-scene photos made it worse. Seeing the headless torso wearing a lacrosse jersey put a personal touch on the grisly scene. Two fingers on his left hand were missing, and blood smeared the palm. This was the kind of stuff I never mentioned to Mary Catherine.

I stared at the sergeant and finally said, "How's this not all over the news?"

"We reported it as a random attack with few details to keep the media quiet and allow us to talk to as many people as possible before something leaked out. That's one of the things I need you to help us on. I want you to head out to the high school he attended and see what you can find out. Kids are much more likely to talk about it if they think it was a random attack rather than some kind of targeted brutal slaying. I want us to get a handle on this as quickly as possible."

"I didn't know we could fudge the facts to the media."

"I didn't know you cared."

"The truth is usually the best course. Even if it terrifies people."

"This comes from the mayor's office. He thinks it could cause an all-out panic. They're afraid it might even hurt tourism."

"God forbid." I shook my head. "It might produce leads, too."

"Stories like this usually are just a distraction to the investigation."

He was right. I took the file and got to work. Every detective on the squad seemed to have a piece of it. I wasted no time heading down to the high school, which was north of Holy Name.

The cover story we were using was that the student, Gary Mule, had been the victim of a random knifing. I had to find out what a fifteen-year-old could do to deserve something like this in a psychotic's mind.

P.S. 419 didn't resemble Holy Name. It had no playgrounds or anything that felt kidlike. It could've been a jail. It could be considered in the same neighborhood as Holy Name, although it was a good walk from my kids' school. It had the standard New York City public school facade: five-story brick exterior and a lone entrance where parents could drop the kids off and pick them up. My guess was that a lot of the kids at the school were on their own when it came to transportation.

The school bucked the trend—it didn't have a name like School for Future Leaders. I'd prefer to see honesty in naming schools. Maybe something like School for Disaffected Youth.

Security had certainly changed since I was a kid. I had to show my police ID to a camera before someone in the office buzzed me through a steel gate. There was even a full-time police officer assigned to the school. But that's not who met me in the hallway before I reached the office.

An officious assistant principal in a surprisingly tight dress and anything but a schoolmarm air approached me.

"Detective Bennett?" the attractive fortysomething woman asked.

"And you are?"

"Toni DiPetro. I'll be your contact for everything related to this incident."

"And why wouldn't Officer Chapman help me?"

"The school board thought it was best if I lead you through the hallway and emphasize that we're attempting to keep this off the radar for as long as possible."

As we strolled the hallways, I asked general questions about problems they'd had on campus. I also noticed that none of the kids paid any attention to us. Even when the classes changed, they floated around us like we didn't exist.

I finally found a quiet area where I could start asking more pointed questions. "Miss DiPetro."

"Please—call me Toni."

"Okay, Toni. Has any of the faculty expressed any theories about why something like this would happen to a student? Because I gotta tell you, I've been doing this a number of years, and this shocks even me."

"Do you work much in the public school system?"

"No, ma'am."

"I think if you did, you might not be shocked by it. Teachers are expected to do more and more, and much of the parenting authority has been ceded to us by the parents. In the media they call it teacher accountability, but really it's a lack of parent accountability. There's no respect anymore. I'm afraid I find the violence in this case shocking but not exactly the murder itself. Does that make sense?"

She had a cute way of raising her voice at the end of sentences, like she was asking questions rather than making statements.

I nodded and said, "I understand. I see it in police work as well. So all that being said, do you have any theories?"

She leaned in close and said, "I've heard rumors, but I can't have them associated with me."

I nodded.

"The student was involved in selling drugs. Everyone knew it. Everyone knows he was killed as part of a drug hit, no matter what we're peddling to the public."

"A drug hit? On a fifteen-year-old?"

"That's not all. It was a specific hit man. I've heard about him for months now. I don't have a name or any concrete info."

I said, "Do you have anything at all?"

She nodded. "He's a New York City high school student. That's how he's able to move so freely without raising any suspicion."

CHAPTER 10

IT WAS HARD to shake Toni DiPetro. I finally explained that I couldn't have her present during my interviews with students, and she pointed me to a couple of areas where I might find kids willing to talk to me. It made sense that kids in the library might be more studious and less involved in criminal activity than others. Still, I realized, asking questions out of the blue might not be the best approach, especially since I was an adult male dressed in a suit. I could always change it up if it didn't work.

There was a study area behind the library where kids were allowed to have drinks and snacks. A cute young woman, maybe sixteen years old, sat reading a giant textbook and holding her nose only a few inches from the pages. I approached her slowly, and before I even pulled out my badge and identification she said, "I have nothing to say to the police."

"Really? You're not even going to let me ask a question?"

"Do I need to refer you to my dad's attorney?"

"How do you even know I'm a cop?"

She didn't miss a beat as she flipped a strand of blond hair out of her face. "If you're a lawyer you would be dressed in a better suit. And if you're a teacher you wouldn't be wearing a suit."

I took that as a cue to move on. The assistant principal had provided me with a list of several names. I made a quick cell-phone call and asked her to summon those kids to an administrative office. Clearly I wasn't going to get anywhere just wandering the halls.

The first kid I met in the comfortable office, which had a wide couch and a TV on the wall, was a stocky Latino named Robert Hernandez. He had dark curly hair parted down the middle and a teenager's attempt at a beard, with stubble sprouting between a moderate case of acne.

I identified myself, and he seemed friendly. He just shrugged and said, "This is about Gary, right?"

"It is. Is there anything you could tell me that might help us catch who killed him?"

"Not a thing. In fact, I don't want anyone to see me in here talking to you for too long, so if it's okay, can I go?"

"Your friend's life meant that little to you?"

"No. It's more like *my* life means that much to me. You're not gonna find anyone to talk."

"Are you worried about reprisals from a gang?"

"These guys are beyond a gang. You can see gang members coming. These guys use people you would never expect. I'm sorry. I can't stay." He sprang up and darted out the door before I could try to persuade him to stay.

The next student was a lanky senior with long greasy hair and a voice that couldn't decide if it belonged to a kid or an adult. He wore a loose plaid shirt over a Nirvana T-shirt, and I understood exactly the look he was going for. His name was Jimmy Hilcox, and I quickly realized that no one at his house had ever taught him the meaning of the word *respect*. That deficiency almost never worked out for kids as they got older and entered society. It didn't work out that well for society, either.

He was more sullen than Robert Hernandez and, for the most part, wouldn't acknowledge me. He didn't even admit that he knew Gary Mule, despite the fact that I'd been told they both played on the lacrosse team and had three classes together.

Finally the dour young man looked at me and said, "Why do you even care what happened?"

"I care anytime someone is murdered in the city. Especially a kid. It's my job to care. But probably the biggest reason is that I have kids of my own."

"Aren't you worried what might happen to your kids if you push this too hard?"

"I always worry about my kids, no matter what I'm doing. Why? Do you know these guys? Can you just give me a name?"

Now his eyes shifted to me. They ran from my shoes to my head. Then he said, "Did you go to college?"

I nodded. "Manhattan College."

"What did you study?"

"Philosophy."

"What did you want to do before you settled for being a cop?"

Damned if that wasn't a pretty good question. Then I

caught myself. I didn't *settle* for anything. Police work is what called to me after I finished school.

I leveled my gaze at the young slacker. "I've saved lives. I've raised kids. I sleep at night." I paused as the kid stared at me. "Most people are lucky if they can achieve any of those things. One day, when you're not working so hard to be an arrogant little prick, you might realize that."

The kid looked at the ground and mumbled, "If you give me your number I might be able to find a name. But it could take a while. And you can't ever tell anyone."

I didn't hesitate. I'd even take a couple of prank calls if it meant I could catch a lead that would stop this killer.

CHAPTER 11

I LEFT THE school feeling like a wolf who was still hungry for sheep. I needed adult interaction. Someone I wouldn't feel guilty about hitting. Or at least scaring. The kids and Miss DiPetro had me thinking in different directions. That was good for a homicide detective. You've got to keep your mind open.

Traffic was snarled as usual, so I left my city-issued Impala in a garage and decided to walk in my search for the right person to talk to. I had several choices, and they were all on the west side of Central Park. At least they would be this time of day. I didn't care, as long as I didn't have to stop at another school today.

I couldn't face another smart-ass teenager unless it was one I had raised. I knew I could help Brian. I just had to find the right person and think in the right direction. I held out hope that something would happen to save Brian.

That's another ingredient necessary for a good homicide detective: hope. You always have to have a little hope. It's the only way to keep your sanity. It's easy to operate in my world and lose sight of the fact that there are still good people out there.

The next thing important to a good homicide detective, believe it or not, is faith. Faith in God. Faith in family. And faith in yourself. I knew I could help Brian. I had faith that if I could find his supplier, we might be able to cut a deal. If we couldn't cut a deal, at least I'd know who would be made to pay for all the pain he had caused my family.

I found Walter Nussbaum in an Irish bar not far from Columbus Circle on West 57th Street. It was a dark, nasty little hole where I knew he and some of his backward friends liked to hang out. This was not a place tourists wandered into by accident. I pushed through the door and noticed three construction workers at the bar. If they cared who I was, it didn't show on their faces. I felt like a sheriff in an old saloon as I scanned the small room for Nussbaum.

He was sitting alone at a table in the corner, thumbing through the latest copy of *Firearms News*. He didn't look up until I was already halfway across the room. He tried to conceal his shock. He probably didn't realize I knew this was one of his hangouts.

"Hello, Walter."

He didn't offer me a seat, but I took one anyway.

I scooted the chair close to him and said in a low voice, "I don't have a lot of time to chat. What did you find out for me?"

"This is uncool, man. I can't be seen talking to you here."

"Then let's leave, and you can talk to me in five minutes.

But you're gonna tell me something useful, and you're gonna do it soon."

"You don't understand." The young man couldn't even hold a page of the magazine. It fluttered in his hand, betraying his jitters.

"No, Walter, *you* don't understand. I need to know who's using schoolkids to push dope. You said you'd find out."

"It's not that simple." His eyes darted past me.

I heard someone behind me say, "This guy bothering you, Chill?"

I took a quick glance at the two twentysomething shitheads. Bother-me gym rats with thick arms and probably heads to match.

I turned back to Walter and said, "Chill? That's your street name?" I almost laughed out loud.

Walter didn't answer.

One of the gym rats, dressed in jeans and a Rutgers hoodie, said, "You need to leave, old man."

"Old man?" Seamus was an old man.

"We decide who comes in here and who gets to talk to our friends. We don't like the way you look."

I said, "Is it the age thing? I mean, that's got to be some kind of discrimination, right?"

The other guy, wearing a New Jersey Devils jacket, said, "Leave him, Jake. We don't want to explain why we beat an elderly man's ass."

Walter added, "Yeah, guys. Leave him alone. I'm fine."

Now Rutgers stepped in close and poked me in the chest. "I don't care what Chill says. I don't want you here. Scoot." He poked me again. "Now."

I reached up with my right hand and grabbed his extended finger. I cranked it down with a little force. It looked like I used a pair of pliers by the way this punk dropped to his knees.

He let out a cry that sounded like "Let go."

I didn't acknowledge him. I looked at the other guy and said, "Wanna try your luck now?"

The musclehead had no idea what to do. He finally balled his right hand and stepped forward, ready to throw a punch.

I jerked the whimpering guy on the floor in front of me and tripped the attacker. As he fell forward over his friend, I threw my left elbow into his chin.

That was it. No one said another word. They both whined, but they never completed a sentence.

I said, "You two stay right there on the floor until I'm ready to leave. Understand?"

They both nodded.

Now I turned my attention back to Walter. I didn't have to say anything.

He stammered, "Okay, okay." He gathered his thoughts. "There's a group. A new group. They're using different kinds of people to run their product. Using a lot of students. That's all I hear. They're using students to do all kinds of stuff. The students are making meth, distributing, even enforcement. One kid is the muscle. Real ruthless. I'm trying to find out his name. You gotta give me more time."

I growled, "I want this asshole."

Walter said, "I want nothing to do with this guy. You may be a big, scary cop, but this kid is a killer. The worst kind."

40

CHAPTER 12

IT WAS A rare quiet time in our apartment. An apartment an NYPD detective could never have afforded on his salary alone. But Maeve, my late wife, had cared for the man who had owned it in his later years. She had made such a difference in his life that he left the apartment to her in his will. That's the effect Maeve had on people.

With ten kids, I needed a place like this. Close to Riverside Park, close to Holy Name, four bedrooms and a makeshift maid's room, a big living room, dining room, and kitchen. It was as if God knew what our family needed and provided it.

And now, without my oldest boy, it felt empty.

I sat on the couch and gazed out at the city lights. I kept thinking of the kids I talked to and Walter Nussbaum's voice as he told me what he knew. They were all scared.

Mary Catherine plopped down next to me on the

comfortable couch. She snuggled in close. I wrapped an arm around her and appreciated her head resting on my shoulder. We relaxed in silence for a few minutes. I needed this.

Then Mary Catherine said in a quiet voice, "Can we talk?"

"Sure."

She sat up to look me in the eyes. "You know, Michael, I've never told you about some of the dark parts of my past."

"No, but I realize Ireland is not all pasture and friendly folk. People there have their issues."

She nodded. "They have the same issues any modern country faces. I was part of those issues. I've sold drugs before."

That caught me by surprise.

"When I lived in Dublin, I fell in with a bad crowd. I started to not care what I was doing. I shoplifted during the day and sold marijuana and even some cocaine at night. It was turning into a very harsh and nasty cycle." She took a moment to let her mind drift back. "I also got used to the money. And even the drugs."

"I had no idea."

Mary Catherine said, "That was the point. I've kept that part of my past locked away. I started a new life. I came to America. And now I have you. I don't even want to think about some of the things I did."

I was astonished but somehow managed to ask, "How'd you turn it around?"

"My family." She said it like it was an obvious answer. "My brothers in particular. You know the story I told about my brother Ken and how he couldn't come to America?"

"Yeah."

"The man he hit was a drug dealer. It was no simple bar-room fight. He meant to hurt that dealer. He wanted men to be scared of him so they wouldn't try to use me. He gave up his dream to save me."

I stared into that beautiful, delicate face and tried to understand what she was saying. I wanted to understand how to apply it to our family now.

Mary Catherine said, "You're doing all you can for Brian. He has a good, strong family. He'll survive, no matter what happens."

I said, "I keep asking myself why he did it."

"There is no why. It just happened. My family couldn't stop me from entering that life, but they saved me from it. You can't blame yourself for what happened to Brian."

I said, "I'm Catholic; I have to."

We both had a laugh for the first time in days.

CHAPTER 13

I MADE THE tough decision to not allow the kids to come to Brian's trial. I wanted their lives to go on without the spectacle of seeing their brother in court. It wasn't easy to convince them that this was best. Especially Jane and Juliana, who felt they were old enough to understand the proceedings. I wasn't sure if I was doing it for them or for myself. Brian was the only child I could concentrate on at the moment.

It had been some time since he was first arrested, and I kept working on finding his supplier as well as trying to find the killer of Gary Mule. I wasn't happy with my progress in either case. There was something going on in town. Something different and hard to explain. I had battled drug lords. This was scarier, because the killer could be anyone. Even a schoolkid.

A wave of anxiety ran through me as we approached the New York County Courthouse, on Centre Street in lower

Manhattan. The thirteen-story Roman-style government building had been in countless movies, including *The Godfather*. It looked like something out of the twenties. To the south, I saw the federal courthouse, now named for former US Supreme Court justice Thurgood Marshall.

I had been through a dozen trials here over the years, but always as a witness for the prosecution. Being the father of a defendant was a new experience. It was a perspective I had not considered before. But I would in the future.

The high ceilings and ornate murals depicting justice spoke to the age and history of the building. I caught Mary Catherine taking in the enormity of the structure. My grandfather, walking on the other side of her, had been unusually quiet and held Mary Catherine's hand as we approached the courtroom on the fourth floor. For the first time ever he looked frail to me.

The judge wasn't on the bench yet, and Brian's attorney, Stacy Ibarra, met me near the door, then led me into the hallway.

She had been a bulldog of an assistant district attorney, and now those intense green eyes met mine. Instantly I knew this wasn't going to be good news.

The forty-year-old attorney said, "I spoke with the ADA on Brian's case. His name is Chad Laing, and he can be a little bit of a dick. He said there was no deal other than a straight-up plea."

My voice was louder than I meant it to be when I said, "To a class B felony? In front of Judge Weicholz? He's a former Marine. He doesn't know *how* to cut anyone any slack." I saw the look on her face and realized how loud I had become. I took a deep breath and counted to five. Then I said, "This is Brian's first offense. That jerk already charged him as an adult.

I thought New York had moved away from the Rockefeller laws."

"Look, Mike, I'm trying everything I can."

"Can we beat the case outright?"

"There's always a chance. But the narcs saw him dealing, then they found a dozen bags of meth and some X on him. They even have surveillance photos, like he was part of a cartel."

"Can I talk to the ADA?"

"Why?"

"I've met Laing before. He knows my reputation. Maybe we can work something out."

I didn't wait for permission as I pushed my way back into the courtroom.

CHAPTER 14

I MARCHED UP to the prosecution table, where a chunky middle-aged man was berating a young female attorney about something. I waited a moment, then cleared my throat.

The man turned, recognized me, and smiled. Then he caught himself. I was the enemy today. Or at least the father of the enemy.

I said, "Can we talk?"

Laing said, "We shouldn't. This is a little awkward, to tell you the truth."

"I just feel like you're going to be unnecessarily tough on my son."

Now he faced me and stood straight. He was a couple of inches shorter than I was. Maybe six foot one. "Do you feel like we're unnecessarily tough on the suspects *you* arrest? Because all I ever hear from the NYPD is what pussies we are. How we never go for a harsh enough sentence. Sound familiar to you, Detective?"

"Brian's a good kid. He's never been in trouble."

The ADA said, "You mean he's never been *caught* before. What are the odds that the cops saw him on his first day in the business? He had two grand in cash, bags of meth, and refused to talk to the arresting officers. Give me a break. He knew how the system worked."

I kept my cool, but it wasn't easy. "It would be a shame to ruin his life at seventeen."

"What about the kids using the shit he sells? Is he *building* their lives? I'm sorry. He pleads straight up or takes his chances at trial."

"Pleads in front of Judge Weicholz?"

The ADA giggled as he scratched his balding head. "Ironic how you guys all love the hanging judge until it's someone you know in front of him. I have to do my duty."

"You don't have to enjoy it so much."

"I never enjoy it, but it is satisfying. I think this conversation is over."

The door next to the empty jury box opened. I turned quickly and saw Brian being led into the courtroom by a bailiff and a corrections officer. He was wearing his only suit. A simple blue single-breasted. One we'd delivered to Rikers Island just for the trial. He looked like he was going to his confirmation. He looked like a little boy to me. Except his hands were cuffed in front of him through a standard waist chain.

My son was a prisoner.

I had never felt so helpless.

CHAPTER 15

ONCE THE JUDGE entered the courtroom, it was showtime. Mary Catherine, Seamus, and I took our seats on the first hard wooden bench directly behind the defense table. I noticed someone had scratched the words *police suck dick* on the wooden railing in front of me.

Brian sat next to his attorney with his hands folded on the table in front of him like he was a student in history class. I could feel Seamus as tense as a board next to me. This was a new experience for all of us.

I had never spent any time in Narcotics. After my early years working in patrol, I did the usual detective stints and special assignments before I landed in Homicide. But I never did time investigating drug crimes. As soon as the jury was selected and the prosecution got rolling, I realized that this was nothing like a homicide case. It moved like lightning.

First the narcotics detective explained that he and his partner had received complaints of increased meth use in the area. The detective, a young hotshot with a neatly trimmed beard and ponytail tucked into the back of his jacket, explained that there had also been two young women who almost died from ingesting too much ecstasy and not taking in enough water at a club.

The detective had somehow discerned that whoever was selling the ecstasy was also selling methamphetamine. It seemed like a leap in logic to me. But now I was on the other side of the justice equation.

The Narcotics team from the area, who worked out of the precinct, had done a series of surveillances. They also started talking to their informants.

On the stand, the detective said, "That's how we noticed the defendant moving between Amsterdam Avenue and the park near 110th. We also followed him onto the Columbia campus once or twice but lost sight of him. On the third day we saw an actual exchange and stepped in to make the arrest."

When she went into her cross-examination, Brian's defense attorney asked if Brian had offered any resistance. She questioned the detective's experience. He only had a year in Narcotics. She didn't make a dent in his overall testimony.

I considered what the detective said. This wasn't just an accident. Brian had met with the supplier somewhere near Columbia University.

The twelve-member jury looked like the city itself. Three African Americans, two Asians, two Hispanics, and five housewives from the Upper West Side. They all seemed to listen intently and would occasionally look over to the defense table at Brian.

It was as if they were trying to convince themselves that this clean-cut young man was really involved in such a nasty business.

The subsequent witnesses were dry compared to the dashing detective. A crime-scene tech showed some photos that had been taken of Brian on the street, and a lab tech explained how the pills and meth were tested.

Compared to a homicide case, this was easy. And these guys got paid the same as I did.

Brian's defense attorney hit the lab tech with a barrage of questions, but she couldn't shake the professional young woman. The lawyer questioned the tests performed on the drugs and the chain of custody. Every lawyer did that. This was her only shot. There was no way she would let Brian on the stand, and she didn't have many witnesses of her own.

Seamus asked me questions during the entire process. The usual things someone might ask. "How do we know the narc is telling the truth?" "Is the judge going to be fair?" "Is Ms. Ibarra the best possible attorney?"

Eventually I groaned in frustration.

Then he asked me a realistic question. "When do we get to talk?"

I considered it.

Finally, I said, "We aren't witnesses. If he has to be

sentenced, then we can talk. Maybe then that collar of yours will come in handy."

Seamus looked at me with clear eyes and said, "And maybe my faith will come in handier."

I had been put in my place.

CHAPTER 16

BY THE NEXT morning at ten o'clock, the prosecution had rested. Ms. Ibarra called an expert to the stand to refute the lab findings. He explained that because of the nature of homemade hallucinogens, there was no way to determine exactly what effect they would have on people. He tried to question whether what Brian was selling were actually drugs.

It had little effect on the case. The jury looked unimpressed.

My last hope lay in the closing arguments. The ADA closed with a simple and powerful comment. "It doesn't matter what someone looks like. Anyone can be a drug dealer. Black, white, rich, or poor. The temptation of money is just too strong. And the effects of drug use on our city and in our society cannot be denied. The case against Brian Bennett is clear and convincing. Please consider everything you have seen and heard."

Brian's lawyer was equally eloquent, but without nearly as

much to work with. She said, "The prosecution wants you to think that this schoolboy is some kind of a drug mastermind. They want you to think that he is solely responsible for the destruction of Western civilization. I want you to think about what really happened." She turned and pointed at Brian, sitting quietly at the table. His hands still folded in front of him. The lawyer continued, "I want you to ask yourself if you really think Brian Bennett is a threat to society. I think we can all agree there are much bigger dangers out there."

That was a desperate trick I'd seen defense attorneys use when there was nothing to their case. They would deflect the question and suggest the crime was victimless. Today I agreed with the defense. There really were bigger threats in the world than my son.

Then it was done. The judge issued stern instructions to the jury. The bailiff made a few short announcements. The jury retired and filed out of the courtroom.

And I just sat there, considering the worst. Praying for a miracle. I noticed my grandfather doing the same thing. It's odd, but for some reason, even after he became a priest, I never considered Seamus devout. His jokes and mischief always made it feel like he was playing a role. His vestments were just a costume. But today I saw his faith. Raw and powerful. He had a certain intensity I had never really noticed before. And he loved his family.

After the courtroom had cleared, the three of us walked together out to the hallway. No one felt like eating lunch. Mary Catherine and I left Seamus on a bench in front of the courtroom, where he found no rest. Every third person who passed him asked for a word or a blessing.

God bless my grandfather. He didn't refuse a soul. Despite his own personal pain, he took the time to help others. He was like an entirely different person from the one who caused trouble at my house on a regular basis.

A young Muslim woman wearing a hijab stopped, kneeled next to him, and asked for his prayers.

Seamus said, "Are you of the faith, my daughter?"

She looked at him with wide, dark eyes and said, "I believe in God."

Seamus smiled, patted her on the shoulder, and said, "That's all anyone could ask."

That made the woman smile.

It made me smile, too.

CHAPTER 17

WE WERE CALLED back into the courtroom almost before the lunch hour was over. How was that possible? How had the jurors come to a verdict so quickly? They had only spent around forty minutes deliberating.

In the world of criminal justice, the axiom is: "The faster the verdict, the better the chance of conviction." I had heard a number of theories about it. I'm not sure I even believed it. I couldn't at the moment. Not with my son's life hanging in the balance. It clearly meant that there had not been much dissent in the jury room.

I slid onto the hard bench. Brian looked over at me for almost the first time. The terror in his eyes made me sick to my stomach. Mainly because I felt the same thing.

Mary Catherine ushered Seamus in between us, and he reached over to grip my hand.

I saw Brian's attorney reach over and hold his forearm. This was it. Whatever was going to happen would happen in the next minute.

The foreman of the jury, a relatively old, dignified African American man, stood and faced the judge.

Judge Weicholz said, "Has the jury reached a verdict, Mr. Foreman?"

The man's voice was deep and resonant. "Yes, Your Honor."

The foreman read the prepared preamble, but all I heard was "Blah, blah, blah."

There was only one phrase I waited to hear. And when the foreman was done with the preamble, all I heard was one word: *guilty*.

That was it. No lesser charge. Nothing to mitigate it. My little boy had been found guilty of a major felony.

Then I heard Brian sob. And Mary Catherine let out a strangled cry.

The world tilted to the left, then started to spin.

Seamus dropped his face into his hands.

Someone had to stay calm. I couldn't let Brian see me like this. I was his father. I had to toughen up. He needed me right now.

I took a deep breath. Wiped the tears from my eyes. Sat up straight as the judge thanked the jury. I even kept my cool as the bailiff and a corrections officer stepped close to Brian and handcuffed him again through the waist chain.

He was going away.

I moved through the low, swinging gate to enter the courtroom, but the bailiff held up a hand. He knew who I was. He didn't like doing it this way. But he couldn't let me near Brian right now.

Brian looked up at me, and I nodded. He had stopped crying, but I could see the fear in his face. My heart broke when I saw him disappear behind the door at the back of the room. I stood there in silence.

The ADA started to leave.

I turned and said to him, "You feel like a big man now?"

"I feel like a successful man. I did my job."

"You know that boy doesn't deserve prison."

"That's up to Judge Weicholz now."

I looked over at Mary Catherine and my grandfather, both sobbing. I felt the same searing pain. We were putting too many kids away on drug charges. Now it hit home. That's usually not a subject a cop should consider. There had to be a way to fix things. Had to be a way to make the courts stop hammering young men who made a mistake.

I gave the ADA a hard look as he left the courtroom. His young co-counsel followed him like a pack mule, loaded down with files.

I turned to Mary Catherine and Seamus. "Let's go, guys. We still have a family to take care of. There's nothing more we can do here."

I left a chunk of my heart in that courtroom.

CHAPTER 18

THAT NIGHT WAS one of the worst of my life. Including the night I lost my wife, Maeve. I tried to focus and pay attention to the other nine children, who needed me, but all I could think about was Brian.

My degree in philosophy and my life as a Catholic made it possible to know how I felt, but they didn't do shit to make me feel better.

I know Jesus said a good shepherd would leave his entire flock to find a single lost sheep. Right now, my lost sheep was all I worried about.

Seamus was in the same boat. His voice cracked when he led the prayer over our pizza. He said, "Dear God in heaven, please help us understand what happened to Brian. Please help us live our lives the way you intended us to. Please guide us through this difficult and sad time. And dear God, we all ask that you protect our dear brother Brian."

It's hard to explain, but the prayer eased my pain a little. Just a little.

After dinner, I plopped on the couch, listening to the sounds of the apartment as the kids went about their business. I could hear Mary Catherine's lyrical accent as she coaxed the kids into doing their homework and preparing for bed. She rarely had to bark an order. Although she did occasionally. She had a certain way with the children—and with me—that made us want to do things to make her happy. It was a gift she didn't even know she possessed.

When I was lost in thought, Chrissy jumped onto the couch and gave me a kiss. If that wasn't one of God's blessings, I don't know what is.

Then Shawna cuddled up next to me.

Over the course of the next hour, each kid found his or her way to me with a hug and a few quiet minutes. It wasn't random. I saw the pattern. The youngest first. Each visit lasted a little longer than the one before it. I knew Mary Catherine was behind the crowd's show of support. I appreciated her thoughtfulness and the kids' love.

Finally, the kids were all in bed, and I was still sprawled on the couch. I noticed that Seamus had made it a point to speak to each child as he or she went to bed.

I heard him say good night to Mary Catherine, then he appeared in front of the couch.

He said, "It was a tough day all around. We'll feel it for a long while."

I nodded.

"But you have duties that far exceed those of most men. A family, people to protect, a city to watch over. Don't let life devour you, Michael. You're better than that."

I had nothing I could say. I stood up and embraced this irascible old man, whom I loved. A long hug. I felt like I did when I was a child and Seamus would comfort me. Then I said something to him that I don't say enough. I said, "I love you."

He gave me a crooked smile, shuffled to the door, and headed back to his quarters behind the rectory at Holy Name.

A few minutes later Mary Catherine snuggled in next to me. Her arm around my chest felt like a warm blanket. She lounged for a few minutes silently, then said, "You know, Michael, it's not your fault. If you have to blame someone, blame Brian. It's his fault. He has to take responsibility. He made a mistake. A bad mistake. That doesn't make him a bad person. It makes him human."

"I'm afraid prison might turn him into a bad person. It's a hard life, and it can change a person."

"He's stronger than that. He'll survive and build a life when he can. You'll see. One day you'll be proud of him and just as close as you are now."

I didn't say a word.

Mary Catherine said, "Trials and hardship are part of life."

"But it just feels so awful."

"As it should. We'll get through it."

All I could say is, "How?"

"As a family." She kissed me on the cheek. "Something might happen. We might find Brian's supplier. That could lead to something. You don't have to be a cop to ask questions. Give it time."

She kissed me on the lips.

I felt like I was able to breathe for the first time since I heard the verdict.

CHAPTER 19

I HIT THE streets again. I had to. We all had lives to live. There was nothing I could do for Brian right now, but there was still a killer responsible for a student's death on the streets. That's why I found myself across the river in the Bronx. I sat on the low metal bleachers at a Little League ballpark by Yankee Stadium.

The temperature had dropped, and I pulled my Windbreaker tight around me. I knew the butt of my Glock was obvious. Just like I was. Everyone in the area knew a cop was sitting in the ballpark. A ballpark in the Bronx. That's probably why he wanted to meet me all the way up here. He wouldn't see anyone he knew.

I waited, wondering if the call had been a prank. He said he had some good information, and something in his voice made me believe him.

Jimmy Hilcox looked completely different in sweatpants and a letterman's jacket pulled over his lacrosse jersey. I guess on days he played sports the grunge look didn't work out that well. Seeing him reminded me of Brian when he would come home from after-school sports. Everything reminded me of Brian lately.

The young man sat down next to me without a word. I had kids. I knew how to just sit quietly for a few minutes.

Finally Jimmy said, "No one can ever know I talked to you about this."

I raised my right hand and mumbled, "Swear to God."

He said, "I've heard a couple of people talk about Gary's murder. He was selling cocaine on the side and made some really good money. Most of us had no idea. Somehow he got on the wrong side of his supplier. He lost some money or drugs, I don't know which. That's why he was killed."

I considered this. "That's really not anything I couldn't have figured out myself. Do you have any information about the killer?"

Jimmy nodded. "He's a student. He goes to one of those charter schools. It's a school for the medical arts. I think it's called the Roosevelt Medical Institute or some shit like that."

"You know anything about the kid?"

"He's a sophomore. He goes by DiDi, but I heard his real name might be Diego. I don't know his last name. I know he lives somewhere in Harlem around 127th. I heard he's a pretty good student and sometimes does his business out of the library at City College or Columbia. No one would bother a Latin kid at either place."

I could see it was tough for this kid to come to me. He

was scared. But he still had the nerve to do the right thing. That meant something to me. Instinctively, I wrapped an arm around his shoulder and gave him a squeeze. "You got lacrosse practice this afternoon?"

"A game. Against one of the private schools from the East Side."

"You ever play against Holy Name?"

"Yeah. How do you know Holy Name?"

"My kids go there."

"How many kids you got in school?"

"Ten." Then I caught myself. "Nine." I could see he was still nervous. His head twisted in every direction, making sure no one had seen him.

I said, "You did good. Real good. No one will ever know what we talked about."

"And no one will ever play lacrosse with Gary Mule again."

"But maybe I can even that score."

CHAPTER 20

TRYING TO GET information from a charter school was like pulling teeth with a wrench. There was no subtlety in it, and there was no way to ask questions quietly. Everyone was so freaked out about privacy and student rights that they lost sight of the fact that a student in another school was dead.

Finally I was referred to a guidance counselor. She was a big woman who had been at her job as long as I'd been alive. And she was the only one who showed any real common sense.

She had a thick Brooklyn accent, and she said, "I know a lot of the students here. So without going into official records, I can tell you that you're probably talking about Diego Martinez. A very good student. But there've also been some questions about him. A man who's not his father occasionally drops him off in a Mercedes. He has virtually no friends here at the school. And he does live in one of the projects just north of 127th. Does that sound like the kid you're looking for?" She slipped a piece of paper across the desk with the address written on it.

It was good to feel the charge of an investigation shoot through me. I was beginning to feel like myself. At least for the moment. I thanked the counselor and hurried out of the school.

The apartment wasn't hard to find. It was on the second floor of a Housing Authority complex. There were six buildings, each five stories high, with a ratty playground in the center. A rusty five-foot chain-link fence surrounded the weathered and cracked playground equipment. No one was in the center courtyard.

As I climbed the stairs, I could see that the wall was littered with hundreds of pieces of brightly colored used pieces of chewing gum. It was like a colorful tiny rock formation.

I wasn't wearing a tie, and my jacket had no markings on it. I considered the implications of the police showing up at the apartment. If Diego wasn't home, he would know to run. If there were a number of his associates inside, I might not be able to handle them by myself. I considered this problem as I continued up the concrete stairs.

I reached in my wallet and dug through some of the business cards I had acquired over the last few months during the course of my daily life. It's always a good idea for cops to have contacts, but it also helps to have a few business cards you can hold up as your own. I found the one I was looking for.

I took a moment outside the door and just listened. Someone was home. A lot of people were home. I could hear a TV, but I also heard voices. Mostly adult females but some kids as well. I was glad I had the business card.

I knocked on the door and stepped back. A cop would've stepped to the side for tactical reasons, but this made me look like what I was pretending to be. I hoped no one shot through the door for no reason.

The door swung in and a woman around forty with black hair and beautiful eyes looked at me suspiciously. A young boy peeked from around her wide hips.

I gave them both a smile and said, "Hello, ma'am. My name is Tom Miko." I held up the business card. "I'm with the New York City Department of Education. I was led to believe that you have at least one student in a charter school, and I wanted to make sure you were aware of the opportunities available for students to return to New York City public schools. There might even be scholarship money available for outside tutoring and studies."

She looked at me and then at the card, which I was still holding up. She smiled and said, "Do you mean Diego or Sabrina?"

"This is open to any student attending a charter school." I had to make this convincing. I wanted to meet this kid or at least get a look inside the apartment. There was no way this would spook him.

I slipped the card back into my wallet before she could see that the real Tom Miko was a maintenance supervisor for the school board. I had talked to him months ago, when one of his employees backed into my city-issued police car. I have no idea why I kept his card.

The woman waved me into the apartment. I couldn't help

but do a scan quickly to make sure there was no threat right in front of me. The apartment was crowded, but mostly with kids. There were two other women around the same age sitting on the couch, each with two infants in her lap.

Four kids around ten years old sat in front of the TV, and a teenage girl peeked out of the hallway to see who was visiting. I wondered if it was some kind of an unlicensed day-care center. More likely it was just women helping out others in the housing complex and watching their kids while they were at work.

A crucifix hung on the wall next to the kitchen on my right. The Lord's Prayer in Spanish hung on a plaque in the hallway.

Although the place was crowded, it seemed organized, and the children were quite polite and well-behaved. The woman who'd let me in now turned and said, "My son, Diego, goes to the special school for medicine."

Bingo. This was adding up quickly. I said, "Is Diego here? I'd like to chat with him about coming back to our school system."

She shook her head. "No, he no study here. Too much noise. He like to study at the library."

"Which library?" I could feel myself getting impatient. I didn't want to sound desperate.

"He studies at college libraries. Sometimes he goes to main New York City library."

"Do you know when he'll be back here?"

Again, she shook her head. "He study a lot. He very smart. Going to college. Diego going to be a doctor."

I kept a smile on my face as I thought, *Yeah, sure. He's already doing autopsies on live patients.*

69

CHAPTER 21

MARY CATHERINE PROWLED the halls of Holy Name. She was in the newer section of the school, which housed the high school students. It was in the rear of the building behind the much larger elementary and middle school buildings. It may have been newer, but it was built in the timeless, dull beige style that hadn't changed in a century and was common in most countries.

So far, on her mission, she'd only seen a couple of kids she knew. She had cookies that she claimed were for Shawna's class, but she used them as icebreakers with the older kids. Just to ask a few quick questions. She didn't want to be too obvious.

Everyone knew Mary Catherine at the school. It wasn't unusual for her to be on campus. She often volunteered and helped with some of the younger kids' classes. If you had ten students in a single school, there was always something to do, and the teachers were always happy to see you.

Today she'd visited Seamus at his administrative office in the church itself. She was just checking on him because he had been so distraught after Brian's trial. She brought him some of the cinnamon rolls that he loved. When she was done, she left his office and entered the school grounds. No one noticed her slip onto campus. Easy as rain, as her mam used to say. The Irish have a saying for everything.

Mary Catherine sometimes worried that her Michael didn't relate to teenagers as well as he thought he did. He was a great father, of that there was no doubt. But he *was* a father, after all. He looked at everything a certain way. Usually in terms of how it affected his children. All he cared about was safe, happy kids. Sometimes his values, like honor, duty, and ethics, seemed like they came from another era. Occasionally it felt like he had no idea what went on in the world of the modern teenager.

But she felt like she did. When she was growing up in Ireland, all she and her friends did was listen to American music, watch American movies, and act like what they thought Americans acted like. Once she got to the United States, she realized that teenagers here acted like teenagers everywhere. And it was difficult for their parents to understand them.

Even now, she watched MTV shows and other pop-culture entertainment at home. Although the channel was off-limits for the kids, she'd watch it during the day, when the apartment was empty.

She also listened. When Jane or Juliana was on the phone

71

or just talking, Mary Catherine took note. They were both good girls, but apparently not all their friends were.

She was also younger than Michael and felt like she wasn't far removed from the passions of youth—including music, the desire to fit in, and the stupid mistakes kids make without thinking.

She chatted with the few students she saw in the hall, and if they asked about Brian she used it as an opening to ask the questions she wanted answered. Questions she *intended* to have answered. Did they ever think Brian was selling drugs? Did they see him meet with anyone? Are any other kids doing the same thing? It could be awkward, but she had to act. She felt like she might be the only one who could help Brian.

Although the students knew Michael because he helped with their soccer and basketball teams, everyone knew he was a respected detective with the NYPD. He may have taken it in stride, but his job tended to intimidate everyone else. Especially teenagers.

Their view of police work had been shaped by TV shows and movies that made detectives seem tough and unpredictable. Brian's troubles had broken through Michael's tough shell. He just wanted his son back safe and sound. And Mary Catherine intended to help.

The three kids she spoke to all happened to mention the same person. A friend of Brian's. A basketball player. An athlete. And a dope dealer. She knew the boy and wasn't surprised by hearing his name.

His father was a well-known Manhattan dentist, and his mother served on every possible charity board. It seemed that they were always mentioned in the newspaper or on NY1. When Mary Catherine thought about it, she couldn't remember ever seeing them at a school activity or involved with their son.

Now she started looking in earnest for Patrick Marshall.

CHAPTER 22

MARY CATHERINE TRIED to figure out the best place to talk to Patrick Marshall without raising any suspicions. She caught a lucky break while visiting the administration office. She saw that the high school juniors had a study hall scheduled for the next forty minutes.

She checked the library and saw that most of the students were inside, working quietly. But no Patrick Marshall. Then she thought about it. One thing a drug dealer needed to do was use his phone. And one thing that was strictly forbidden on campus was the use of cell phones. She mumbled to herself, "That little shit is on his phone somewhere."

She recalled Seamus telling her that he was always shooing kids on cell phones out of the courtyard at the rear of the school, which connected to the church. It was supposed to be a quiet, peaceful area where the priests could meditate.

Somehow she had a difficult time imagining Seamus meditating.

She walked to the grassy square. There she saw two saplings and a concrete bench between the two buildings as well as a ten-foot-high wrought-iron fence protecting it from the street. And there, leaning on the fence, was a tall, athletic, good-looking young man. She couldn't explain it, but he made her angry. His family was wealthy. God had given him everything, and he still was doing something like this.

Like Brian. She whispered out loud, "Oh, my God." She caught herself. Brian had it all, too. Maybe not as much money, but he had a supportive family. What caused this? Why were kids getting involved with this terrible scourge?

Patrick turned and saw her. He mumbled something into the phone, then jammed it into his pocket.

She said, "Hello, Patrick."

He gave her a weak smile. "Hi. How are you, Mrs. Ben…"

She didn't worry about correcting him. It happened all the time.

Patrick said, "How's Brian doing?"

"Not so well. We're waiting for his sentencing."

He eased over to the concrete bench and plopped down. He just looked down at the ground and started to cry.

Mary Catherine sat on the bench next to him.

Finally Patrick got hold of himself and cleared his throat. He said, "I'm sorry. Brian didn't deserve what happened."

She put her arm around his shoulder and said in a soft voice, "It's all right, Patrick. I know it's not just Brian that's got you down."

He didn't say anything.

She said, "What's really wrong? You can tell me. It will be our little secret."

Again, she just sat there during a long silence.

He sniffled. "Brian got caught up in something like a game at first. He didn't mean for it to get out of control."

"For what to get out of control?"

Patrick hesitated.

"It's all right, dear." She remembered what it was like for teenagers to talk to adults. It was better to just wait.

Finally Patrick said, "Brian wanted to look cool. He didn't want to always be just a cop's kid. He thought he could prove how tough he was. Then it just kept going." Patrick took a moment.

Mary Catherine hoped he wouldn't start crying again.

He said, "This guy who gives him meth to sell scares the shit out of him. He's crazy."

Mary Catherine said, "Who's the guy?"

He shook his head. "I don't know."

"Then why are you out here making calls?"

"I'm calling my girlfriend."

"What's her name?"

He hesitated.

Mary Catherine said, "You don't know your girlfriend's name?" She smiled, trying to lighten the mood. Then, in a very soft voice, she said, "Everyone knows, Patrick. How do you think I found you so easily? You're going to end up like Brian. Just like him."

He said, "Are you going to tell Detective Bennett on me?"

"I told you this was our little secret. This courtyard is almost like a confessional."

He perked up. "Really?"

"Really." Then she added, "But you've got to stop doing this. You don't need to be something you're not. It would kill your parents."

"Maybe of embarrassment. They don't care what I do otherwise."

"You may think that, but it's not true."

He looked down at the ground again and said, "Besides, he'd never let me just quit. Brian couldn't walk away. He's shown us what would happen. People who cross him are tortured or killed. Just like the kid from P.S. 419. We've all heard about how his head was cut off. Even if it wasn't on the news."

Mary Catherine searched for an answer. "What if there was another way?"

"How?"

"Tell me his name. No one will know. I can get it to Mr. Bennett. He can work miracles." She knew Michael's reputation would play into Patrick's decision.

And she was right.

CHAPTER 23

I WAS TRYING not to hit the gas too hard in my city-issued Impala. I was heading up to 116th Street, and the traffic along Broadway was just light enough to make me cocky. I was driving like a tourist—a little too fast and thinking about my destination instead of what was in front of me. To make matters worse, a light freezing rain had fallen across the city, making the roads slick.

I had gotten a tip from a former NYPD sergeant who now worked as a security guard on the Columbia campus. That was one of the perks of being on the force for a while: you knew a hundred former cops who had retired and were working private security jobs all over the city. Anyone who hadn't moved to Florida was the head of security at some foundation or corporation. We were like an infestation of fleas. We just kept spreading out farther and farther.

In this case, it was working to my advantage. I had left the high school yearbook photograph of my suspected hit man, Diego, with the security people near the libraries Jimmy Hilcox had mentioned. It was only a matter of time before someone noticed the young man. That was based on the assumption that he actually studied at the libraries occasionally.

Then I got a call from Todd Schupper, a former financial-crimes supervisor who said he never wanted to look at another ledger book or calculator for the rest of his life. Columbia offered him a job strolling around the campus, and he jumped at it. They also allowed him to take one class per semester for free, and he figured by the time he was seventy he would've earned his degree in Asian history. A subject that had fascinated him since he was a kid.

I made my way to Columbia's main library, known to most as Butler Library. It was actually on 114th just west of Amsterdam, and it was spectacular. The building looked like a Greek temple, with its massive columns in front. Inside, the soaring ceilings, heavy chandeliers, and tall windows had cost a fortune to build, especially in the Depression, when the building went up.

I met my buddy, who was standing near the information desk and chatting with a sharp-eyed reference librarian who looked like she had been there since the building opened.

Todd, heavier than I remembered him, greeted me in a low tone. "Mike, how are you?"

I shrugged. Everyone knew the story about Brian, and I didn't want to go into it again. I just said, "Where's the kid?"

Todd pointed toward the study area, furnished with ten

broad wooden tables between shelves of reference books. I saw Diego, alone, at one of the far tables.

I watched him. I hoped that this was not our killer. He looked like a kid. He had neatly trimmed dark hair and the thin build of a distance runner. The way he stuck his tongue out while he concentrated reminded me of Brian.

Todd said, "You need backup?"

I shook my head. I was already committed to this, no matter what common sense told me about talking to a potential killer by myself.

I said, "I'll be fine."

Todd smiled. "That's what everyone says just before they screw up."

CHAPTER 24

NO ONE WAS sitting near Diego as I approached. A coat and backpack were slung across the back of the chair next to him. I slid into the chair directly across from him. The way he raised his eyes from the book told me that he immediately realized I was a cop.

He said, "Am I not supposed to be here?"

"I don't know what the exact rules are for studying in the library, but you seem to be following them."

I reached across and lifted the cover of his book from the table. *Biology of Humans* by Judith Goodenough.

I smiled and said, "Tough subject, but a great name for an author."

"The book costs, like, seventy bucks, but I can read it here or over at the O'Malley library for free."

"I went to Manhattan College. Spent a lot of time at O'Malley. Should've spent more."

Diego looked at me a second time and said, "Aren't you a cop?"

"You'd be surprised. A lot of cops go to college."

"I didn't mean it that way. I'm sorry, sir. What did you study?"

"Philosophy." I paused for a moment, then said, "I guess that doesn't set me up for a lot of jobs other than being a cop."

I didn't see how there was any way this young man was tied up in the drug business. Let alone capable of doing what I had heard he did.

"My name is Mike Bennett. I work out of the Manhattan North Homicide Squad. Your name's Diego, right?"

He nodded but didn't seem particularly nervous. "Why would a homicide detective come into the library to talk to me? I'm a high school student. I live in the projects north of here."

"I'm just trying to do my job. Probably been some sort of mistake, but I thought I would sit and talk with you for a few minutes before the mistake turned into something worse."

He closed the biology book and shoved it to one side. Then he took a paperback from the table and stuck it in the backpack sitting on the chair next to him. "I brought that with me into the library."

I raised both hands. "I didn't say anything."

"I just wanted you to know I'm straight up." He twisted his head in every direction to make sure no one could hear us, then said, "What did you want to talk to me about?"

"I heard you might be working with a group. A group that can be pretty tough. A group that moves dope through the city and is brutal to the people who sell it for them. That's just what I hear. I wanted to see what you had to say."

"Who says I work for any group? I go to high school. I want to be a doctor."

I studied his face and couldn't see any hint of deception. He looked me right in the eye and kept that calm, polite tone.

"It doesn't matter who says you're in the group. I'm interested in knowing about what you do in your free time. If you ever travel to any of the high schools close by. How you can afford to buy a customized Wenger backpack and a Vineyard Vines peacoat." I looked at the chair next to him with the jacket neatly hung across the back and the backpack open, facing him. "Those are the kinds of questions I'd like answered."

It worked. I could see the change in his face. I was betting he had three-hundred-dollar sneakers on as well. But he kept his calm.

Diego looked at me and said, "Do you get questioned every time you buy something nice? I don't think it's right that I get singled out for having a couple of nice things. What exactly do you think I did?"

"Does the name Gary Mule mean anything to you?"

The kid caught me by surprise. It was such a casual move. No telegraph, no stress. He just leaned over and reached into his open backpack.

That's when I saw the gun.

CHAPTER 25

I MAY HAVE been caught by surprise, but experience and training had taught me not to let it linger. There was no way I could reach the Glock on my hip in time to keep Diego from putting a round into my face. Instead I braced myself and shoved the table as hard as I could. It was heavy and knocked him back, then it started to tip over.

He sprang back, but he still had the gun in his hand. Now I had an overturned table to duck behind as he fired a round. I felt the impact on the heavy wood.

The sharp blast in the hushed silence of the library was startling. Nothing like this had ever happened before in Butler Library. The effect was immediate. I heard screaming and saw students starting to scatter.

Now I had my pistol in my hand, and I shouted for

everyone to hear, "Police, get down. Get down." I crawled to the end of the table and peeked around quickly with my pistol in front of me. Diego was already running away.

There were more screams. I had to trust that the security guard, Todd, was already on the phone calling for help. Right now it was my job to make sure no bystanders got shot, but I couldn't let this kid get away, either. He wasn't just a killer: he was the key to breaking this drug ring and stopping the killing.

I got up from behind the table and started to sprint in the same direction Diego had run. I caught a glimpse of him turning to the right into the stacks of books. Each shelf went eight feet into the air and was loaded with thick reference books. It was like a maze, and he had spent a lot more time here than I had.

Then I lost sight of him completely. I was worried about stumbling into an ambush. That's what I would do—stage an ambush—if I were as desperate as Diego was. I paused at the end of a long line of books. I took in a couple of breaths and focused. I turned quickly to charge up the aisle and immediately saw someone right in front of me.

I raised my pistol and shouted, "Don't move."

I heard a squeal and realized I had stumbled into a student. She was sobbing as she hit the floor, but she somehow managed to say, "There's a man with a gun at the end of the aisle."

I said in a quieter voice, "Run to the front. Do it now." She sprinted past me, and now I could hear other people running away. That was good. At least from my perspective. Tactically. The fewer people I had to worry about the better.

I crept forward with my gun out in front of me, then I saw

movement to my right. I froze and dipped down slightly and realized I could see between the tops of the books and the shelf above them. Diego was in the next aisle, and he was waiting for me.

I crouched down lower and continued to move forward until I was just about even with where I saw Diego in the next aisle. My heart was thumping in my chest, and sweat poured off my forehead. This was not something anyone expected to happen inside the library of an Ivy League school.

I listened but gained no advantage. Then I realized what I could do. I was sure he was still on the other side of the bookshelf, so I stood up quickly and shoved hard against the books just above the level of my head. They pushed through the shelf and started to topple down on the other side of the aisle. I heard someone squawk.

I took the opportunity to bound three steps ahead and turn into the next aisle. My gun was up and on target, and I could see Diego on the ground. But he had anticipated what I was going to do and had his pistol up. He fired one round, which went slightly to the left and struck the shelf right next to my head.

Instinctively I squeezed the trigger twice at the target directly in front of me. It was a simple double tap. *Bang, bang.* For an instant, I could see the look in Diego's eyes. Then he fell back and dropped the gun onto the floor.

I immediately holstered my pistol and dropped to my knee. I reached down and pulled his thick T-shirt up over his stomach and chest to see two wounds just above his sternum. Blood was already starting to pump out. I placed my palms over each hole, hoping to stem the blood flow.

The young man made a gurgling sound and tried to lift his head off the floor.

I yelled out, "I need some help here." A few seconds later, Todd appeared at my side.

He said, "Fire and rescue is on the way. What do you need me to do?"

"Help me stop the bleeding on one of these wounds."

Todd didn't move. He put his hand on my shoulder instead. "Mike, it's over. You did what you had to do."

I looked down and saw that Diego was perfectly still. I felt for a pulse at his chest and then at his neck. No more blood was pumping out of the wounds. He was dead.

I flopped back, and my shoulders hit the bookshelf. I sat there staring down at the teenager I had just shot dead.

From the end of the aisle a woman's voice said, "You murdered him."

My head snapped in that direction. It was a young woman, and she was staring at me. A young man joined her and said, "You shot him for no reason?"

Before fire and rescue and more cops could show up, a small crowd gathered, and they all picked up a similar theme. They thought I had acted rashly and fired my weapon without provocation. They thought I was some kind of monster.

Once someone was there to secure the scene and Todd was leading me toward an office where I could gather my thoughts, I kept hearing people say, "Murderer." "Killer."

Todd kept his arm on my shoulder and said, "Don't worry about these ignorant morons. One thing I've learned working here is that I'm never surprised to see smart people acting like idiots. They have no idea you just saved their asses."

At the moment their taunts didn't bother me. The fact that I had to shoot a kid around Brian's age was enough to make my legs weak. Once we got in the office, all I could do was drop my face into my hands.

CHAPTER 26

IT DIDN'T TAKE long to get the scene secured and order restored in the library. Harry Grissom, the lieutenant who ran our squad, showed up and sat with me for a while. Even though he asked me a few questions, I realized he was carefully avoiding asking why I had been interviewing a potential homicide suspect alone without telling anyone where I had gone.

Harry was a veteran and had seen more than most cops should. Someone had told him that the crowd had immediately turned against me after the shooting, and he took a minute to talk to me about it.

He rubbed his cheek where a hint of gray stubble was poking through. "You know, Mike, people say stupid things without thinking. They think they know what police work is like from watching TV, but they have no idea. They don't know the risks we take or the satisfaction we feel when we make an arrest. We've already recovered the gun the kid had, and crime scene is digging a bullet out of the bookshelf and table. The security guard saw everything, and so did the librarian. For all the bullshit these assholes are spewing, not one of them witnessed anything. So you gotta let it roll off your back."

All I could do at this point was just nod my head weakly.

Harry said, "What can I do for you, Mike?"

"I need to tell his mother."

"What? Are you insane? We'll have someone go talk to her."

"I just feel like it's something *I* need to do."

It took some persuading, and it was way outside any guidelines Homicide had, but forty-five minutes later, I found myself at Diego's apartment, near 127th Street. This time I had the lieutenant and a detective named Susan Ruiz with me. We climbed the hard concrete stairs, and I knocked on the door I had visited a few days earlier.

The same woman answered the door and immediately recognized me. She smiled and said, "Diego is studying. But I told him about your offer to leave the charter school."

I held up my badge and said, "I'm afraid I misled you. I'm a homicide detective with the NYPD." I had intended to just tell her what had happened, but when I saw her face, I had to take a moment.

The woman said, "I no understand. Why did you lie? Why do you want to speak to my Diego?"

A couple of kids gathered behind her to see who was at the door. She stepped forward slightly, and I could see how worried she was.

I said, "I'm afraid I have some bad news."

"What? What is it?"

"Diego was shot and killed by the police on the Columbia campus."

She stumbled back a little bit, but quickly gathered herself. "What? Why did the police shoot my boy?"

"It wasn't just the police, ma'am. Diego pulled a pistol and fired at me. He left me no choice. I had to shoot him." After a few seconds of silence, I said, "And I thought it was the right thing to do for me to come here and tell you what happened."

I felt Lieutenant Grissom and Detective Ruiz slide in close to me for support.

A woman came behind Diego's mother and wrapped an arm around her just as she started to cry. Then she started to wail.

I just stood there wondering why I had thought this was important.

Then, without warning, she looked me in the eye and slapped me hard right across the face. My left cheek burned with the blow. I had to hold up my right hand to keep Detective Ruiz from stepping between us.

Then Diego's mother said in a very calm voice, "Get out. Get out of here. You've done enough. You're a liar and a killer. God will punish you for what you've done."

Even after the door slammed, I just stood there for a few more moments.

CHAPTER 27

I TRIED TO stay upbeat with the kids when I got home. Of course they knew what had happened. It was on the news, and there was the usual string of phone calls and friends from the office who stopped by to check on me. It was a police ritual carried out across the country after an officer is involved in a fatal shooting. Shootings are tricky: they can have their effect psychologically days or even weeks after the tragedy.

It wasn't until after dinner, when I had a few minutes to think, that it really hit me hard.

I had shot a teenager. That was not something a few drinks and a baseball game would wash from my brain. I kept seeing Diego and hearing him make that horrible sound as I tried to stop the blood from pumping out of the two bullet wounds I had put in his chest.

I had a phantom pain on the left side of my face where his

mother had slapped me. Harry Grissom had told me she was out of line, but I knew she wasn't. She was a mother who'd lost her son. I understood all those mothers who went on TV and told people how great their children were even after they'd been caught doing terrible things.

One young man, shot by a security guard, was seen on video shooting a young mother in front of her infant. And that night the robber's mother was on TV talking about what a good boy he was and how he could never do anything like that.

I got it. No parent ever wanted to admit that his or her child had some horrendous character flaw. Who knows what led Diego down a different path? I couldn't figure out why Brian felt like he needed to sell drugs, either. In that sense, I shared a lot with Diego's mother.

I helped Bridget with a project about the Civil War, which of course she enhanced by making an interactive map, complete with pop-up paper cannons. It was a pretty good representation of Pickett's Charge at Gettysburg. She had facts and figures written behind pull tabs on the map. And right at the Union line she had written "The high-water mark of the Confederacy." That was the exact phrase I had been taught as a child in school—it means the farthest north Robert E. Lee had led his army.

Then I tried to help Trent with a book report on Jackie Robinson. I had felt the book might've been targeted for kids older than he was and was pleasantly surprised at how well he'd understood it. I sometimes worried that he would lose touch with his African American heritage after being raised in an Irish American household. However, he clearly understood the importance of Robinson's entrance into major-league baseball. He also learned about the struggles that Robinson went through and the raw, naked hatred he endured.

Trent turned from the report and said, "I'm checking out a book about Jesse Owens tomorrow. Did you know that he was in the Olympics before World War II and forced Adolf Hitler to admit that the Germans weren't the master race?"

I smiled with pride at my sixth grader. "I don't know if Hitler ever said it out loud, but Jesse sure made him look like a doofus. A bigger doofus than he really was." The smile Trent gave me lifted my spirits more than I thought anything could.

After eleven, when the kids were no longer up to distract me from my thoughts, Mary Catherine joined me on the balcony.

She shivered and wrapped her robe tightly around her as she snuggled up next to me and put her arm around my waist. "You'll catch your death from a chill out here, Michael Bennett."

"You're from Ireland. I would've thought you were used to a cool breeze."

"Cool breezes are pleasant. This is a nor'easter."

"That's what they say in Boston. Here in New York we don't acknowledge anything those people say. It's just a cold wind from the north."

Despite the fact that she was shivering, I realized she had something to say or she wouldn't still be standing there. Without admitting I was wrong or that it was too cold to be standing on a balcony, I turned to her and followed her into the living room, where we both sat on the couch. Only then did I realize how cold it had been on the balcony.

Mary Catherine didn't rush into it. We just sat there

together, holding hands like teenagers. I had explained to her what had happened almost as soon as I got home, and, mercifully, she hadn't asked any questions since.

Finally she said, "Michael, if I had something important to tell you, is it possible to get you to promise that you won't do anything rash and will keep yourself under control?"

"That is an oddly worded request. What about me and the way I'm acting makes you think I might lose control?"

"It's about Brian's trouble."

I sat up. "Did something happen? Is Brian okay?"

"Yes. Brian is fine. But I may have found out some information about the man Brian was working for."

"What? How?" I took a moment, cleared my head, and said, "Tell me what you know."

She said, "I need your word of honor that you will keep control."

All I said was, "You have it."

"One of Brian's friends talked to me at school. He was very hesitant and doesn't want me to mention his name or anything about him. He said that Brian worked for a man named Albert. He's a drug dealer from the Bronx who uses high school students as employees."

"Do you have a last name?"

"No, but he lives somewhere near Fordham Heights and is called Caracortada."

"What the heck does that mean?"

"I looked it up, and I think it means 'Scarface.' That matches up with the description I got. He has a scar on the left side of his face."

"It also goes along with every dope dealer I ever met who

wanted to emulate Tony Montana from the movie *Scarface*." My mind was racing with possibilities. "How on earth did you find any of this out?"

"I know enough about police work to say you never divulge a source."

I looked at that beautiful face, carefully moved a strand of blond hair, and tucked it behind her ear. That sincere and earnest personality often showed in her expression. She had made up her mind.

She would never tell me where she got this information. Now it was up to me to do something with it.

CHAPTER 28

THE NYPD POLICY for an officer-involved shooting dictated that the officer remain at home, off duty, for at least seven days after the incident. That was if it was a "good shoot" and the officer was ready to come back to work. There had been instances of officers staying at home, or "on the bricks," for months while investigations dragged on.

My shooting involved several good witnesses, the bullet hole next to my head, and a suspect who had been tied to a brutal murder of a high school student. No matter what people inside the library thought, it was a good shoot.

I hadn't been completely idle during my time on the bricks. I had given the information Mary Catherine had found out, even if she wouldn't say how, to one of my friends in a Manhattan North narcotics task force.

Now I sat in the front seat of Tim Marcia's car in Fordham

Heights, not too far from the Bronx Zoo. We had the heat up in the roomy unmarked NYPD Tahoe. It was cold and messy outside, and snow fell on and off as ice built up on the sidewalks.

Tim was a sergeant in charge of a Manhattan North narcotics task force that was trying to stem the growing tide of heroin in the city after a crackdown on prescription drugs.

The fifty-year-old veteran looked like a cop, with a caterpillar of a mustache and sharp, intelligent eyes. But he knew his business.

As we waited for some of his detectives to get into place, he said, "Working narcotics is like being the Dutch boy who plugs a hole in the dike. As soon as one hole is plugged, another leak springs close by." Then he turned to me and added, "At least this time we might be able to help one of our own.

"This is where your friend Caracortada lives and works. His real name is Albert Stass."

"What kind of Latin name is that?"

"He was born in Uruguay. Maybe his grandparents were German. A lot of Germans fled the country before and after the war. Not just Nazis." We watched as a kid left the apartment building. Tim continued. "He's worked with the Sinaloa cartel and spent time in a Mexican prison. His release is a little shady because his sentence was commuted from twenty-five years to just under two." He gave a couple of quick instructions on the radio. Then he looked at me. "Luckily, the duty judge lives in the real world and agrees with what our surveillances have uncovered. Now we get to squeeze Mr. Stass."

We found his apartment on the second floor. I insisted that

it be just the two of us at the front door. The other detectives were either downstairs or outside.

I took a moment to dust the snow that had accumulated on my shoulders during our short walk into the building. Even with the gray skies outside, I had something resembling hope growing inside me. This was the first proactive thing I'd been able to do for Brian since this whole mess had started.

As we stood on either side of the door, I noticed that Tim looked concerned. I said, "You got something to say?"

Tim said, "I've got to go in first."

"Why?"

Tim looked serious. "Because Mary Catherine called me and told me to look out for you. I'm more afraid of an angry Irish woman than I am of this asshole."

I nodded and said, "I know the feeling."

CHAPTER 29

TIM KNOCKED ON the door. We both had our pistols in our hands, down by our sides. There was no one in the narrow hallway, and we stood off to either side of the door. I was shocked to see the handle turn and the door open almost immediately. As soon as I saw the scar on the face of the man who opened it, I knew we were in the right place.

But before we could officially identify ourselves, the door slammed shut. Tim muttered, "Shit."

I tried the handle. It was locked, and without thinking I threw my weight into the door. The lock held, but the hinges broke off. That was common when people spent a fortune on a lock but ignored the rest of the door.

We both darted into the room and stepped away from the door. In police work, putting your silhouette against an open door is a sin. It's called the fatal funnel. You're a target to anyone in the room. So now I was crouched low, to the side of the door, with my gun up. I scanned the entire room and heard Tim yell, "Bedroom."

We hustled past the tiny kitchen to the open bedroom door. I carefully peeked around to see as much of the room as possible, then Tim bolted in with me right behind him.

It was empty.

I said, "He's here somewhere." The room was messy, but there were no mountains of laundry or closets for him to hide in. Then I noticed slight movement in the corner. A doggie door had been built into the wall. Rocking back and forth gently. It couldn't be.

I said, "Tim—on the rear wall to the left of the bed."

Tim advanced carefully with his pistol up in front of him. "I'll be damned."

We moved in closer to the doggie door. Both of us were big men. This was not something I wanted to do. Not something I normally *would* do. But this was the asshole who had turned my son into a drug dealer. I had to take the risk.

Even as I crouched down, I heard Tim say, "No. Wait, Mike." I ignored him as I poked my head through the door flap and saw that the adjacent apartment was dark. I crawled on through the door, then put my back against the wall. To my surprise, Tim squeezed through the doggie door as well, cursing under his breath the whole time.

I took a moment to let my eyes adjust to the dark. Then we moved through the apartment.

Tim said "Holy crap" as we passed a table stacked with plastic bags of methamphetamine and three pistols sitting casually on the end. Clearly Albert Stass could've armed himself while running through this room. We paused at the door that led into the living room.

I stayed behind the cover of the wall and peeked around quickly and saw nothing. Then Tim and I entered. It was empty except for a table with a stack of cash on it.

Tim looked at me and said, "This guy is a magician."

A voice came over the radio and said, "Sarge, are you looking for a skinny Latin man in his underwear running through the snow?"

Cops and their sarcasm. It's what kept us sane.

We raced out the front door and down the hallway, then down a flight of stairs. The others had positioned themselves on the far side of a snow-covered baseball field. They understood how important it was for me to be in on this arrest. I appreciated their discretion.

It wasn't hard to sprint along the sidewalk and then cut into the field not far from the running man. He looked shocked to see me when he turned his head.

I shouted, "Keep running. It only means you'll be more tired when I arrest you."

He had a small automatic pistol in his right hand, but he showed no interest in using it as his pace slowed. He tossed it to the side and kept running in his bare feet, wearing nothing but his tighty-whities. It had to be uncomfortable in the cold.

I could've shouted for him to stop. Tim was right next to me now, jogging along at a comfortable clip. But as the man started to slide to a stop so he could turn and run between some bleachers, I launched myself.

My shoulder struck his ribs and banged him hard against the bleachers. We both crashed on the frozen ground. He was facedown and didn't struggle as I twisted his arm behind his back. In a single fluid motion—one I had practiced over the course of a long career and hundreds of hours of training sessions—I holstered my pistol and pulled my handcuffs from my belt.

After I had him cuffed, I left him lying on the icy ground. When I stood up, Tim said, "Nicely done. All by the book. This is a good arrest no matter how you look at it."

I saw the irony: this hard-core drug dealer would be housed in relative comfort while the legal system slowly churned; meanwhile, the kids he had working for him killed and *were* killed every day.

Life plays mean tricks. If you're a cop, you see a lot more of them than most people.

CHAPTER 30

IT WASN'T UNTIL I was in the elevator in my apartment building that I realized how tricky it might be to explain what happened to Mary Catherine. She didn't want me to go on the arrest in the first place and had told my friend Tim Marcia to keep an eye on me. I decided to leave out the details, including crawling through the doggie door and chasing an armed, desperate man on foot. Instead I was just going to say, "We made the arrest without incident." Almost the same thing the official report would say.

But I felt lighter. I thought we might have some ammunition when it came to Brian's sentencing. If anyone could persuade this guy to talk it was Tim Marcia. Besides, between the drugs, guns, and money in his apartment, he had to realize that we could bury him *under* the jail.

As I slipped my key into the door I was looking forward to

telling Mary Catherine about the arrest. It came from information she had found. She would be happy that she had given us what we needed to make the bust.

That plan changed when I opened the door to a scene of absolute chaos inside. Kids were screaming and crowded in the dining room. Shawna was weeping on the couch, and Juliana was on the wall phone in the kitchen.

Before I could ask what was wrong, I heard Juliana say on the phone, "This is Juliana Bennett. My grandfather is having a heart attack, and we need an ambulance right now." She gave our address and answered a couple of questions from the dispatcher.

Even in the immediate crisis, I recognized how calm her voice was and how quickly she had gotten out the important information.

I rushed to the spot where Mary Catherine and a couple of the children were crouched around Seamus. He was propped up against the wall and had an odd, waxy complexion as he gasped for breath. He started to pant like a dog.

I felt a stab of terror at the sight of the man who had been a rock for me my entire life. He had suffered heart issues before, but nothing that ever looked like this. I dropped to one knee, shooing Trent away from his great-grandfather, and felt Seamus's neck to get an idea of his pulse. I could barely feel his heartbeat as it erratically shifted and paused.

He turned his pale eyes up to me and tried to say something.

"Just keep quiet, Seamus. It's going to be all right. Help is on the way."

He tried to speak again and made a feeble attempt to

motion me closer with his right hand. I leaned in with my ear right next to his mouth. I could hear his ragged breathing as he tried to gather the strength to speak.

I caught a few words, including "love" and "proud of you."

I patted him on the shoulder and said, "I know. I know, Seamus. I love you, too." I was trying to block out the kids around me, who were all scared and not sure what to do or how to react.

Then Seamus grabbed my shirt and pulled me back to him. "Brian broke my heart. I don't know that I can take it anymore."

It was right then that I knew we couldn't wait for fire and rescue or an ambulance. Seamus didn't have that kind of time left.

CHAPTER 31

I ONLY HAD one choice, so I picked up my grandfather and followed Mary Catherine as she opened doors and sent kids ahead to call for the elevator. I trusted that one of the older kids would know to stay at the apartment with the younger ones and found myself racing to my car with Mary Catherine, Jane, and Trent. That was a good team to have on my side.

Mary Catherine said, "Are you sure we shouldn't wait for help?"

"Not at this time of the evening."

We got to my police car, and I laid Seamus in the backseat, where Mary Catherine could hold him. I got behind the wheel and hit the gas. We spun through the parking garage and out to the street in a matter of seconds. Even I was shocked at how fast I was driving. But this was Seamus. I couldn't let anything happen to him.

I took 96th to Broadway with the lights flashing and siren blaring. I resisted the urge to keep looking in the backseat and focused on the traffic in front of me. Once I was on Broadway, I knew it was twenty or so blocks up to Mount Sinai St. Luke's hospital, right near the Columbia campus. I'd be fighting more traffic, but it was a direct route.

I grabbed my NYPD radio and said I was transporting an apparent cardiac victim in need of immediate assistance. Out of nowhere, a marked cruiser pulled out in front of me with his full array of lights flashing and gave me an escort. God bless the NYPD.

We pulled into the emergency room, and Mary Catherine ran inside to get help. I carefully lifted Seamus from the backseat.

He managed to say, "There's no way you're carrying me in there like a baby. At least find a wheelchair."

Before Seamus had finished the sentence, Trent came running up with a simple, old-style wheelchair, and I placed Seamus into the seat. Just as we got through the door there were orderlies and a nurse waiting for us. We followed them up to a small room where a young internist met us.

He talked in a soothing tone to Seamus, trying to get some answers and assess his overall situation. Nurses hooked sensors to his chest, and instantly I started to see the EKG representation of his heartbeats on a monitor.

Mary Catherine, Jane, and Trent were wedged in tight against me in the corner. No one had really noticed us.

Then it happened. It was a jolt to my system, and I

don't know how badly it scared Mary Catherine and the kids.

A loud tone erupted from the EKG. The doctor shouted some instructions using acronyms I wasn't familiar with. But it was clear to me that Seamus had flatlined, and now they had to take drastic measures to save him.

CHAPTER 32

I STOOD IN silence in the corner of the cardiac treatment room, clutching Mary Catherine, Jane, and Trent to my side. The doctor shouted "Clear" as he placed paddles on my grandfather's bare chest. It was like something out of a movie.

A jolt of electricity shot through my grandfather, but the horrible tone coming from the EKG machine only faltered for a moment, then continued. One of the nurses checked Seamus's mouth and airway and repositioned his head.

The doctor yelled, "Clear!" Once again Seamus's body spasmed as electricity shot from the paddles and coursed throughout his body.

Jane turned and buried her face in my chest as she started to weep.

Trent squeezed my hand so tightly that my fingers turned purple.

And Mary Catherine just stared at the horrific scene in front of us. I realized that she had a special bond with my grandfather. At first I thought it was just their shared Irish birth, but over time I realized it was much more than that. She had rescued the family he loved so much during their darkest hour. She had been loyal and kind, and she treated Seamus like he was her own grandfather.

And Seamus loved her like she was part of the family. No matter how hard it might be for me to imagine life without my grandfather, Mary Catherine would have a harder time adjusting.

But I wasn't willing to give up yet. I bowed my head and prayed with all my heart. Like any good Catholic, I often said prayers from memory. Simple prayers to ask God to look over my family or help solve some of the world's major problems. It wasn't that I didn't mean those prayers—it was just that, at the moment, nothing seemed more urgent or necessary than God's intervention on behalf of my grandfather.

Silently I said, "God, please help us right now. I need that old man. *You* need that old man here. He definitely makes things easier for all of us. You must know you have no more loyal servant. That is why I ask you to please help us now and let Seamus Bennett live with us on earth a while longer."

As I finished the prayer, the room was suddenly quiet again. The tone from the EKG stopped. The doctor appeared less frantic. A nurse inserted something into Seamus's mouth that ran down his throat. She wouldn't do that if he were dead.

God had heard our prayers for our favorite priest.

CHAPTER 33

ALMOST A MONTH after Seamus's heart attack—or, as he took to calling it, his "return from the dead"—I found myself standing in the same small break room on Rikers Island where I had visited Brian before his trial.

Between visiting Seamus in the hospital, attending Brian's sentencing, and visiting him here, I felt like all I did was sit in small waiting rooms.

We had been chatting for a few minutes as I filled Brian in on everything that had happened. We were all still recovering from Seamus's heart attack as well as Brian's sentencing.

The judge said that the arrest of Albert Stass could not be tied to Brian because Stass had refused to talk and there was nothing directly relating the two arrests. Then the judge said, "But I recognize the service the defendant's father has provided to the city of New York. I also recognize that the defendant has a chance to turn his life around."

Suddenly I started to feel hope that Brian might be coming home soon.

Then the judge looked at Brian and said, "Therefore I will not sentence you to the maximum twenty-five years in state prison for a class B felony. Instead you will serve a term of between five and not more than ten years at a state prison chosen by the New York State Department of Corrections and Community Supervision."

That was as big a blow as Seamus's heart attack.

Brian seemed resigned and was happy to be leaving Rikers Island, no matter where he was headed.

When I sat down in the chair next to him, Brian said, "I know I'm responsible for Seamus's heart attack. I know the stress of my arrest and trial is what led to it."

"Don't be silly. He's a man in his eighties. He didn't always take care of himself. There's no way it was your fault." Even as I said it, I didn't believe it. I realized that the stress of the last couple of months had taken its toll on the old man. But Brian didn't need to know that.

Brian started to cry. He turned in his chair and gave me a hug. "I'm so sorry, Dad. I'm so sorry I got involved in this. I just didn't want any of you to get hurt, and that's what they told me would happen. The guy you arrested, Caracortada, was just one of them. They said if I ever talked, they'd come after you and the family. I couldn't let that happen. I didn't want anyone to get hurt."

Brian sniffled and wiped his nose on his sleeve. Suddenly I found myself crying as well.

"It's okay, son. You just made a mistake. We all do it. I admire you for being worried about your family." Then I really started to cry. I couldn't speak. I put my head into my hands and just started to sob. I couldn't help myself. This was my little boy. I taught him how to ride a bike. I helped him with his first math homework. And now I was about to lose him. For a long, long time.

I felt his arm across my shoulder, trying to comfort me. Then I heard Brian say, "It's gonna be all right, Dad. Really."

I sat up straight and wiped my face. I'd come here to support my son, and now he was the one helping me. I turned to him and said, "I love you, Brian. You'll never know how much I love you."

"I love you, too, Dad."

Then the door opened and two uniformed corrections officers took my son away from me. I watched silently as he was led back to the main cell block.

At the end of the long hallway I saw the steel-bar door slam behind him. The sound echoed in my ears.

PART TWO

PART TWO

CHAPTER 34

I COULDN'T HELP but feel that winter was darker and lasted longer than usual. Now, as summer approached, our lives seemed to be getting back to normal. Despite Seamus's objections, we'd moved him to our apartment a few blocks from his quarters at the Holy Name rectory.

He had fussed that he didn't want to be any trouble. Then the old priest said that he didn't want his great-grandchildren to look at him like he was an invalid. Finally, Mary Catherine talked to him quietly, as if he were a horse she was calming down. After she reasoned with the old coot for several minutes, he decided to take up residence in the downstairs bedroom.

Mary Catherine and I discussed getting away from the city for a few weeks. The kids needed a change of pace, and I needed some time. Time to think about what I wanted to do with the rest of my life. Maybe it was my philosophy degree working on my attitude, but I was starting to think there was more to life than police work.

Going through the criminal justice system on the other side had opened my eyes. Maybe I could do just as much good for society in a different position. I didn't know, but I was keeping my options open.

Mary Catherine quickly warmed to the idea of a vacation, and a call from an old friend working as a cop in Maine gave me an idea. One evening I was on the phone, and Mary Catherine heard me say, "Really? The house is right on the lake? In moose country?"

Before I hung up, Mary Catherine said, "Where? Where is there a house like that?"

"Maine."

"I've never been to Maine."

"You've never been to Pennsylvania, either. That's hardly a recommendation for a place to spend three weeks away from home."

Mary Catherine asked, "Who was telling you about the house?"

"An old NYPD buddy who works in a town not far from Bangor." I thought about it for a moment and added, "I guess every town in Maine is not too far from Bangor."

Mary Catherine said, "Do you think Seamus is able to travel?"

From the couch in the living room, Seamus called out, "I can travel anywhere you can travel."

I smiled and said, "At least we know his hearing is still in pretty good shape."

Seamus's shout from the couch attracted some of the kids the way a dead fish in the water attracts sharks. They circled us, and Eddie said, "Are we going somewhere?"

I smiled and patted my teenage mathlete on the head. He was a constant stream of motion and didn't even stop when he asked this question. He just motored on into the living room to keep his great-grandfather company.

Chrissy shouted, "Can we go to Disney?"

Fiona said, "Yellowstone." And was immediately seconded by her twin, Bridget.

I listened to the input. Even my quiet one, Jane, suggested Philadelphia for all its historical sites. Of course Ricky suggested New Orleans because his newest interest in cooking was Cajun food. It was also the home of his hero, Emeril Lagasse.

Mary Catherine gave me a quick sly smile and shouted, "Let's go to Maine." Then she jumped up and down, and her excitement was contagious. Soon she'd convinced the younger kids that Maine would give them the greatest adventure ever. They even chanted, "Maine, Maine."

The Bennett family was going on a vacation.

CHAPTER 35

IT WASN'T WHAT you'd call directly on the way to Maine, but we all agreed we wanted to visit Brian now that he'd been assigned his permanent home at a prison.

I had kept visiting Brian at Rikers right up until he was transferred to the Gowanda Correctional Facility, in the extreme western part of New York State, around thirty miles south of Buffalo. As far as prisons go, it was about the best I could hope for. The state had a youthful-offender program, and Brian was able to call home a couple of times a week.

As we pulled down the long entrance road, the sight of the thick chain-link fence topped by spools and spools of razor wire was jarring to the senses.

Chrissy said, "Why is all that funny-looking wire on top of the fence?"

Before I could answer, Jane said, "They don't want birds sitting on the fence and pooping everywhere."

I looked up in the mirror to catch Jane's attention and gave her a smile and a wink.

Ricky said, "I wonder how they feed everyone."

From the front seat, which I had rigged especially for him, Seamus said, "Poorly. The people who cook here have nothing close to the commitment you bring to the kitchen, Ricky."

That made the young man smile.

As everyone filed out of the van, Shawna said, "Look." She pointed at a single window on the first floor of the administration building.

A lone figure stared out through the metal bars.

Shawna said, "It's Brian."

Everyone turned quickly, and before I could ask how she knew it was her brother, the figure in the window waved.

We had to visit in shifts of three. I had already called the prison and asked about the policy. They worked with me and asked us to come on a day that was not a scheduled visiting day. That's how Brian knew we were coming and was able to wait for us at the administration building.

The final group to visit was just Mary Catherine, Seamus, and me, although I had actually sat in on all the visits. The corrections officers seemed impressed that we had such a large family and that all the kids were committed to seeing their brother. We were the only visitors that day.

It was a standard visiting room at a large, medium-security correctional facility. There were three separate visiting stations, and we were kept apart by a counter built on top of a low wall, as well as a glass partition. A corrections officer stood directly behind the inmates' area. The partitions on each side made it feel like a booth.

Seamus had been almost bursting with excitement at the prospect of seeing his great-grandson. He dominated the conversation as he listened to the activities Brian was involved in, which included finishing high school.

The old man said, "Just keep your head up and do what's right."

"I'll try, Gramps."

Seamus got a little agitated and said, "You've got to do better than try, Brian. You've got to *be* the better man. No matter what happens, rise above it."

Brian was very solemn when he said, "Yes, sir."

Seamus said, "Make use of the chapel. Tell the chaplain that your great-grandfather is a priest in the city. Tell him to call me at Holy Name. He'll do it as a matter of professional courtesy. I want him to know what a great kid you are."

Brian smiled and said, "Thanks, Gramps."

We finished up, and there were tearful good-byes all around. I felt like I needed to help Seamus when he was slow to get up from the chair. Mary Catherine and I led him down the long, unremarkable hallway. I turned back one last time to see Brian standing behind the wide counter, waving to us.

It felt like I had a hole in my heart.

CHAPTER 36

IT WAS LATE in the afternoon by the time we all piled into the van. With three large suitcases strapped on the luggage rack on the roof, we had a little bit of a *Beverly Hillbillies* vibe heading east on I-90.

I polled the audience, and the overwhelming response was that we drive straight through to Maine and our new home away from home.

Mary Catherine caught the look of concern on my face as I calculated the twelve or so hours between now and arrival. She leaned over and said, "I'll help. It'll be fun."

And so we were off on our adventure to the town of Linewiler, Maine.

The crowd wanted a ghost story, and all I could think of was "The Legend of Sleepy Hollow." The story of Ichabod Crane was enough to scare some of the younger kids. I tried not to be too dramatic in my retelling, but Mary Catherine put her hand on my shoulder and said, "Maybe we should try another story."

Trent said, "But it's got to be a ghost story. Something scary."

Eddie chimed in, "Yeah, Dad. Not a short story we read in second grade."

Fiona said, "Hey, we're reading it now. In eighth grade!"

Eddie kept his smug smile as he said, "We all move at our own pace, Fiona. I'm sure everything will turn out fine for you."

It was hard for me to suppress a smile. I love the interplay between brothers and sisters. God knows I provided enough brothers and sisters for that to happen.

Then it was Seamus who started a story. I was a little surprised, but I appreciated his Irish accent and serious tone as he shifted in the front seat to look back at the faces of his great-grandchildren.

He said, "It started a long time ago. Way before any of you were born." He looked directly at Mary Catherine and said, "Even before you were born."

He had the kids' complete and undivided attention.

"I was called from the church in New York down to Washington, DC, where strange events were occurring around a little girl." He searched everyone's faces to make sure they were paying attention, then snuck a quick glance at mine.

"The girl's mother was a famous actress, and no one had been able to tell her why the girl was acting so strangely. Not doctors, not psychiatrists, not neurosurgeons."

Finally I had to interrupt him. "Seamus, are you trying to

pass off the plot of *The Exorcist* as something that happened to you?"

The old man just shrugged, like he'd been caught stealing a cookie. "I doubt they've ever heard it before."

Once it had turned dark and we had grabbed a quick bite to eat, everyone started dozing off in the van. Seamus was one of the first to fall asleep—and his slumber might have been the most obvious. His head rested on the back of the reclined front seat, and his mouth dropped open. At least his wheezing snore assured me that he was alive during the trip.

By eleven o'clock, I was the only one still awake in the van. Mary Catherine sat on the first bench seat with Chrissy's head in her lap and Fiona's on her shoulder. It was a perfect picture of three pretty girls, even if all three of them had snoring issues of their own.

The trip felt longer than I anticipated, even though we were on the final leg. I had to stop in Portsmouth, New Hampshire, just to stretch my legs and grab a quick cup of coffee. As I tried to quietly slip out of the van, Mary Catherine popped awake and crawled across my seat to join me.

She said, "I dozed off for just a moment. I hope you don't mind."

I chuckled, thinking about the four-hour nap that lasted "just a moment."

We sat and chatted for a few minutes over coffee and a doughnut. I hadn't seen her so excited about something in a long time. She really needed to be out of the city.

She was still awake and taking in the scenery as we passed through the town of Linewiler. The sun was just coming up, and pine trees lined the road on both sides as far as the eye could see. The lush greens and blues of the lakes interspersed through the forests were like an anti–New York City poster. It was beautiful.

I saw the mailbox on the main road and made the turn to our rented house. It was an old Victorian home, and it sat right on the edge of a lake that had three different streams flowing into it.

It didn't take long for the first kid to stir and start to wake the others.

From the back of the van Ricky said, "It looks like a haunted house."

Bridget said, "We should name it."

Mary Catherine had the perfect name: Mildew Manor.

CHAPTER 37

FOR A CHANGE, everyone chipped in on the effort to unload the car and get us settled into the house. I realized that part of it had to do with each kid wanting to claim a particular bedroom. But this was not a Manhattan apartment. This was a real live house that had an incredible six bedrooms plus a foldout couch in the living room.

I stepped out onto the front porch with Mary Catherine and draped my arm around her shoulder to pull her close. We just stared out across the beautiful lake. The only other houses were almost a mile away on the other side. White pines and candlewood pines lined the lake, making an almost impenetrable wall of forest. It was spectacular.

Eddie stepped out onto the porch, followed by the other kids. He held a laminated sheet he'd found in the kitchen containing facts about the house.

My brainiac, who was normally subdued, couldn't hide his excitement. "The house was built in 1904 and includes a full acre on the lake."

Chrissy asked, "What's the lake's name?"

Eddie hesitated with the pronunciation, then gave it his best shot. "Lake Nimicadiota." He paused for a moment and added, "It means 'Fish Lake' in some Native American language. But no one knows exactly who named it."

Seamus said, "We'll call it Lake Nim."

Mary Catherine looked at Eddie and said, "Does that paper give us any other facts about the lake?"

"There are three separate streams that feed the lake, and in the summer it rises from the melting snow in the foothills. All three streams have trout, and the lake itself has an abundance of bass and other freshwater fish."

I smiled at the way he so carefully read the information off the page.

Ricky jumped up and down and said, "Trout—that's great."

It was good to see Ricky take an interest in something other than cooking.

Then the young man said, "You can sauté trout in olive oil, and it's supposed to be phenomenal."

Seamus said, "You can pan-fry or deep-fry them, too."

Now Trent stepped in. "You like to fish, Gramps?"

"Back home—I mean in the old country—I fed my family many a time with my skill at fishing. We would stand in the icy waters of the streams coming down from the hills, and I could fill my bucket with fish."

I had to say, "I thought your dad was a baker. Didn't *he* feed the family many a time?"

Seamus just gave me a sharp look. Then he said, "We all had to feed the family."

Mary Catherine stepped into the brawl. "I fished back in Ireland, too."

Shawna said, "Did you have to feed your family?"

"No, darling. But we used to camp, and I liked to fish. In fact, I could fish your Gramps under the table."

CHAPTER 38

IT WAS LIKE a duel in eighteenth-century France. The fishing contest was on. Old Irish against young Irish. It couldn't have been more exciting if one of them had slapped the other across the face with white gloves.

I couldn't believe how quickly the kids got ready and found all manner of fishing rods in the garage. They each set about a task. Fiona grabbed some bread from the pantry. Ricky and Eddie dug for worms at the edge of an overgrown garden. And I checked the structural integrity of the dock, which ran from the shoreline more than seventy-five feet into the water, where it opened onto a wide platform.

The family divided into two factions. Those who wanted to see if Seamus was telling another of his tall tales and those who wanted to see what Mary Catherine was bragging about. It was fun from everyone's perspective.

Out on the dock, I was impressed with the way Seamus handled the rod. He pulled in two decent bass before I had the first bite on my line. Then he started explaining to Ricky the subtle nuances of casting and reeling the worm in slowly.

Then Trent hooked something that made his reel whine as it swam out to deeper water. Trent put on an odd accent and said, "That's a big fish."

Eddie immediately said, "Aye, that's a twenty-footer."

Trent came back with, "Twenty-five. Three tons of him."

I laughed out loud when I realized my sons were doing a scene from *Jaws*. I smiled as the boys worked the line until whatever they were pulling in broke free.

Then I heard a shout from the shoreline. My natural instinct as a father made me race down the dock toward shore. As I leaped onto solid ground, I saw Juliana up to her knees in the cold water and Mary Catherine standing on the shore.

Just as I skidded to a stop, I realized they were helping a squealing Chrissy pull in what appeared to be the winning fish. She tried turning the handle of the small kids' reel as the rod bent nearly in half under the weight of the fish.

Mary Catherine gently coaxed Chrissy to walk backward and helped her with the rod. Ultimately it was Mary Catherine who pulled the giant lunker onto shore.

It was a catfish unlike any I had ever seen. It had to be six inches across at its head and almost two feet long.

Chrissy looked down at the fish and said, "We aren't going to eat that, are we?"

By now Seamus had walked up, and he chuckled as he said, "Of course we are. Catfish is even tastier than cat."

Chrissy was suitably horrified, while the rest of us laughed in the warm sunshine.

These were the days I lived for.

CHAPTER 39

OUR FIRST DINNER at Mildew Manor looked like a feast from a medieval lord's castle. We pushed two tables together and covered them with a long tablecloth. On top were baskets of bread, a platter piled high with roasted corn on the cob, and plates heaped with trout, bass, and, of course, catfish.

I was impressed with Ricky's ability to cook the three kinds of fish in different ways. He sautéed the trout, fried the catfish, and baked the bass. It was a wonder to behold, and he never looked happier.

As we sat down, a couple of the kids looked ready to pounce on the bounty we had placed on the table. But the sight of my grandfather at the end of the table as he cleared his throat froze everyone in place.

He bowed his head, and everyone followed his example. In what we liked to call his prayer voice—a serious and solemn tone he rarely used in other situations—Seamus said, "Dear Lord, thank you for allowing us to all be here together and experience the wonders of nature and the beauty of this land. And thank you most of all for giving each of us the ability and insight to realize what a great day this was and how important each of us is to the family. And, dear Lord, please protect our sweet Brian as he works to overcome the obstacles placed before him. Amen."

In unison, the entire table followed with "Amen."

The trout went first, then the bass. I noticed a hesitation among the kids to try the breaded catfish. It wasn't the typical entrée served on the Upper West Side of Manhattan.

I winked at Seamus, who immediately understood what I wanted to do. We both reached for a piece of catfish and then pretended to fight over it. That drew the attention of the kids, and before I knew it, all the pieces of fried catfish were being devoured. It was such a big hit that I wondered where I would be able to buy catfish in the city when we got back.

As the meal wound down and we looked out over the lake and the setting sun, I knew I had to treasure these moments with my family. How many times had I let something like this slip past me because I was focused on work?

As amazing as the whole day had been, I couldn't help but think how much better it would have been if Brian had been able to join us.

I thought back on my grandfather's prayer. I needed to have the insight to appreciate how great a day like this could be. I also felt a touch of sadness at how rarely days like this happened.

CHAPTER 40

AS DARKNESS CLOSED in on Mildew Manor, I realized I was exhausted. I had only grabbed a couple of hours' sleep since we'd left the city and visited Brian.

Now I found myself strolling hand in hand with Mary Catherine around the edge of the lake. This was anything but tiring. We walked at a leisurely pace, and I enjoyed hearing the sounds of the forest at night. Sometimes I forgot that, growing up in a place like New York City, I didn't have a chance to hear those sounds on a regular basis.

We walked about a quarter of the way around the lake on a path made of pine needles and maple leaves that had been blown toward the lake from deeper in the forest.

I turned and looked back at the house, which was now about half a mile away. The ghost stories must've had an effect, because every light in the house was on.

We stopped at a little clearing and, like magic, Mary Catherine pulled a blanket from the big bag she seemed to carry everywhere.

I said, "What all do you have in there?"

She smiled and said, "Anything you ever need. Haven't you noticed?"

"I notice everything."

"Have you also noticed that we haven't had any alone time for quite a while?" She reached up on her tiptoes and kissed me on the lips.

I said, "I'm sorry. It's been a rough time lately."

"I'm not complaining, just commenting."

I took her in my arms and said, "Comment on this." I kissed her. I couldn't have loved her any more. I started to speak, but she put her finger to my lips.

She smiled and said, "I don't need you to talk. I just need you to look pretty."

Somehow I found my second wind and wasn't nearly as exhausted as I thought.

CHAPTER 41

WHEN I WOKE up the next morning in the king-size bed, I didn't want to admit that my back was a little sore from making love on the blanket by the lake. It was never a good idea to admit something like that to your younger girlfriend.

As I stood in the kitchen, secretly stretching out my back and legs, I heard a car pull into the front yard.

Mary Catherine looked up from her coffee at the kitchen table. "Are you expecting any visitors?"

Before I could answer, I heard Shawna open the front door, and I heard a woman's voice. I knew exactly who it was.

Mary Catherine followed me into the living room to greet our guest, who was still standing in the doorway, chatting with Shawna.

Sandy Coles turned her attention to me and said, "She doesn't remember me at all."

I stepped across the living room and gave my former partner from the Forty-Ninth Precinct a hug.

I said, "She was barely a toddler when you fled the city." I stepped back and was amazed that this pretty, hard-nosed cop, who stood almost six feet tall, hadn't seemed to age at all in the past eight years. I couldn't help but say, "You look amazing."

Then Mary Catherine cleared her throat.

I jumped to it and introduced them. I didn't even stumble over the word *girlfriend* when I introduced Mary Catherine. I said, "Sandy is the one who found the house for us."

Mary Catherine said, "So this is your old NYPD buddy?"

Sandy said, "Back in the Forty-Ninth, Mike and the other guys in the squad always treated me as an equal. Unfortunately, that meant I had to put up with all their juvenile jokes. We've been buddies ever since."

I appreciated that she had the sense to realize the pickle I was in. She rescued me further by saying in a grave tone, "Mike, I could really use your help."

I saw the pained look on Mary Catherine's face. She was afraid she was going to lose me to some new investigation.

Sandy said, "The town is going to be mobbed for the Fourth of July parade. We have three of our officers out with the flu and two others on vacation. We could really use some help keeping the crowds in check and making sure no one does anything stupid."

"All you need me for is crowd control?"

"That's it, Detective. Are you too good for it anymore?"

I could read the relief on Mary Catherine's face. But I still waited until she gave me a little nod of her head.

Sandy said, "It'll earn this beautiful family of yours seats in the reviewing stand right in the center of town."

I said, "I'm sure I could handle just about anything that walks in your town. Except maybe an errant moose."

Sandy laughed and said, "That'd be funnier if I hadn't had to chase off more than my share of moose over the years."

It was awfully good to see her again.

CHAPTER 42

ON THE FOURTH of July, all the kids could talk about was the parade. They had been to all kinds of parades in the city. Parades for the Yankees, gay pride parades, parades celebrating every possible nationality, and, of course, the obligatory Saint Patrick's Day parade. Seamus was generally in charge of getting everyone excited about that.

Today I was already arguing with the old man about whether he would use a wheelchair.

He said, "I don't need a wheelchair. I can walk as well as anyone."

"But Seamus, we don't know what the crowds are going to be like. It may get hot by the time the parade gets going. It just makes good sense for you to make use of the wheelchair we toted along."

"It also makes sense for me to get some exercise."

Jane stepped up next to her great-grandfather and said, "What if I promise to stay right next to him the whole day?" She looped her arm through his, and the old man beamed.

I couldn't say no to that. It was one of the sweetest gestures I'd ever seen one of the kids make toward their great-grandfather.

As we were about to leave the house, the wheelchair was in its normal place by the front door, but Seamus had something else in his hand.

I blurted out, "What the hell?"

He held up the black top hat and smiled. Then he slipped it on his white head. "Quite dashing, don't you think?"

"If you're the guy from Monopoly."

"The brim will keep the sun off my face, and if we're in the reviewing stand people might think I'm in charge."

"Well, there's no arguing with that logic." It was all I could do to usher my grandfather to the van and pacify the kids who were already in their seats, ready to go.

After I got the family settled in the comfortable reviewing stand, I swung by the police staging area, and Sandy gave me a vest to put over my shirt that said PARADE MARSHAL. My only real connection to the police, though, was the portable radio she gave me. My job was simply to keep people from wandering into the street, and if I saw something serious, I was to get on the radio.

I started my job as a volunteer for the Linewiler Police Department. Sandy had recruited several others. Two were retired cops living in town, and one was an off-duty firefighter. I imagined it was hard for most men to say no to her.

I tried to enjoy the parade, watching the homemade floats

and listening to the bands as they marched by. The theme, of course, was the pioneer spirit of Maine and national pride. More than one float looked like it had a papier-mâché Paul Bunyan on it. When I asked, I was told it was just a woodsman. Of course Paul Bunyan was not from Maine.

I stuck fairly close to the reviewing stand and noticed how many people came up to introduce themselves to my family. It took some people a few seconds to realize that all the kids were in one family. Looking at it from their perspective, I could see why they might be a little confused. But this was the new millennium, and kids were being adopted by an increasing number of families in the United States.

The other thing I noticed was how well the local cops were treated by the people from the town. It was nothing like New York, where the cops had to be on edge and in survival mode almost all the time. The townspeople were calling the cops by their first names and slapping them on the back.

New millennium or not, that was something I wasn't used to.

CHAPTER 43

AFTER THE PARADE, everyone headed to the historic firehouse on the north side of town. It was easy to find because the parade ended directly in front of it.

Sandy had stepped into the reviewing stand and sat next to Mary Catherine. I saw them whispering and giggling, then Mary Catherine told me the entire family was going to a clambake at the firehouse.

We walked, as a family, almost half a mile to the firehouse. Seamus was given a ride in a golf cart by a heavyset Kiwanis Club member. With his top hat on and riding in the comfort of an electric cart, he really did look like a parade official.

I noted that every storefront was filled and businesses seemed to be prospering in the small town. They had three separate schools: an elementary school, a middle school, and a high school. And it didn't take long to hear people boast about the high test scores and the number of kids who went on to college.

I sat on a picnic bench with Seamus safely tucked in next to me. I was keeping a close eye on my grandfather, but aside from looking a little tired, he seemed okay.

I lost track of some of the kids, but mainly it was because they had gone off to play various games. Trent was playing baseball at a diamond across the street. Bridget and Fiona were playing a kind of hide-and-seek game with some local girls. Even Eddie and Ricky were playing soccer in the open field next to the firehouse.

Somehow the atmosphere had gotten me to drop my usual guard-dog attitude toward the kids. Is this what the real world looks like? Is this what normal feels like? It sure seemed nice. Friendly people, comfortable atmosphere. A guy could get used to this.

I looked over at Mary Catherine as she tried some clams coming right off the grill. She laughed at something a woman said, and I realized this was the best possible place we could've come for vacation.

Maybe this could be more than just a vacation spot. If a tough cop like Sandy could find her work rewarding in a little town like this, why couldn't I?

The idea intrigued me so much that I even started to worry about the one sticking point. What would happen to Seamus? Would he be able to transfer to a church up here? We couldn't just leave him in the city with none of his great-grandchildren close by. Who would listen to his wild stories?

Then there was Brian. I had no idea what would happen to

him. But maybe Maine would be a good place for him to get a fresh start when he got out of prison.

Sandy walked over and said, "Your family seems to be enjoying themselves."

"You were right, Sandy. This place is perfect."

"Almost. We do have problems, just like everywhere."

"Like what?"

"Heroin use is up. Way up. It's cheap, and there are a dozen dealers with connections in the city. But it's nothing a big-city cop like you couldn't handle. That is, if you had a mind to help."

"This place has a drug issue?"

"Every place has some kind of drug issue."

She gave me a lot to think about.

CHAPTER 44

MARY CATHERINE JOINED me at the picnic table, bringing a plate of clams and two bags of potato chips.

With a broad smile she said, "Isn't this wonderful?"

Seamus muttered, "I think it would get boring after a while. It's a nice vacation, but that's it."

I looked at her and said, "The kids seem to love it."

Mary Catherine said, "Everyone is so friendly. I've already met half a dozen women who want me to join one club or another. I keep having to explain that we're just visiting."

Sandy sat on the bench directly across from me. Her blue eyes found mine, and she reached across and took hold of my hands. She said, "I'm so glad you guys came."

I caught the look Mary Catherine slipped me. What did she want me to do? Jerk my hands out of Sandy's? Instead we both listened as Sandy said, "You could probably lease the house you're staying in year-round, if you're interested."

Mary Catherine snaked her arm around my shoulders and gave me a hug. "It's certainly nice here, and people are friendly. Maybe too friendly."

The dig went right over Sandy's head as she looked me in the eye and said, "It's time you get that family out of New York. They can always move back when they're adults if they miss it that much. They should at least have a chance at a normal childhood."

I said, "I was raised in New York, and my childhood was normal."

"That's what every New Yorker says." She winked at me.

I noticed a young lady slowly making her way across the firehouse yard to a table not far away. She dragged her right foot as she walked, and when she sat down I noticed that the right side of her face seemed to sag slightly.

She sat by herself as various people brought her plates of food and drink.

I asked Sandy who the girl was.

She said, "It's a little bit of a sad story. Her name is Sadie, and her mom passed away last year."

Mary Catherine said, "Who takes care of her?"

"The whole town. Technically she lives in a group home, but really she's as close to homeless as we have here in Linewiler. She likes to be off on her own. No one really knows where she sleeps a lot of the time."

I watched the teenager as she nodded her thanks to the people who brought her food and drink. She had dark stringy hair but a beautiful smile and a pretty face. I wondered how someone ended up in her situation. Where was her father? I don't know why, but this young woman intrigued me. She could've been one of my daughters. The idea of them being alone and fending for themselves sent a chill through me.

CHAPTER 45

LATER THAT NIGHT, Mary Catherine asked me on another walk around the lake. After what had happened the last time we walked, I couldn't refuse, no matter how tired I was.

I was still smiling about how much fun the kids had at the cookout. Even Seamus had begun to enjoy himself.

As we walked down the path, with the water on our left, Mary Catherine hooked her arm through mine. She laid her head on my shoulder as we walked and said, "I could definitely get used to life in the country." After a few more steps, she said, "Maybe not in the winter. I imagine that the snow here comes up to your chin."

I chuckled and said, "Maybe *your* chin."

We sat on the blanket she pulled from her miraculous bag and stared out at the calm water. Once again, I could see the house from where we were and felt relieved that every light was on. At least I knew where the kids were.

We chatted about nothing for a few minutes, then Mary Catherine worked in a bombshell of a question very casually. "I see the way Sandy and you talk and the way she looks at you. Did you guys ever date each other?"

She looked me right in the eye. I'd been hoping that this would never come up. It was really a nonissue. But I answered honestly.

"I don't know if *date* is the right word. We had a minor little nothing a thousand years ago. We never took it very far and have never talked about it since."

"You agree that she's still beautiful."

This sounded like a trap. I wasn't sure how to respond. "I guess she's pretty. But she doesn't hold a candle to you."

Mary Catherine smiled and said, "I appreciate that, but I don't want you to think I'm falling for an old line like that."

"A guy has got to try."

My cell phone rang. Actually, it played the theme to the movie *Shaft*, a tune that Ricky had installed on my phone. I glanced at the screen casually and saw that it was Sandy Coles. Mary Catherine saw it, too.

I looked at her and said, "Why do I feel I definitely should not answer this call?"

CHAPTER 46

I TOOK NO chances after Mary Catherine's question and immediately put the phone on speaker. I didn't even give the customary warning to the caller that I had done so. I wasn't worried.

"Hello, Sandy. What's going on?"

"Hey, Mike. I'm sorry to bother you at this hour, but I was wondering if I could impose on you again. I need another favor. A police favor."

I was silent for a moment and looked at Mary Catherine, who was shaking her head emphatically. I couldn't pretend to misinterpret that signal.

Then Sandy said over the phone's speaker, "You can say no, Michael. No one expects you to give up your vacation."

I winced when I heard her call me Michael. Only Mary Catherine called me Michael now. Occasionally Seamus did, when he wasn't calling me a jackass or an imbecile. Both were terms of endearment for him.

Sandy said, "This really is important. Not just crowd control at a parade."

"What do you got?"

"A couple of missing teenagers. I mean really missing. Disappeared from the local hangout and left their car running. There's a patrol officer over there now, and she says she needs as much help as we can send."

I was silent for a few more moments.

Then Sandy said, "These aren't criminals, Michael. These are decent local kids. Both of them are supposed to go to college in a couple of months. I'm really worried."

I could hear the strain in her voice. I knew what looking for a missing kid could do to a good cop. Failing on a job like that was worse than not finding a killer. At least psychologically.

I looked over at Mary Catherine, who whispered, "So go. Go save the state of Maine, Michael. Go save the world for all I care."

Mary Catherine wasn't happy, but I knew that she understood the issue.

I said in a clear voice into the phone, "When can you pick me up?"

Sandy said, "I'm parked in your driveway now."

CHAPTER 47

THE SPOT SANDY was talking about was up in the hills on the other side of town. It looked like what I imagined lovers' lanes looked like across the country. In New York City, we had other places to take our girl-friends, like the rear seats of theaters or Central Park. Nothing as isolated as this. I could understand its attraction for kids. For one thing, you could see a vehicle coming up the winding road for ten minutes before it got there.

It was a wide space just off the road, intended to be a scenic overlook. Instead kids could park here at night without too much fear of getting in trouble.

We found the young patrol officer standing by a new Dodge Challenger. It was sporty with wide tires and looked more like something a middle-aged man who missed the muscle cars of his youth would drive.

The officer, a tall, athletic-looking young woman with straight brown hair tied in a ponytail, was all business as we approached.

"Someone called in about an hour ago because the Challenger was sitting here running with no one in it. I ran the plate, and it comes back to Tom Bacon."

Sandy said, "The contractor?"

"Yes, ma'am. I haven't called the house yet. I thought it best that we check the area. I think they might've walked up the path across the street higher into the hills."

I looked into the dark woods and decided I was happier stepping away from the overlook. My fear of heights became more acute the closer I stood to the edge. But with the railing and a couple of cars around, it didn't bother me too much.

Sandy looked at me and said, "You up for a little hike through the woods?"

I just nodded, relieved to be backing away from the precipice.

Sandy gave me a Windbreaker that said POLICE on the back. She handed me a big Kel-Lite, like the one I used to carry on patrol. It lit up the woods and can be used as a club if need be.

Sandy said, "You carrying an off-duty weapon?"

I patted my hip, where my small Glock 27 rested.

She raised her right hand and said, "Do you swear to uphold the law, blah, blah, blah?"

"Yes?"

Sandy smiled and said, "Good. You're now an authorized reserve officer with the Linewiler Police Department. Your powers will lapse after one year."

I just stared at her.

She slapped me on the shoulder and said, "It's good to have you as a partner again. Now, let's go find us a couple of missing teenagers."

CHAPTER 48

I WASN'T MUCH of a woodsman. That's not one of the skills you develop when living in a big city. I could figure out what subway someone had taken and what neighborhoods to avoid, but tromping along a narrow trail surrounded by woods was not my usual preference.

Sandy, on the other hand, was raised in New Jersey and used to play in the Pine Barrens. She constantly reminded us what we were missing when we all worked together in the Bronx.

Now I understood what she was talking about. She noticed a freshly broken branch along the trail and pointed out that someone had been through there in the last couple of hours. She also was able to identify where someone had stepped by looking at the disturbed leaves lying on the ground. It was an impressive skill that I wouldn't have believed unless I had seen it myself.

Occasionally we would stop on the trail and scan the woods with our flashlights. Once I picked up the eyes of an animal. Two red glowing dots in the distance.

I mumbled, "What the hell is that?"

Sandy matter-of-factly said, "It might be a bear. But it's probably just a fox or a badger."

I swung the light back that way to judge how far the eyes were off the ground, but I couldn't find it again. That did not make me feel more confident in any way.

As we continued I kept hearing a rustling sound and had the distinct impression that we were being watched. I moved closer to Sandy and whispered my suspicion.

She was a pro and barely broke stride, but she turned her head to get a good view behind us. She said, "Maybe, but I don't care right now. We gotta find these kids."

It was unnerving, and I dropped behind a little. I turned once, quickly, and swept the light to the side of the trail. I caught a glimpse of something. I didn't know what. Maybe a bright color. I hurried to catch up to Sandy.

I could feel the trail continue to rise as we marched along, finding signs every few hundred feet that someone had been there before us. I didn't want to admit to Sandy that the woods were freaking me out a little bit. Maybe I had imagined being watched. I reached back and felt the weight of my pistol on my hip. When I do that in New York City, it gives me a feeling of security. In Maine, the idea of shooting a charging bear with my small pistol gave me a feeling of powerlessness.

Finally we stepped out into a wide clearing that gave us a beautiful view of the valley below us. We emerged from the woods onto the rocky flat that extended more than fifty feet.

Sandy walked right to the edge. She motioned me over. I knew it was a drop-off, and I wasn't thrilled about getting too close. Finally she looked over her shoulder and said, "Come on, you little girl. Take a look at this."

I crept closer to the edge and could see it was a sheer cliff. Eventually I was able to stand next to Sandy and look straight down. I fought the urge to grab her arm to feel more stable. I always disliked heights, and this was just crazy. *Scary* wasn't the word that came to mind.

It felt like we were above the clouds, even though I knew it was just a little fog between us and the ground. I could just make out the stream below. Way below us.

Sandy said, "You don't think they could've ended up going over this cliff, do you?"

I took a step away from the edge and said, "Who knows? I've heard that the suicide rate has been climbing steadily."

Sandy said, "I know. The kids see something romantic in it. But not two of them at the same time. They wouldn't just step right over the edge."

She said it more as a hope than a fact.

I said, "Let's head back to the car. The woods are freaking me out."

As we started back down the trail, relief washed over me. I no longer felt like eyes were on us. I took the lead and followed the same trail down until I found a split. I didn't notice it on the way up.

"Let's look this way."

Sandy noticed some trampled brush and said, "Good spot, partner." Just as if I'd seen a suspect in a crowded bus station.

We followed the cutoff for fifty feet, then I froze.

On the ground in front of me was a green Nike athletic shoe.

The homicide detective in me kept me from picking it up. I inspected it where it was.

Sandy stepped around me and scanned the area. "Look here." She shone her light on the ground.

In the pine needles, I could just make out the outline of a spot where someone had lain on the forest floor. I hoped it hadn't been a dead body.

CHAPTER 49

SANDY BROUGHT IN some officers from the state police to help search the area for the missing teens. So far no media had shown up, but it was just a matter of time before they did.

The kids who called in the report told us who had been in the car. The driver was Thomas Bacon Jr., known in town as Tom-Tom. He was there with his girlfriend, Tricia, who was a star on the high school's track and lacrosse teams.

Even though it was quite late, we had to talk to the parents. The first place Sandy drove was the missing girl's house. Sandy didn't know her personally. She said a lot of houses outside the city limits fed the high school in town.

Tricia Green lived in a well-kept trailer park not far off US Route 2, west of the city. We pulled to a stop on the gravel in front of the trailer, and almost immediately the front door opened.

An attractive African American woman around forty was already calling outside. "Tricia, you're more than two hours past your curfew. That means you're grounded for the weekend, and I don't care…" She saw that she wasn't talking to her daughter.

The woman stared at us for a moment and saw that we were both wearing police Windbreakers. She gasped and put her hand to her mouth. "What's wrong? Is my baby all right?"

Sandy stepped forward quickly and said, "Mrs. Green, I'm Sandy Coles from the Linewiler Police Department. We don't know anything about your daughter. That's why we're here. We found Tom-Tom Bacon's car abandoned on Hillside Road, and someone said he was there with your daughter. Have you heard from her?"

The conversation went exactly like every conversation with a panicked parent goes. I just listened as we headed inside and sat on the vinyl sofa while Mrs. Green made us each a cup of coffee.

She was a lovely woman and clearly proud of her daughter. There were pictures of the beautiful lacrosse player all over the walls.

Mrs. Green caught me looking at the photos and said, "My Tricia has a track scholarship at Auburn and is going to play lacrosse at the club level."

Sandy said, "Auburn is a great school. You must be very proud."

Mrs. Green nodded.

Then Sandy carefully navigated the more sensitive questions. After the normal questions about the last time Tricia called and where she liked to hang out, Sandy said, "Has your daughter ever expressed any need to hurt herself?"

Mrs. Green took the question in the right way and said, "No. Never."

"And she has been seeing Tom-Tom for a while?"

"Since the beginning of the semester. He seems like a nice young man, and his family is certainly prominent."

"Have you ever suspected that your daughter or Tom-Tom uses any kind of drugs?"

That caught Mrs. Green by surprise, and she hesitated to answer. Finally she said, "Kids today are curious and try a lot of things. But you can't be an athlete at Tricia's level without taking care of yourself."

Sandy was masterly in the way she got more information, such as the name of Tricia's cell-phone carrier and other personal tidbits. Then she assured Mrs. Green that we were doing everything we could to find her daughter.

Sandy stood, and Mrs. Green followed us outside to the car. I knew what Sandy was doing and admired the way she had asked important questions before this most important aspect of the meeting.

Sandy reached into the car and brought out the shoe we had found. She showed it to Mrs. Green and said, "Is this Tricia's shoe?"

Mrs. Green gasped. Slowly she nodded. A tear welled up in her eye.

Sandy said, "It doesn't mean anything by itself, but I wanted to make sure we were on the right track. Give us some time, and we'll find the kids."

As we headed out of the trailer park, I noticed a small

figure leaning on the fence surrounding it. I realized it was the girl I had seen at the clambake. The homeless girl named Sadie.

She gave me a sharp salute.

I didn't know what to do except return it. I was rewarded with a pretty smile as we pulled onto the road. Then I noticed she was wearing a dress with a bright pattern on it. Maybe she got around faster than I thought.

CHAPTER 50

IT WAS THE middle of the night by the time we pulled up in front of Tom Bacon's house. It was a beautiful redbrick ranch house built directly on a lake, not far from the center of town.

Sandy had called ahead, and Mr. Bacon had the door open before we even pulled to a complete stop in his wide driveway, which led to a three-car garage. A Range Rover and a new F-150 pickup truck sat in the driveway.

Mr. Bacon was tall and carried extra weight around his midsection. He looked like the stereotype of a successful businessman. His red face hinted at how much he drank most nights, but he was stone cold sober as he approached us.

He gave no greeting, and his first words were, "Is someone going to take care of my son's car, or do I need to go up and get it?"

Sandy said, "Can we ask you a few questions first?"

The heavyset white man turned and signaled us to follow him into the house. I started to wonder if there might be some racial overtones to this disappearance. Many people mistakenly thought the majority of racially motivated crimes took place in the South. They didn't seem to take into account places like Boston, where resistance to school integration was as strong as anywhere in the country. There were still a number of hate crimes committed across the Northeast. I was hoping that wasn't the case here.

The house was quiet, and the only lights on were in the living room, at the front of the house. I caught a quick glimpse of a spectacular view through the windows at the rear.

Mr. Bacon said, "Let's try to keep it down if we can. I've got two other kids asleep upstairs, and they have school in the morning."

I noticed photos on the wall, just as there had been at Tricia Green's home. The difference was that almost every photo showed Mr. Bacon either holding a rifle and standing over a dead animal or holding up a giant dead fish on the back of a yacht. There was one photo of the whole family, and I saw that his wife was clearly a second wife and not that much older than Tom-Tom. The two younger boys were only three or four years old in the photo.

Now we had to ask some awkward questions about his first wife, including whether his son might want to travel to see her.

I wondered where else a kid like that might go. I forgot how hard a missing-persons case could be.

CHAPTER 51

THE MORE TOM Bacon spoke, the more I realized he was sort of a dick. He owned a prosperous construction company and lived with his *third* wife, not his second. He tended to look at me when he spoke, as though Sandy didn't matter. More than once, I redirected his attention to the real Maine cop in the room.

Bacon said, "I wouldn't worry too much about Tom-Tom. He'll show up. He and that skank from the trailer park are just off having a good time. Maybe he even went over to my ex-wife's house. She doesn't have the same rules I do."

Sandy said, "Rules about what?"

"Drugs, for one thing. She lets those kids do anything they want. That's how my daughter, Tom-Tom's sister, ended up pregnant when she was only sixteen. Now she and her little brat live with my ex-wife. I never would've let that shit happen here." Then he looked at me. "But you know how judges are during a divorce. The wife always gets everything."

Sandy said, "Are you saying that Tom-Tom and Tricia use drugs?"

"That's exactly what I'm saying. Can't you hear? Like all the kids now, they got interested in crazy shit. In my day, we used to smoke a little pot, but they're dead set against inhaling any smoke. That doesn't keep them from trying stronger shit like ecstasy or even heroin. That's the new rage. They all like the feeling smack gives them."

Sandy said, "But Tricia and your son were both on the school sports teams. Tricia played lacrosse, and they both ran track. How can you do that if you're using heroin?"

"They would time it. They don't use much during the season. But this time of year, no one's playing any sports. Tom-Tom works for me a couple of days a week, but he can dig ditches with his head clouded. I can't speak for what happens to that girl. I heard she's so fast she got a scholarship to some school down south."

I mumbled, "Auburn."

Bacon said, "Good. As long as it's far away from here."

I thought about everything Mr. Bacon had said. I couldn't believe they had a real heroin problem in the high school here. All I could think was, *Shit: heroin up here in moose country?*

CHAPTER 52

ON THE RIDE back to Mildew Manor, Sandy seemed distracted. After a long silence she said, "I guess our little town isn't as perfect as I wished. That had something to do with my calling you about the rental house."

I'd suspected as much. "If you have such a drug problem, why didn't you call in the state police or maybe even the DEA?"

"Because I wanted to have my former partner back me up. Someone I could trust. The house you guys are renting has been abandoned for the last four years. I know the real-estate company that bought it. After they fixed it up around Christmas and rented it for a few weekends, I persuaded them to give you a great rate during the summer. I'm sorry, but this was all orchestrated by me."

I didn't like being deceived, but on the other hand, I had to admit that Sandy had been brilliant in orchestrating our vacation. And it wasn't like the kids weren't enjoying themselves.

Sandy said, "The locals used to call your place the Ghost House because they would occasionally see lights floating around inside and hear strange noises. I think it's more likely that some homeless people were in there every once in a while."

I said, "The Ghost House. I like it. That's a name that'll scare the shit out of the kids."

Sandy laughed when she realized I wasn't angry about being manipulated. She pulled into the driveway but left the engine running. "The problems started a few years ago. A couple of people moved in from out of state, and all of a sudden we started getting slammed with heroin. What happened to the days of kids smoking a little pot?"

"I have a friend who runs a drug task force in the city. He was telling me that once they started concentrating on getting prescription painkillers off the market, heroin exploded. He says it's like trying to plug a leak in a dike. There just aren't enough resources to do everything."

Sandy let out a laugh and said, "I guess it doesn't matter how big your city is. Everyone's got the same problems." She leaned over and kissed me on the cheek. "Thanks, Mike. You're a lifesaver."

It was my hope that Mary Catherine hadn't looked out the window and seen that kiss. That little nothing.

PART THREE

CHAPTER 53

I TRIED NOT to think of the next day as a workday. I was still on vacation, after all. But that didn't change the fact that Sandy Coles picked me up in a police car precisely at nine so we could be on our way to interview some kind of local heroin dealer.

The Linewiler police had treated the area where we had found Tricia Green's shoe like it was a crime scene. But there was no information or leads on the missing kids, and Tom-Tom Bacon's father was no longer as nonchalant about his son's disappearance as he had been the previous night. He was yammering about calling a state senator so we could get more help.

That didn't change Sandy's attitude about the investigation in any way. She didn't care if the kids were rich or poor, just that they were in danger. It was sort of her role with the

Linewiler Police Department. Mostly detective, partly assistant chief, and always trying to help people. That's all anyone could ask of a cop.

And it didn't take much for me to agree to go with her. At least I felt like I might help out if things didn't go as planned with the dealer. There was no such thing as a rational and reasonable drug dealer if his back was against the wall. And they always believed their backs were against the wall.

The dealer's house was on a winding unpaved road in the foothills about five miles from town. For more than a quarter mile, I noticed abandoned cars and old appliances stacked up in some semblance of order. It looked like the place was a junkyard. Except there were woods all around it and no signs. From a police perspective it would be a nightmare to search.

Sandy caught me up on the dealer, Dell Streeter, as we approached the house.

"He moved into this place around four years ago. He came from somewhere along the border in Texas. He did seven years in a Texas state prison for manslaughter. That's why I needed you to come along."

I said, "What's he been like since he lived here?"

"He got in one fight in town. He punched a guy in a sports bar. Even though the guy had a shattered nose and a bunch of missing teeth, something scared him bad enough to prevent him from pressing charges. No matter how hard I pushed."

"This guy sounds like a sweetheart. And I love what he's done with the property."

Sandy pulled up to the gate closest to his driveway. I noticed there were two goons sitting on the porch. I guess they were protecting the rusting washer and dryer that stood to one side of the driveway. Or maybe they were worried someone would try to steal the gas stove that rotted right in the center of the front yard.

One of the goons, a muscle-bound redneck with tattoos running up his left arm, stepped inside the house. A moment later, a tall, lean man with a weather-beaten face came onto the porch. He had thinning blond hair and was around forty-five years old. He squinted at the car, then motioned for one of his men to open the gate.

He looked like a cowboy from a 1970s western. Not as dashing as the old-time cowboys, because he had a definite edge to him.

I took an instant dislike to him when we got out of the car and he said, "Howdy. You have ten seconds to state your business here."

I had to ask, "What happens after ten seconds?"

"Then somebody's ass is gonna get kicked."

I said, "If that's the way you want it. But I'm on the tired side, so if you want your ass kicked, you're going to have to come down to me."

It was gratifying to hear my partner laugh at one of my cracks.

I was glad I'd come along.

CHAPTER 54

SANDY DEFUSED THE situation quickly. She held up her badge and said, "Mr. Streeter, I'm Sandy Coles with the Linewiler Police Department. You remember me, don't you?"

He walked along the porch toward us, the hard heels of his cowboy boots making a loud knock against the wooden planks every time he took a step. "You're the one who tried to convince people I sucker punched that dude in the sports bar."

"I never said you sucker punched him. You hit him from behind without provocation."

"I had plenty of provocation. He said the Cowboys were the worst team in the NFC."

I noticed him look over his shoulder at his smirking goons. I guess I wasn't the only one who liked people to appreciate his jokes.

Sandy said, "I'm not looking to cause you any problems.

We're just trying to find a couple of missing teenagers. Tom-Tom Bacon and Tricia Green. Someone said they might've stopped by here."

"You mean the kid with the Challenger?"

"That's right."

"Never seen him before." That made his goons laugh out loud.

Now I stepped closer to the porch. I'd had enough of this shit kicker's attitude. "Why don't you save the Clint Eastwood bullshit for someone who cares? We're just here looking for the kids."

Streeter said, "Just who in the hell are you?"

"Michael Bennett, NYPD."

"Would you looky here? We got us a real big-city cop. Well, Mr. NYPD, in case you haven't noticed, you're not in the city anymore. And if you don't watch your manners, you can earn yourself an ass kicking. And we'll be happy to step down there to deliver it."

Streeter took a step and dropped two feet down off the porch to the ground. Both his men took the stairs by the front door and backed him up. He looked over at Sandy and said, "That goes for you, too, Detective Coles. Last I checked, this house wasn't in your jurisdiction. You got no warrant. And you're on my property."

That's when I punched him in the face.

CHAPTER 55

I'LL GIVE DELL Streeter credit. He took a good shot in the face and stayed on his feet. At least for a second. Then he dropped down to sit hard on the ground. Neither of the men behind him knew what to do. They started to help him up, but he shoved them away.

Once he was on his feet again, he looked at me and said, "I'll give you that one. I didn't expect it, and you've got a pretty good punch. But I've got a good memory, and you're not someone I'm gonna forget."

Sandy urged me back in the car, no matter how badly I wanted to smack this guy again. Once we were through the gate and back on the long, curving road, she said, "I don't see how that was helpful, Mike. We could use his help, not his anger."

"Sandy, you know as well as I do that guys like that are

never going to help the cops. They only understand one thing. At least the next time he might show us a little more respect. Besides, I don't think I can get fired from this job."

"I'm just so frustrated. That asshole knows something. We're going to have to talk to him again soon." Just as we rounded a wide curve around a massive mound of granite, Sandy had to slam on the brakes to avoid two pickups pulled across the road.

Sandy calmly looked straight ahead and mumbled, "This can't be good."

"On the bright side, we're going to get to talk to Streeter sooner than you thought."

Just then, a Dodge Charger pulled up behind us. Streeter and his two henchmen climbed out of the car. If you counted the two men in the pickup trucks, the odds were not in our favor. I reached toward my pistol.

Sandy turned to me and said, "Keep your cool. Let's try not to pull our guns unless we have to. Remember, we're looking for missing teenagers. We won't help them by being on suspension for a shooting. It won't help them if the media is focused on us instead of them."

I climbed out of the car with Sandy, and we immediately faced Dell Streeter. I tensed and left my hand resting on my hip. I hoped there was no way this crazy Texan wanted to get into a gunfight with the cops.

Streeter smiled and said, "Told you I don't forget easy. Especially when it's only been a couple of minutes. Now it's time for a little payback." He held up his hands, and so did the two men who were with him. "Just a good old-fashioned fistfight, if you're up for it."

He stepped closer, but before I could make a move, Sandy swung her left foot up quickly and caught the man at Streeter's side in the groin. Then she turned quickly and threw a hard roundhouse punch at Streeter's head. He ducked and kicked Sandy off her feet. She went down hard. She rolled to avoid Streeter's boot in her ribs.

I moved fast and charged Streeter, but his other goon tackled me from my blind side. It felt like a bus hit me as I went down on the nasty road, too. The solid man with strong legs knocked the wind out of me. The way he stood over me made me think he had played some football in Texas.

I started to rise to my knees, but the man kicked me across the side of my head and knocked me back on the ground. I slid down the loose gravel of the unpaved road a few more feet. Blood started to leak from my nose, and my right hand bled from road rash.

Then Streeter kicked Sandy. No cop wants to see his partner kicked. I sprang up, focused on Streeter again. I barreled toward him. But before I could deliver a blow, the muscle-bound goon threw a punch and caught me squarely in the head. I tumbled back onto the ground. This time I was dazed when I went down. It's a terrifying feeling when you know your gun could be exposed if you're unconscious. Training and habit taught me to reach down and hold my gun in its holster.

Then I heard Streeter call off one of his men as he stepped forward to kick Sandy again. It was the guy who had been on the ground holding his balls. Obviously he wanted some revenge. He looked annoyed at his employer as he stepped away.

Streeter said, "I just gave you a little dose of Texas justice. Next time you come to my house you show a little more respect."

I struggled to get to my knees. The pebbles under my kneecaps sent new tendrils of pain through my body. I couldn't even feel my nose, and my left eye was swelling up.

Sandy made it to her feet and squared off against Streeter again.

The Texan chuckled and said, "I like that fighting spirit. You do your department proud. But don't be stupid, Detective. I run this county now. The sooner you figure that out, the better off we'll all be."

CHAPTER 56

IT WAS MORE embarrassing than painful to sit in the upstairs bathroom of the Ghost House while Mary Catherine tended to my wounds. In terms of police work, they weren't particularly serious. A split lip, some sore ribs, a couple of gashes near my right eyebrow. Nothing that needed stitches.

Sandy sat across from me, having already been inspected by Mary Catherine. Maybe this jerk-off dealer had some respect for a local cop and didn't throw any real punches or kicks to her face. But she probably had a cracked rib. Sandy wouldn't admit to anyone that her ribs bothered her. Most cops knew there was not much you could do for a cracked rib. It hurt to breathe. It hurt your pride. And in the end, you had to just suck it up.

Mary Catherine and Sandy started to chat like I wasn't even in the room. Always a good feeling when two women talk about you as if you didn't exist.

Sandy said, "One time we were called to a domestic in the South Bronx. Mr. Manners over here starts talking to the wife, who had stabbed her husband with a fork in the shoulder. I was talking to him while the fork was still sticking straight up in his flesh. I hear Mike saying, 'Ma'am, you need to calm down. Why did you stab your husband with a fork?'"

I stayed silent because I'd heard the story a thousand times.

Sandy could hardly contain her smile. "The woman says to Mike, 'I didn't stab my husband with a fork. I stabbed him with a goddamn butcher knife.'

"Mike looked over at me and the man, then said, 'I can see a fork sticking out of his shoulder.' The woman says, 'That ain't my husband. That's my boyfriend.' Then Mike asks, 'Then where is your husband?'

"The woman looks right at Mike and says, 'I already told you. I stabbed him with a butcher knife. He's in the bedroom on the floor.'"

Mary Catherine was mesmerized and ceased putting the necessary Band-Aids on my face. "What happened next?"

Sandy laughed as she said, "Mike stepped into the bedroom, and sure enough, that was the start of his homicide career. We almost left the apartment with the woman's dead husband lying on the floor. There was still a butcher knife stuck right in his throat. Mike turned white as a ghost. It was hysterical."

It's funny, but I don't remember it being quite so amusing

at the time. Not only had I almost overlooked a homicide, it was also the most blood I had seen up to that point in my life. But the story made Mary Catherine laugh, and her laugh always made me smile.

Mary Catherine said, "Has he always been so clueless with women?"

"If you mean not having any idea what they're thinking, yes. He never knew when women were flirting with him or what kind of effect he had on them."

Mary Catherine started to laugh again. "He's that way with a lot of things. Sometimes the kids and I just point Michael in the right direction and tell him what to do. He really can be quite helpful when he sets his mind to it."

Sandy said, "His manners hide his shortcomings quite well. I think Seamus had a lot to do with shaping his personality."

When we were done and back downstairs, Sandy stopped in front of Juliana, who was almost as tall as Sandy.

Sandy gave her a spontaneous hug and said, "Oh, my God, I remember when you were bouncing around the apartment in New York. Your mom thought about tying your feet together. Look at you now. Such a beauty."

Chrissy scampered up, looking for some attention. Sandy immediately went down on one knee and brushed some light hair out of Chrissy's face. "You have some great role models to follow in this family," she said. "Juliana and Jane are crushing high school and headed to good colleges somewhere. And you couldn't have a better role model than Mary Catherine. You're one lucky little girl."

Sandy looked up at me. I didn't have to say anything. I

knew I was one lucky man. And for some reason it was important to me that the whole family like Sandy. Especially Mary Catherine. And they clearly did.

No matter what happened the rest of this vacation, I knew it would be worth it.

CHAPTER 57

THANKS TO THE efforts of Seamus and Mary Catherine, somehow a giant pot of Irish stew ended up on the stove. This dish was one of the kids' favorites and a sly way for Mary Catherine to slip some vegetables into their diet. Thank God no one was an avowed vegetarian in the family. I couldn't remember a meal in which meat wasn't the main focus.

Sandy fit right in at our double-size table, and it didn't take long for someone to ask her about the house we were living in.

The pretty, engaging woman had all the kids yearning for her attention. She immediately picked up on Eddie's brains and Juliana's calm demeanor. It was like she had been in touch with the family every day for the past eight years.

She told a few stories about our early days on the NYPD. Nothing too graphic, but I always ended up being the dumbass in the story. I didn't mind, as long as the kids were happy and laughing.

Bridget said, "Tell us more about Linewiler. Have you ever been in this house before?"

Sandy lowered her voice and said, "I know you guys call this Mildew Manor, but before that, it was known in town as…" She paused for dramatic effect and spat out, "The Ghost House."

I was surprised to see the teenagers a little more spooked by the term than Chrissy and Shawna were. They were both listening intently.

Jane asked, "Was anyone murdered here?"

"No."

Trent asked, "Did somebody die here?"

"Not that I know of."

Eddie said, "Then why is it called the Ghost House?"

"Because no real-estate agent could sell it, and it remained empty for several summers."

That brought laughter from Mary Catherine, Seamus, and me, but the kids looked disappointed that there wasn't any sinister meaning to it. Then Sandy said, "I don't actually know where the name came from. It started as a rumor, and the name just sort of stuck. I know some homeless people stayed here sometimes, and that probably scared the local kids. But you don't have anything to worry about with your dad, Mary Catherine, and Gramps around."

Chrissy, who was sitting right next to Sandy, said, "Why don't you have any kids?"

Sandy gave her a smile and said, "You've got to find the right guy, and I'm telling you that's not easy to do. I hope to have a child one day. I guess I can't wait very long. But until then, I hope your dad shares you guys with me just a little bit."

I had to laugh and say, "Share them with you? Why don't I *leave* them with you? They can go to school up here in Maine, and I'll come visit sometime around Christmas."

I was prepared to field questions and comments from the crowd when someone knocked on the front door.

Seamus said, "A little late for a visitor."

I saw the look of concern on Sandy's face as we both stood at the same time to go to the front door. I motioned for Mary Catherine and the kids to stay where they were. Maybe my little scuffle with Dell Streeter had gotten under my skin more than I realized.

Sandy stood to the side of the door, ready to take action if necessary, when I opened it.

I was surprised by our guest.

It was Sadie, the homeless girl I'd seen at the clambake and around town.

She didn't look as frail as I remembered. She focused those dark eyes on me and said, "Are you still looking for Tom-Tom Bacon and Tricia?"

"Yes, I am."

"Then I have something important to show you. Can you drive me?"

Sandy stepped from behind the door and said, "We both can."

Sadie nodded her head and said, "Good, because there's some people who'll be mad I'm telling secrets."

CHAPTER 58

I SAT IN the backseat with Sadie, where I could face her, and turned Sandy into our chauffeur. She knew exactly what I was doing. We'd used the technique effectively back in New York. People were much more willing to talk to you if there wasn't the barrier of a seat between you.

I studied the girl carefully as we headed to the woods on the other side of town, not far from where Dell Streeter lived.

I said, "Can I ask you a question, Sadie?"

"You want to know why I'm like this?" She jiggled her right leg and right hand. "It's from a stroke. That's why I slur my words a little bit, too."

"Are you getting any kind of treatment?"

"Some. I see a social worker who makes me go to the doctor. She's nice, but she has no idea what life is like on the streets."

"When did you have the stroke?"

"Around two years ago, when I was fifteen. Before my mom died."

I mumbled, "I'm sorry to hear your mom died."

"Don't be. You didn't have anything to do with it. She overdosed. But we did use to live in your house."

"The one we're renting on the lake?"

"The same one. The Ghost House."

From the front seat Sandy said, "So you've heard it called that, too?"

Sadie giggled. "*I'm* the one who started the name. First I came up with a rumor that it was haunted to keep people away, then I made sure everyone called it the Ghost House in town and at school."

I smiled and said, "You used to live there?"

"My mom and I squatted there when it was abandoned. By making up the name and rumors, I kept people from bothering us. It was pretty nice for a while. Just my mom and me. She was hooked on heroin by then, and I picked up the habit, too. That's what caused my stroke. I just got too high one night, and it happened. Turned out I was the lucky one. My mom OD'd down in Brunswick. No one even held a funeral for her."

"What are you going to show us tonight?"

"Some of the things I saw when I was high. When no one thinks you're paying attention. When people look right past you like you're just a piece of furniture."

"Does it have anything to do with Dell Streeter?"

"Anything about drugs has something to do with Dell Streeter. My mom used to call him the devil on earth."

CHAPTER 59

AS WE PULLED off the highway onto one of the side streets, Sadie sat up and gave directions to Sandy. She had us turn onto an unpaved road and then into a clearing in the woods.

There was something about this odd young woman. Almost a feral quality that made me interested in what she had to say. The thought crossed my mind that she was leading us into some kind of trap. But only for a moment. I'd made my career out of reading people. This girl had nothing left to hide.

It didn't really matter at this point, because I was willing to do just about anything to find the missing teenagers. The fact that I went into the woods and looked over cliffs should've been enough to convince anyone that I was serious about this.

We stood by the car for a moment and got acclimated to the dark. There was almost no moon in the sky. There were no towns to produce any serious ambient light. It gave me the chance to look up at the stars and see them in a new way. They were bright and bold and not washed out by city lights.

I turned to Sadie. "You watched us last night when we were looking for Tom-Tom and Tricia, didn't you?"

She smiled. "I see everything that goes on around here. No one sees me." She pointed toward the woods and said, "This is something I've never told anyone."

I still had the Kel-Lite Sandy had given me so I could search the woods for Tom-Tom and Tricia. Sandy had a hand-held spotlight that illuminated the woods for a hundred yards. It was like daylight had come at ten thirty at night.

The bright light only made the rest of the woods seem darker and spookier. My Kel-Lite barely poked a hole in the darkness.

I turned to Sandy and said, "How far are we from Dell Streeter's junkyard?"

"Maybe a mile as the crow flies. Just under two miles if we had to take the roads. Why?"

"I wouldn't want to run into any of his lackeys by mistake."

"Why not?" I could see her smile even in the darkness.

"We didn't do so well this afternoon when we *knew* we were running into them. Don't worry: I haven't forgotten what happened. I just don't want it to happen again."

We stood in a clearing and scanned the dark woods with our lights one more time. I didn't like the gloom beyond the edge of my flashlight. It felt like the forest was alive with creepy growls and screeches.

Sadie wasn't discouraged or scared in any way. She limped away from the clearing into the woods. I was surprised by how fast she moved. Sandy and I both hustled to keep up as she slipped through the darkness, barely touching the tree limbs.

Sandy whispered to me, "Is this crazy that we're just following her?"

"My instinct says to do it. She seems to have an inside track on everything."

"I hope you brought your gun."

I said, "I hope I did, too."

Sadie heard us and said, "You won't need a gun. Nothing but ghosts up here."

"Just like there were ghosts at my house when you lived there?"

"No. There really are ghosts up here. This is no rumor." She kept moving and disappeared into the darkness.

CHAPTER 60

AFTER A FEW minutes of marching through the woods with Sadie, we came to a stop in a clearing. It was around the size of a basketball court. Just an odd shape in the middle of the forest. Two boulders forced the trees to grow at odd angles on the edge of the clearing.

Sandy and I both swept the area with our flashlights quickly. If anything was going to happen, it would happen right now. I don't know why I was jumpy, but things were getting weird and I was stuck in the middle of the woods. If that isn't a reason to be jumpy, I don't know what is.

Sadie walked directly over to the larger of the two boulders, turned, and sat on top of it. It appeared as if it was a regular resting spot for her. She just looked at us, not saying a word.

I stepped over to her and said, "Is this what you wanted us to see?"

She nodded and gave me a sly smile.

"Am I missing something? I don't see anything out of the ordinary here."

"I think that's why they like this spot. That's why they use it."

"Who likes it? What do they use it for?" I was starting to feel like this girl was playing games with us. But I still had the feeling that she was onto something. She just didn't have that many opportunities to play games like this. I had to be patient. The same as if she were one of my own kids. Hell, she *could've* been one of my own kids.

Sadie finally said, "This is where they do it. Here and in the woods around the edge." She spread her arms to show us she was talking about the place where the forest ended. "No reason for anyone to come up here. Nothing really to see. No hiking trails. Tourists don't care about just another patch of woods. This is where they like to bury the bodies."

Sandy's head snapped up, and she said, "Who likes to bury the bodies? How do you know that?"

"Because this is where they buried me. At least they tried to." She pointed to a shallow dip in the grass and said, "Right over there."

I stepped over and inspected the ground. Grass had grown over the spot. The fact that there was a ridge around the hole, and the size of it, made it look like a grave. But that didn't make sense. I turned to Sadie and asked, "Why would someone bury you?"

"They thought I was dead. I probably looked dead. I was over at Dell Streeter's house and got so high I guess I just passed out. They didn't want to answer any questions, so Dell and one of his boys brought me up here, dug a grave, and planted me."

"Why would they just dump you?"

"They told me it was bad for business to have dead customers. This was just after my mom died. They said it was a good thing she died in Brunswick because no one would care where she got the stuff."

Listening to Sadie tell her story, I realized just how smart she really was. She understood exactly what had happened and why. She wasn't feeling sorry for herself. I sensed that she was mad. Maybe it just took her a while to stand up for herself.

Sandy said, "How'd you escape?"

"Before they were done throwing dirt on me, I woke up. I think I scared the shit out of them. I started coughing up dirt. I remember sitting right there and starting to cry. I thought I really was dead and they were doing the right thing."

I took a minute and walked to the edge of the trees, using my light to check the ground carefully. Not far from where Sadie said her grave had been, I saw two uneven ripples on the ground. They had been there awhile. Grass was growing over them. Maybe it was the power of suggestion, but they looked like graves to me.

Sandy stepped up close to me and said, "We're going to have to go over this place carefully in the morning. I need to call in some crime-scene people."

I sat down on the boulder next to Sadie and put my arm around her shoulder. She didn't seem too upset. I wanted her to know she wasn't alone. Her body felt slight next to mine. I wanted to hug her and give her a good meal. It was the kind of thing any parent would have done.

We sat in silence for a few moments until I said, "Once they realized you were alive, what happened?"

"They let me go. But they told me if I ever talked to anyone about this, I'd be one dead bitch."

Sadie turned and looked me in the face.

She said, "Guess I'm a dead bitch."

CHAPTER 61

SANDY AND I made some quick plans as we headed back to my house. We couldn't leave Sadie alone, and we couldn't search the field at night. The solution was simple. Who would notice one more kid at my house?

It was late by the time we slipped in the house. My sleeping angel, Mary Catherine, sprawled on the foldout couch with Shawna and Chrissy snuggled up on either side of her. The TV was still on.

I led Sadie quietly up the stairs. Now I found out where her disability caused her problems. The stairs were difficult for her to navigate. She was fast when she was moving forward and from side to side, but going up and down was a challenge.

We finally made it to the second floor, and Jane stepped out of her bedroom to meet us.

I whispered, "Jane, this is Sadie. You think you could help her find some clothes and a bed to sleep in?"

Jane didn't question anything about the odd situation. She smiled and said, "Since both Eddie and Ricky are asleep in your bed, I know their beds are open." She took Sadie by the hand and said, "We'll have you fixed up in no time."

I ended up sleeping on a cot in my own bedroom. Ricky's persistent sinus problems made him snore. He sounded like someone trying to start a chain saw. I slept in fits all night. Two separate times I got off the cot and made a run through the house to make sure everyone was safely in bed.

Jane had taken the second bed in the room with Sadie. I couldn't believe how compassionate and caring my children had become. And I couldn't have been more proud.

When I finally fell asleep soundly, I managed to miss the boys waking up and the crowd gathering for breakfast in the kitchen. I was almost the last one to the party. Most of the older kids sat around the table, chatting with Sadie.

Sadie was wearing one of Jane's sundresses and appeared to be right at home.

Mary Catherine was hustling around the stove, flipping pancakes and trying to be part of the conversation. As I stood at the door listening, I heard her say, "I have an aunt named Sadie. She's not as pretty as you, but she's one of my favorite aunts."

That made our guest smile.

Mary Catherine caught sight of me and lifted her eyebrows. I knew the look. She was asking me what the hell was going on without saying a word. If she was upset in the least, she didn't show it.

Chrissy was at the end of the table, nibbling on one of the first pancakes that had come off the stove. When there was a break in the conversation, she asked Sadie, "How did you hurt your leg?"

Sadie looked at the little girl and said, "It's really my brain that's hurt."

"Then why do you walk funny?"

Everyone at the table was horrified for a moment until Sadie broke into a big smile and started to laugh. Then she said, "That's a really good question, Chrissy. And as smart as I think I am, I've never asked anyone to explain it to me completely."

Chrissy had a broad grin on her face and said, "Glad I could help."

I guess everyone felt comfortable around this family.

CHAPTER 62

AFTER BREAKFAST, I met Sandy at the clearing Sadie had shown us the night before. Now it was a full-scale crime scene, with a photographer methodically working from one end to the other.

A K-9 handler, using a golden retriever as a cadaver dog, searched the area. I noticed two small flags marking the ripples on the ground I had noticed the night before.

Sandy walked over to me and said, "We have at least two older graves over there." She pointed to markers a dozen feet away. "The investigator from the medical examiner's office marked those when we were still pulling equipment out of our cars."

There was something missing at the scene. It took me a few seconds to realize what it was.

I turned to Sandy and said, "There's no media here. That

wouldn't happen in New York. They monitor our radios and have stringers hanging around a lot of the precincts. Back home, we'd have news trucks and photographers getting in our way."

"One more advantage to Maine," said Sandy as she instructed a young crime-scene tech to get ready to uncover the graves.

As I watched the scene unfold, I realized that someone would notice us up here working. I'd have to keep a close eye on Sadie. It was never a good idea to take a threat against a kid too lightly. She seemed happy with my family at the house right now. That worked for me, too.

I walked over to the spot where the medical examiner's investigator and a crime-scene tech were carefully uncovering the graves that had been identified. The investigator from the medical examiner's office was around fifty and had a big ruddy nose and a belly straining against a short-sleeved button-down shirt. He wore a New England Patriots clip-on tie. Anytime I saw someone in a tie like that I knew it meant that he was loosely following a dress code from his office. I assumed he was wearing the tie as some sort of protest.

The investigator looked at me and said, "Who the hell are you?"

"Mike Bennett. I'm working with Sandy Coles."

"You the NYPD guy?"

I nodded.

He stuck out his hand. "Bob Carbone. I retired from the Boston PD. I'll save you the effort. Yes, I know what I'm doing. No, I don't need any help. And yes, I do think Boston is a much better city than New York."

He immediately turned and focused on the graves once again.

I either liked this guy immensely or thought he was a dick. I wasn't sure which.

After more than an hour, the two bodies at the markers had been uncovered. Another grave had been found not far from them in the woods. We had stumbled into something serious.

Sandy, Bob Carbone, and I met at the back of Sandy's car, where a plain blue portable canopy had been set up.

Carbone's accent was so thick it was distracting as he said, "We got two adult males from the first graves. Pretty good deterioration because they were just in open soil, but we should be able to identify them."

Sandy said, "How long have they been there?"

He shrugged. "Maybe two years." He turned and pointed in the direction of the third grave. "That one is a female around twenty years old. She hasn't been there as long as the others. Maybe six months to a year."

I said, "Any idea how they died?"

"No obvious trauma, but that doesn't mean much. We'll have to get the medical examiner's full report. An autopsy should tell us a lot."

The tubby former Boston cop was starting to explain that he wanted to excavate the bodies completely and transport them when I heard someone shout from the far end of the clearing.

All three of us started to trot that way. The uniformed K-9 officer was trying to pull his golden retriever away from something. Two of the crime-scene techs were standing next to him.

As we got closer, I saw that they were looking at something on the ground. My stomach tightened up as I realized they had found two more graves. These were new. Even I could tell that. The dog had become so excited that he had uncovered the end of one of them.

I could clearly see the exposed feet sticking up out of the dirt and pine needles. One foot had a dirty white sock over it. The other was wearing a bright green Nike athletic shoe.

It was Tricia Green. Shit.

CHAPTER 63

SANDY AND I raced back to the Ghost House. Everything Sadie had told us was true. Now we needed to see if she could help us put the pieces together and make a case against Dell Streeter.

As soon as I stepped in the front door I found Sadie sitting on the floor with Bridget, working on some sort of epic arts-and-crafts project involving pinecones, an old sheet, and a lot of glue.

"What are you girls up to?"

Bridget looked up at me with the kind of smile she only had when satisfying her addiction to arts and crafts. "I'm showing Sadie how we can make portraits of animals using just pinecones and pine needles."

Sadie looked up and smiled. She didn't say a word, but I could tell she was enjoying it. She had never experienced a family life like this before. Just the thought of it made me a little sad.

It took a few minutes to get Sadie away from the other kids. We ended up in the downstairs bedroom, where Sandy and I sat on mismatched chairs while Sadie faced us from the edge of the bed. She didn't seem nervous at all.

This was the sort of thing you approached slowly. You couldn't do a straight interview. We intended to just let Sadie unwind once we started talking. We would let her tell things at her own pace.

Before we even told Sadie what we'd found in the woods, Sandy started asking her questions about growing up. Not just to put her at ease but also to understand her thought process. This sort of thing was vital to cops if they wanted to make a case that would go to a jury.

Sadie told us a little about her childhood. She said, "I remember when my mom worked at the Target in Bangor. We had fun together. Then she hurt her back, and the doctor gave her pills. Then she started using. She called it mud or sometimes smack. But I knew what it really was. She used to say it was like taking a vacation.

"She did more and more. She got it from Dell Streeter. I thought he was taking care of my mom. When she got really bad, he let us live at his house. After a while, she realized he was bad for both of us. She said he was the reason she was hooked. When she died, he didn't want me around at all."

Sandy and I listened as this train wreck unfolded. I still had a hard time understanding how things could go so wrong for people.

Sadie said, "I heard about two guys who used a bad batch of

mud at Dell's house. They both died, and instead of involving the police, Dell and his buddies just buried them in the field. I guess that's what they did with me, too."

I let her sit there for a minute to make sure there was nothing else she wanted to tell us. Then I got down on my knee in front of her so we could look at each other eye to eye.

I said, "Would you be willing to make a statement? Maybe testify in court later, if you had to?"

She thought about it, then nodded. "Yeah. I can do that to someone who tried to bury me alive."

I said, "I'll keep you safe."

She smiled and said, "No one can keep me safe after I do this. Dell Streeter knows everyone. But I'll do it anyway."

CHAPTER 64

THE PENOBSCOT COUNTY district attorney didn't seem thrilled with the idea of using a disabled teenager and former drug user as the sole witness in what could turn out to be the biggest case in the county's history. The pudgy assistant district attorney, with a perpetual sweat forming on his forehead, virtually ignored my presence during the meeting.

He kept adding things to Sandy's arrest warrant and throwing up unnecessary roadblocks.

Finally we had what we needed. We headed straight to Streeter's compound, where a couple of county sheriff's deputies met us. This was the second arrest in a row that I was looking forward to. The last arrest I made was the asshole who had Brian selling drugs for him. I recognized the connections between the cases—drugs, young people, dealers with no conscience. It may have been swaying my judgment, but at this point I didn't care.

We rolled into the front yard and hustled up to the porch before anyone knew we were there. Just as Sandy started to pound on the front door, it opened. One of Streeter's goons stared at us, slack-jawed. It was the guy who had punched me in the head.

I grabbed his shoulder and pulled him through the door onto the porch. I saw the gun stuck in the small of his back and jerked it out with my right hand. He balled his hand into a fist and lined up on my face.

I raised my knee and struck him in the thigh. The jolt to his system made him drop his hands and bend over. Then I drove the same knee directly into his face. He sprawled onto the porch, and I looked at the uniformed sheriff's deputy with us. The young deputy just nodded, understanding he was supposed to watch the man on the ground.

Now we fanned out into the house quickly with our guns drawn.

Sandy covered one side of the wide living room and I the other. I was looking down the hallway when another goon came out, clearly not expecting to see anyone in the house.

He started to call out when I stuck the gun right in his face. I whispered, "On the ground—now." I pushed the barrel of my pistol against his temple, and he got the message. I patted him down quickly when he was on the ground, but he had no weapons.

Then I heard Sandy shout, "Police—don't move."

When I looked up from the man on the ground, Sandy had her pistol pointed down the other hallway.

I stepped closer with my gun raised. Dell Streeter was standing in the other hallway. He was in jeans but had no shirt or shoes on.

Sandy said, "Keep your hands where I can see them."

Streeter forced a smile and showed us that his hands were empty. "I hope you have a good reason for burglarizing my house and threatening me with guns. I guess we call that home invasion."

Sandy said, "Walk toward me slowly."

I saw Streeter's eyes dart back and forth. He had to be wondering where his bodyguards were.

When he was in the living room, Sandy shoved him to the ground. I covered him while she holstered her pistol and jerked his left hand behind his back. She slipped the handcuffs from her belt and had him secured in a couple of seconds.

From the ground, Streeter griped, "Those cuffs are awful tight."

Sandy didn't answer as she jerked him to his feet. She said, "Dell Streeter, you're under arrest."

"Let me put on some clothes before you take me anywhere."

Now we were leading him out the door past his two goons, who were being watched by the sheriff's deputies.

I said, "Unlike restaurants, we'll still give you service without a shirt or shoes."

As we got to Sandy's car, the dealer said, "Let's see how funny you are when they let me go and I have your jobs."

I said, "You can have my job, but I don't think you'd like

210

it. Seems like all you ever get to deal with is jerks." I inadvertently slammed his face into the roof of the car when I tried to get him into the backseat.

Sandy didn't mind the blood that leaked out of his nose onto the upholstery.

CHAPTER 65

DELL STREETER, STILL shirtless, sat in a chair with his hands cuffed behind his back. There was no one else in the Linewiler detective bureau. That was the way Sandy and I wanted it.

It was time to have a serious talk with the Texan.

Streeter said, "Where's the bright light? Are you going to use the phone book to beat me so there are no bruises? Who's going to be the good cop and who's going to be the bad one?"

Sandy said, "You've seen a lot of movies."

"I've had a lot of cops talk to me. And I'll tell you right now I've got nothing to say."

"Most drug dealers don't."

"Drug dealer! I run a successful appliance repair service."

I said, "If you're so successful, how come you live in that shithole?"

"Less for crooked cops to steal. Plus I like the tax breaks for having a home office."

Sandy played it cool, sitting on the edge of a nearby desk. "I don't think you appreciate the situation you're in."

Streeter said, "Why don't you explain it to a simple country boy like me?"

I leaned in close and said, "Right now we can tie five bodies to you."

He chuckled but kept his mouth shut.

"You think this is funny? You think it's a joke?"

He grinned. "Yeah. I think someone is playing a joke on me. I'll laugh tonight. When I'm home."

"You could get life for this, easy."

"Life is never easy. You should know that. I did a little research on you after our first meeting. You couldn't even keep your own kid from selling dope. Who are you to threaten me?"

Even with his hands behind his back, it felt like he had slapped me. I had to get hold of myself. I had never punched anyone in handcuffs. I wanted to go my whole career being able to say that.

Streeter said, "I just want to make sure you get me in front of the judge for my arraignment before the end of the day."

"Why is that?"

"Because the Rangers are on ESPN tonight, and I intend to watch it from my living room." He gave us a smirk. He was daring me to do something drastic.

Sandy said, "There's always a way to help yourself in a situation like this."

"A situation like what? Like being kidnapped illegally by

the police?" He looked back at me and said, "I'm starting to understand why so many people shoot the cops. You deserve it."

Sandy said, "We've got someone talking to your two flunkies in another room."

"So?"

"No telling what they're saying right now."

"The same thing I'm about to say."

I said, "What's that?"

"The magic words: I want to talk to my attorney."

He gave us another smirk, because he knew he'd just shut down this interview.

At least I made it through without punching a guy in hand-cuffs.

CHAPTER 66

LATE THAT AFTERNOON we found ourselves sitting on a hard bench at the Penobscot Judicial Center. It may not have been as expansive and historic as a New York City courthouse, but it had the same sense of power. There were still people sitting around us, upset that a relative had been arrested. There were still well-dressed attorneys waiting at the side of the courtroom to step forward when their clients were called.

Dell Streeter sat with the other two men facing Judge Lauren Furtado. A young, skinny man had been arrested for shoplifting, and an older, tired-looking man had been arrested for failure to pay child support.

Courtroom activity was pretty much the same everywhere.

When Dell Streeter's case was called, a woman dressed in a sharp Armani pantsuit stepped confidently to the podium.

She was probably around thirty-five, and her hair fell to her shoulders.

She announced herself as Arlene Greenberg.

Sandy knew her and clearly wasn't a fan.

The lawyer wasted no time once the preliminary items were handled by the judge.

The lawyer said, "Your Honor, I move that this case be dismissed and that my client Mr. Streeter be released immediately. Based on the affidavit submitted by Detective Coles, I see very little probable cause. In fact all I've seen and heard about today is outrageous police conduct."

The lawyer turned and looked back at Sandy and me sitting together in the front row.

She said, "I have affidavits from two of Mr. Streeter's friends who were beaten mercilessly by the police. They say the house they all share was trashed. Mr. Streeter himself has told me he was held in a freezing room and deprived of a shirt. He was ridiculed and threatened. It was the closest thing to torture I have seen in my entire career."

I was stunned to see the ADA sitting at the prosecution table and not saying a word or objecting as the lawyer spit out these lies.

Judge Furtado said, "What do you have to say about that, Mr. Albanese?"

The pudgy ADA slowly rose to his feet and said, "I…well…um. I certainly would never condone that sort of behavior."

I wanted to jump up and shout that this was bullshit. I fidgeted in my seat, and Sandy read my mind. She put her hand on my leg to keep me seated. She knew me pretty well.

The well-dressed defense attorney said, "Your Honor, this entire case is based on a statement from one witness. A witness who has a history of drug use as well as a mental and physical disability. Mr. Streeter is a businessman and has worked from his house repairing appliances without any complaints for several years."

Now the ADA stood up and said, "We *do* have five bodies."

The attorney shot back without waiting for the judge to say anything. "But nothing tying them to my client."

Now the judge looked at the ADA and said, "Is this true, Mr. Albanese?"

The ADA took a painful amount of time to answer. It made whatever he said look fabricated. Finally he said, "Technically, for now, we have not developed forensic evidence to tie the bodies to the defendant."

The judge said, "Do you think it might be best to wait until you have evidence? I see that Mr. Streeter owns his house and has been a resident of Maine for almost three years. Would it be such a big risk to withdraw the charges and investigate further?"

The ADA nodded and said, "I see what you're saying, Your Honor. At this time the state would like to withdraw the charges."

Judge Furtado banged her gavel and said, "The court is in recess." Then she looked directly at the nervous ADA and said, "Get your case in order, Mr. Albanese."

Sandy and I just sat there. Speechless. I was focused on the smirk on Dell Streeter's face as he turned from his attorney to look at me.

He was free to go. Unlike most defendants, he wasn't even

going to process through the rear of the courtroom. He was talking to his attorney and getting ready to walk out the front door.

Sandy said, "This stinks."

I said, "I know. But we can't just give up."

Sandy said, "No—I mean it smells like a payoff. We had things that tubby little ass could've mentioned. He could've explained that we had forensics being developed in the lab. DNA lab work takes time. This isn't some stupid TV show. There's no magic machine to analyze everything."

All I could say was, "I know."

I watched helplessly as Dell Streeter hugged the attorney and passed through the low swinging gate into the gallery.

He strutted right up to us and said, "Gonna take a lot more than that to stop me. I heard there might be an investigation into how I was treated."

I said, "If I were you, I'd worry about other investigations."

Streeter chuckled. "I sure hope that little scurvy cripple girl doesn't fall down and hurt herself. I guess it might save us some tax dollars. She's never going to contribute to society anyway." He winked and then strolled right out the front door of the courtroom.

I had a serious urge to pull my pistol and put a bullet in the back of his head. It might even have been worth it.

PART FOUR

CHAPTER 67

THREE DAYS AFTER the nasty court scene, life was back to normal at Mildew Manor—or, as we now called it, the Ghost House. The case against Dell Streeter wasn't closed. It would move ahead again as the police gathered more information. If I thought I could add anything, I intended to help. I made that clear to Sandy.

On this bright, beautiful Sunday morning, Mary Catherine and I had woken before anyone else. As the kids got older, I found that happening more and more. We decided to make use of the beautiful weather and spectacular scenery and walk along our favorite path by the lake.

Mary Catherine knew her nature pretty well and spotted a blue jay. Then she explained the difference between a blackbird and a crow. When a fish jumped, she was quick to point out that it was a trout.

The morning was perfect as I held her hand and just strolled along. She made me feel alive and connected. It was hard to explain, considering how much my life had changed in the past decade. A few years ago, there was no way I could've predicted that I'd be walking with this beautiful Irish girl along a serene lake in Maine and have a huge horde of kids waiting for me. And that I would love every minute of it.

I happily listened as Mary Catherine told me about her camping trips as a child in Ireland. I guess, like most Americans, I didn't think about the Irish, or any Europeans, going on camping trips. For some reason it felt uniquely American to me. But her stories were similar to all the stories I had heard about camping. Leaky tents, falling in icy rivers, raccoons stealing your food. Somehow I didn't miss the fact that I had never camped as a child.

Then she stopped and took my other hand as well. We were facing each other with the perfect lake and forest background surrounding us. There was something on her mind.

Mary Catherine said, "No pressure, Michael. I'm not one of those women. But I want to get to the point, and I do have a question."

I stared at her, not sure if it was wise for me to say anything at all. Better to let it just unfold.

"Michael, do we have a future? A real future together?"

"This isn't about Sandy Coles, is it?"

"No, Michael. Not in the slightest. This is about us. About the chances of our spending our lives together. I love you. I know you love me. But life is complicated. No one knows exactly how other people see the future. You don't have to answer me this second. I just wanted you to know what I've been thinking about."

Now I knew, and it made me nervous. I don't know why, but the idea of a long-term serious commitment scared me. Mary Catherine was perfect in every way. It was me. It was my shortcomings that kept me from answering her.

Whatever the reason, I stayed silent. I was an idiot and instantly regretted it.

Mary Catherine was right. Life really is complicated.

CHAPTER 68

BY TEN IN the morning, we had somehow whipped our brood into shape and gotten everyone dressed properly in time for mass at the local church. Seamus had met the young priest in charge of the tiny Catholic church in town. They had started talking at the firehouse clambake, and the priest invited Seamus to celebrate mass at one of the day's services.

Seamus understood his limitations and that he was still recovering from his heart attack. He chose to celebrate the family mass and was treated like a rock star from the moment we arrived at the church.

We all sat in the third row. We took up the *entire* third row. Tom Bacon and his family and friends filled the pews in front of us.

The young priest acknowledged the Bacon family and gave a good sermon about the need for strong families. Although he mentioned what a good boy Tom-Tom had been, the priest never mentioned Tricia's name. He also said more than once that Tom-Tom had "passed away." There was no mention of the circumstances.

The young priest ended by saying that everyone should cherish time with their loved ones because no one knows when we'll ever see them again.

Mary Catherine started to cry. I had a lump in my throat.

Then it was time for Holy Communion. Seamus was introduced as a "distinguished priest all the way from the Holy Name parish in New York City." I could see that it sounded great to others. But I still saw the old man who made fart noises when I tried to discipline the kids.

Seamus was impressive. That's coming from someone who's used to hearing his accent and seeing him dressed as a priest all the time. The local people loved it.

It was always a moving experience to hear my grandfather celebrate Holy Communion. His accent seemed to hit just the right syllables, and his tone changed perfectly as he recited Jesus's words from the Last Supper: "Take this, all of you, and eat of it: for this is my body, which will be given up for you. In a similar way, when supper was ended, he took the chalice, and, once more giving thanks, he gave it to his disciples, saying: Take this, all of you, and drink from it: for this is the chalice of my blood, the blood of the new and eternal covenant, which will be poured out for you and for many for the forgiveness of sins."

Seamus had told me how powerful those words were to him when he considered the sacrifice Christ made for all mankind. And today, as I looked up at him preparing the communion, it really moved me.

Mary Catherine and I had been holding hands for the entire service. It was a natural thing for me to do, and I didn't notice it. That is, until Trent and Juliana both looked over at us and said, "Awww." Like we were teenagers on our first date.

Mary Catherine smiled at the kids and squeezed my hand.

This was the way I always dreamed my life would be. Why hadn't I jumped to dispel Mary Catherine's questions about our future? She was everything I wanted and needed in a partner.

Was there something I couldn't understand that was holding me back? Was I still too in love with my late wife, Maeve, to move on?

I was in the perfect place to pray for guidance on the issue. But that didn't mean I wasn't still an idiot for not telling Mary Catherine exactly how I felt about her.

As the service ended, I gathered everyone together so we could pay our respects to the Bacon family. Tom and his wife and ex-wives had formed an impromptu receiving line and accepted everyone's sympathy.

When my turn in the line came up, I took his hand and mumbled, "I'm so sorry."

When I tried to move on, Tom wouldn't release my hand.

He said, "You should be sorry and ashamed. That maniac killed my boy, and a lot of people in town think he's responsible for other missing kids. No one is happy. They think you and Sandy Coles took money to let him go. Or are you just incompetent?"

"What are you talking about?"

He released my hand and said, "You'll find out. We're not gonna stand for this."

"Stand for what?"

"Injustice. That Texas redneck is going to pay for what he did. You and the local cops have a lot to answer for, too."

I wanted to answer this crazy accusation when Mary Catherine gently tugged on my arm to move away.

She whispered, "Let it be, Michael. He's crazy with grief."

As usual, she was right.

CHAPTER 69

LATER THAT EVENING, after a nice dinner with the family and another group fishing event, I tried to relax on the couch with Mary Catherine. She knew me better than anyone. That's why she understood how much Tom Bacon's comments bothered me. The fact that we hadn't found the teenagers alive was bad enough. The idea that others thought we hadn't tried our hardest made it hurt that much more.

I tried not to be distracted and to give my full attention to Mary Catherine and Chrissy, who was nestled in on the other side of Mary Catherine. We had watched a Disney movie about some princess in a cold, icy land. I really didn't pay that much attention. Now we were trying to get everyone calmed down for bed.

I allowed the older kids to sit out on the dock and just do what teenagers did. That group didn't worry me much.

My phone rang, and I knew before I picked it up off the table who it was. I wasn't expecting the phone to ring, but only one person would call me at this time of night.

I looked at Mary Catherine as I held the phone to my ear and said, "Hello, Sandy. What's gone wrong now?" I meant it as a joke, but as soon as I heard her voice, I knew it wasn't funny.

"Mike, I need some help."

"What's wrong? Are you okay?"

"I am for now. But there's a crowd growing outside city hall. They're upset with how things went with Dell Streeter at his arraignment. Tom Bacon has got them riled up. A couple of them are armed."

"I'll be there in ten minutes."

Mary Catherine understood instantly what was going on and gave me a kiss on the lips. All she said as I slipped out the door was, "Please be careful."

"I always try to be careful." I gave her a wink, hoping it might lighten the mood. It didn't do much.

Once I was on the road, racing down Route 2 toward town, all I could think about was Sandy having to face an angry crowd. As I pulled into the lot, I could see around ten people in front of her. She was at the top of the five-step stairway leading into the tiny city hall.

I was shocked to see several men holding rifles and several others with handguns in holsters on their hips. Then I remembered I wasn't in New York City anymore. Maine is an open-carry state. No one was breaking any laws. At most, some local jurisdictions made it illegal to discharge firearms within the city limits. It was still unnerving.

As I walked up to the rear of the crowd I heard a heavyset man wearing a neatly trimmed beard and holding a Remington 30-06 rifle yell out, "How can you tell us you're doing everything you can when Dell Streeter is free to come and go? Who knows how many people he's killed? My Marjorie disappeared two years ago. That might be her body they haven't been able to identify yet. And you want us to be calm?"

Sandy kept her cool and looked directly at the man. "Look, Anthony, all I can tell you is we're doing the best we can. No one around here has ever seen anything like this. The case against Dell Streeter isn't closed. We're trying to develop more evidence against him."

Anthony said, "That's not good enough."

Sandy said, "Arguing about it out here isn't going to help anything. What if we all go over to the firehouse and sit down and try to discuss it?"

Someone shouted from the middle of the crowd, "There's nothing to discuss. Dell Streeter needs to pay for what he did."

Then Tom Bacon said, "I don't think you'll be able to do much to stop us, Detective Coles."

That's when I said from the rear of the crowd, "I bet both of us together could stop more than half of you. Anyone want to try your luck?"

I could tell by the way all the heads swiveled toward me that I had caught everyone by surprise. I could also tell that no one wanted to try his luck.

CHAPTER 70

IT ONLY TOOK a few minutes to get everyone settled in the training room of the firehouse. The fire chief didn't look like he appreciated being woken for something short of a three-alarm fire. But when he heard what Sandy had to say and saw the group of armed men milling around in front of the station, he opened the side door.

Most of the fifteen folding chairs set up in the training room were filled by the crowd that had been outside. They weren't all men. There were four women. Each of them was armed as well.

I leaned against a table that held half a dozen CPR dummies and let Sandy run things.

The guy who'd spoken outside, Anthony, said, "For all we know, you take your orders from Dell Streeter. You're not doing us any good here. I'm not even sure why we have our own police department. The state police could cover the town more effectively. Maybe we don't even need them."

One of the women said, "Aside from writing a few tickets and harassing us about stupid shit, the cops here don't do anything. Here's the first chance for you to be useful, and you blow the case."

Sandy, ever the professional, let the woman finish her thoughts. Then Sandy said, "As I said before, the case against Streeter is not closed. It is an active investigation. I promise you we're working on it day and night. I haven't spent five hours at home since those kids went missing."

Tom Bacon said, "But you've had time to visit your boyfriend out at the Ghost House. A couple of people have seen your car out there."

"I've stopped there. I think I ate a meal or two with his family. But I've been focused on this case. And frankly I don't appreciate the innuendo in your comments."

This was not the same town I'd seen at the Fourth of July parade. The town that greeted all its police officers and showed them respect. This town had fallen into an anti-cop mind-set. This had nothing to do with a police shooting, either. Suddenly I realized how much people needed a reason or an excuse for the tragedies they suffered. The cops were convenient scapegoats.

Sandy tried to reason with the crowd, but people were done listening. I watched silently as everyone started heading out the door.

I stepped over toward Sandy. The bearded asshole named Anthony looked at me and said, "I know how New York cops are. I watch the news. Someone got to you guys. Someone has paid you off."

I looked at him and shook my head. "That's right, Anthony. I accepted a freezer full of venison and moose jerky just to let a killer walk free." As I walked past him I muttered, "Jerk-off."

Anthony said, "What did you just say?"

I turned around until we were nose to nose and said, "I called you a jerk-off. I did that because you're *acting* like a jerk-off. What are you gonna do about it? You can't fire me from the Linewiler Police Department."

The man shifted his hand on the rifle he was holding.

I stared him down and said, "You move that hand on that rifle one more time and you'll lose it."

I heard car doors slam and tires squeal as people pulled away. I realized that I had not helped the situation dramatically. I also knew that the people of Linewiler were not happy.

I figured I could live with both those situations.

CHAPTER 71

THE NEXT MORNING I met Sandy at her office. She didn't say why she needed me, and I didn't ask. She was my partner. She had been since the days we both worked the Bronx.

We sat in the conference room at the police department with a uniformed sergeant, the chief of police, and the chief assistant district attorney. The chief ADA was a beautiful Latin woman named Addy Villanueva. A graduate of the University of Maine, she was petite but fiery. No one would mistake her for shy or quiet. Her long dark hair flipped from side to side as she talked to us about the calls her office had been getting from various politicians.

She said, "One of your residents, Tom Bacon, had the US congressman call our office and demand action on the case. The ADA who handled the Streeter case in court for you has called in sick, and no one can get in touch with him. Two different county commissioners called my office and demanded to know what was going on. My boss, who is an elected official, told me to make sure things wouldn't get any worse. I don't see how they could."

Sandy said, "I guess it's worse if some vigilante does something crazy, like shoot Dell Streeter."

I liked her casual tone. It was an old police trick that helped put people in their place and keep situations calm.

The ADA said, "Is that a possibility?"

Sandy shrugged and said, "Based on what I saw last night, yes."

The beautiful ADA said, "We can't let that happen. *You* can't let that happen."

Now I cut in. "Do you expect the police of this department to provide protection to a guy like Dell Streeter?"

She stared at me for a moment. She was trying to decide if she even needed to answer an outsider like me.

I said, "What's the use of Streeter's bodyguards if they can't scare off a few vigilantes? Seems like a waste of money to me."

The ADA didn't appreciate flippant comments. That was all I had right now. She gave me a dirty look but still didn't answer.

I kept going. "So I guess you're saying he needs police protection. Police resources that could be used to make a case against him instead of protecting him."

"That's exactly what I'm saying. And don't give me that bull about resources. Everyone works with less. The town has an overtime budget for emergencies. I'd call this an emergency." She took a moment to catch her breath. She looked right at me

235

and said, "Are you telling me the NYPD has never been in an awkward position like this?"

"Not one that touches so many people personally. Not one in which everyone involved knows everyone else. And certainly not one in which everyone in town gets to carry a gun."

The ADA stared me down with her dark eyes and said, "The gun politics of Maine are none of your concern. If the Linewiler Police Department wants to accept your help, that's okay with me, but don't try to do things the NYPD way. We're not in New York. We're in Maine. We have our own way of doing things."

"I've seen that firsthand. And so far, I'm not terribly impressed."

CHAPTER 72

THAT NIGHT WE were sitting at our extra-large dining table. Seamus had just said a moving prayer. The old man never failed to surprise me. Just when I think he likes to play the part of a priest as much as he actually likes being a priest, it feels like he opens a connection for me directly to God.

Seamus said, "Thank you, Lord, for this wonderful meal. Give us strength in this time of crisis. Let us see the pain of others and through that understand their actions. No one here on earth can judge us. No one here on earth can truly hurt us. With faith and love, please show us the path. And, as always, please protect our precious Brian."

It made me think about how I felt when Brian got in trouble. What I had considered doing to get him out of trouble. How it felt when the judicial system didn't work the way I thought it should. These Linewiler people were going through the same thing, but with a slightly different perspective.

Sadie sat between Bridget and Fiona. She seemed to have fallen right in with the family and was accepted by all the kids. Somehow her face looked fuller and her eyes more focused. She still had that winning smile and laughed easily at some of the stories being told.

I listened to the kids talk about their day. It hurt me a little bit to know I was missing out on so much of the vacation. Jane had taken Shawna and Chrissy on a hike into the hills west of the house. She had packed a lunch, and they were gone almost all day. It sounded amazing to me.

The twins and Sadie had collected pinecones and smooth pebbles for some sort of arts-and-crafts project that was going to be undertaken tomorrow. There was no question that Sadie would spend another night at the house. I had no problem with that.

The boys had gone fishing, and Eddie had devised a way to lure fish into a submerged net and ended up catching half a dozen catfish. Then they built a little pen on the edge of the lake where the catfish were waiting if we needed them for dinner. It was ingenious, and I was sorry I couldn't see Eddie's mind at work that day.

Mary Catherine tried to soften the blow by telling me that the kids were taking advantage of their chance to spend time in nature and that they couldn't wait for me to come with them.

Seamus said, "Aye, it's a fine vacation. I spent the day comfortably in the rocking chair on the back porch. It let me keep an eye on the kids and catch up on my reading."

"What reading?"

Mary Catherine said, "I finally got him to pick up a Michael Connelly novel by telling him that Connelly was an Irishman. Once he started reading about Harry Bosch, he couldn't put the book down."

I may have missed a day with the family, but I was starting to enjoy the evening. The dinner Mary Catherine had made was excellent. Some kind of casserole with vegetables and ground beef in a dark, garlicky gravy. Everyone gobbled it up, including Sadie. I was happy to see her eating so well.

Then a burst of noise made me jump. It sounded like an explosion. The sound of shattered glass filled the room, and I instinctively covered the two kids closest to me. There were shouts, and Chrissy cried out like she'd been hurt.

It took me a moment to realize that one of the front windows had been knocked out. I rose to my feet and looked over the table. "Is anyone hurt?" I kept my voice even and calm. No one really answered me. "Guys, is everyone okay?"

Everyone nodded, and I gave a quick extra look at Seamus to make sure the shock hadn't affected his heart.

I slowly stepped forward into the living room and found a red brick lying on the thin throw rug.

"Son of a bitch," I muttered in a low voice.

I reached for my car keys on the table by the door. Someone was going to pay for this. As I grabbed the door handle, I felt Mary Catherine's hand on my arm.

"It's all right, Michael. No one's hurt. We need you to stay here with us."

I thought about what she said as well as the tone she used. She was right. I needed to stay here.

I looked over at the table and saw that the kids were still terrified. Suddenly I wasn't sure I liked Maine as much as I thought I did. Nothing like this had ever happened to us in New York City.

CHAPTER 73

THE NEXT MORNING, I used a pane of glass I found in the garage to fix the shattered window. Seamus and I went to work before any of the kids were awake. I appreciated his steady hand holding the glass in place while I used some sketchy, dried-out caulk to seal it in.

Seamus said, "Not exactly the vacation you were looking for, is it?"

"No, I guess not."

"But in adversity, God often shows us what we really need."

"What's that supposed to mean?"

"I don't want you feeling sorry for yourself because your vacation isn't what you expected. I want you to see what good could come from it."

"Sometimes I swear you're from the Far East. You're absolutely inscrutable."

He gave me that charming crooked smile and said, "The Irish have always been inscrutable. We just call it mystical."

Later, after my grandfather showed me the wonders of sitting in a rocking chair, looking out over a lake, I couldn't ignore the sunshine or how much fun the kids were having jumping off the dock. This was, after all, my vacation.

I stood up, pulled off my shirt, and said, "To hell with worrying. I'm going swimming with my kids."

Seamus clapped his hands and said, "That's the spirit."

That was the day I taught the kids the difference between a cannonball and an *atomic* cannonball.

The wake of my splash washed Ricky onto the floating dock, much to the delight of all the kids. Even Sadie was cautiously hanging on to a float in shallow water, taking part in the family fun.

Then I saw a speedboat sitting on the lake off in the distance. I hadn't noticed it putter into position. It'd come down from the wide North River, which entered the lake between the forest in the foothills.

I couldn't see who was piloting the boat. It looked like a man. The engine was off, and he was just drifting. I imagined him staring at us.

I tried not to let my paranoia get the best of me. But the longer he watched us, the more angry I became. I stepped off the dock into the old rowboat that was moored alongside. It was clunky and awkward. We'd used it to fish a couple of times, and the kids liked to sit in it and rock back and forth. Now I was on the middle bench with both the oars firmly in my hands, and I pulled with all my might.

The rowboat was surprisingly agile and cut through the

water directly toward the speedboat. If nothing else, I wanted this idiot to realize I was paying attention. No one could watch my family without my taking some sort of action.

As I got closer, I heard the speedboat's motor roar to life. The operator was a middle-aged man with short dark hair. I didn't recognize him. He hit the throttle, and the boat jumped to life. He made a sharp U-turn and came past me at close to full speed. The wave from his boat soaked me and threatened to swamp my rowboat.

Then the speedboat made a pass toward shore. Not too close to the kids, but aimed directly at the house. He made another sharp turn, and the maneuver kicked water up onto the yard. It also destroyed the pen the boys had made for the catfish.

They shouted at the man as he pulled away from shore and headed directly at me again. He buzzed my rowboat, and this time the water was so deep that when the stern of my boat dipped, the lake almost flooded over the sides.

The man turned the boat and headed back toward the wide stream. He gave me a jaunty wave as he disappeared behind a clump of trees. I could hear the motor for another twenty seconds after he was out of sight.

Even if I wanted to, I knew I couldn't ignore what was going on in this town. I had to help Sandy with this crazy case and these ungrateful townspeople.

CHAPTER 74

I WAS ANTSY. I was supposed to be on vacation and enjoying my family, but instead I found that the only thing I could think about was the mess in Linewiler. For my entire career, I could never relax when a partner was working. It didn't matter who that partner was. Apparently it didn't matter *where* that partner was, either.

Mary Catherine, bless her heart, understood exactly what I was feeling and gave me a nod to let me know it was okay to leave for a few hours.

Sandy was happy to see me when I pulled up in the front yard of Dell Streeter's compound.

She gave me that familiar wide grin. "Look what the cat dragged in."

I said, "This is some shitty duty. Protecting a dope dealer

from irate townspeople. Sounds like the plot of an old horror movie."

Sandy said, "I have my extra blue light on the roof so there's no mistaking that this is a police car. We're sort of acting like a big dog. Anyone who sees us doesn't want to fool around."

"It's too bad you have to waste any time protecting this scumbag."

Sandy just shrugged. She was always better than I was at accepting a situation and just moving on. She had kept me from saying stupid things to the bosses before, when we worked the streets together.

She said, "The lab is working overtime. I pray to God we'll have something to link him to the bodies soon. Until then, we can't let anything stupid happen. Every politician in Maine has made it clear they don't want this to be on the news."

"I hate to be cynical, but guys like Dell Streeter ruin neighborhoods and towns all the time. I can't say I'd be too upset if the town decided it had had enough."

Sandy said, "You saw that crowd at the fire station. What's scary to me is that I know all those people. Until last night, I never had a reason to think they could do something crazy, like shoot someone for revenge. Now I have to rethink everything I believed. Now I have to look at my neighbors with suspicion. It's the exact reason I left New York."

"We could call in sick and forget this whole nasty business."

Sandy laughed and said, "You always could cheer me up, Bennett."

"Seriously, why is the town's only detective sitting on a midnight shift?"

"The truth is, a couple of the patrol officers refused to do it. They're close with some of the angry residents. And some of the cops are locals and have known the families their whole lives. I didn't want to take the risk that they would allow something to happen."

As usual, her reasoning was sound.

Dell Streeter stepped out onto his porch and performed an exaggerated stretch. He smiled and waved at Sandy. Then he looked more closely and saw me in the front seat. He casually came down the steps and across the yard to the car.

"Oh, great," I muttered.

Sandy dutifully rolled down her window. Dell leaned down as if he were talking to a couple of his neighbors on their way to the grocery store.

"Howdy, folks," said the Texan.

Neither of us answered.

Streeter said, "How funny is it that we kicked your asses the other day, and now you're supposed to protect us? Life can be a hoot, can't it?"

Sandy said, "Sometimes I just can't stand how much fun it is."

He looked past Sandy to me and said, "How about you, Mr. NYPD? Are you having a good day?"

I turned my head to face him and calmly said, "You know, Dell, guys who run their mouths too much always regret it later on."

"I might agree with you, except the man I've tried to model my life after has proved too many people wrong about that."

"Who have you modeled your life after?"

Streeter had a broad grin when he said, "Jerry Jones, of course."

As soon as he said it, I had to agree. The answer was obvious.

CHAPTER 75

WHILE SITTING IN the front seat of Sandy's car, I dozed off. That's not accurate. I fell asleep. Deep sleep. For some reason I was dreaming about the movie *Jaws*. I guess the boys' little impromptu skit about fishing had stuck in my head.

I awoke to Sandy shaking my shoulder.

She said, "Jesus. I was about to check your pulse."

"Sorry. You know how vacations can wear you out." I looked around and wondered why she bothered waking me. "Is everything okay?"

"I don't know. It's just a feeling. There hasn't been any activity at the house for a few hours. And I thought I saw a vehicle on the back road."

"When did you see the vehicle?"

"About two hours ago. That's when everything went silent."

I looked around the yard and said, "I see Streeter's pickup truck and the other two cars that were here before."

Sandy said, "I have no idea how many cars are parked in the back or in that run-down barn. They could've used any of them if they wanted to sneak away."

"Why would they sneak away? We're protecting them. It's not like we're on a surveillance of the house."

"I don't know, but it makes me nervous." Sandy's ringtone was a pleasant chime. She picked the phone up off the seat and said, "Hey, Charlie, what's up?"

All I heard from Sandy was a couple of "Uh-huh"s and a "No shit?"

She put down the phone and looked at me. "One of the men who was at the meeting last night was just shot outside a sports bar in town."

"You think it could be connected to Dell Streeter? You think it might actually *be* Dell Streeter?"

Sandy said, "I can't just sit here and guess. Let's go knock on the door."

"I don't want to talk to that snot again. But if there's a chance to make some kind of a case against him, I'll do whatever you want."

We hopped out of the car, and I followed her up the stairs to the porch. We stood there and listened for a minute. There was not a sound or vibration coming from the house. I looked across the compound to the dirt road that ran on the other side of the property. It was dark, and I couldn't see much. It was around one in the morning, and the clouds obscured the moon.

I said, "What do we do if no one answers? Do we kick in the door? How do we justify it?"

Sandy looked at me and said, "For a guy who always flies by the seat of his pants and rarely worries about consequences, you're starting to sound like an old man."

This time I stepped up and pounded on the front door. There was no way that sound wasn't going to wake someone up.

Still, there was no answer and no activity in the compound. I tried looking in the windows, but heavy curtains blocked my view.

Sandy said, "What do you think?"

"I think we can articulate it by saying there was a shooting in town and we had to verify his safety inside the house. Who can argue with a safety check?"

"I like the way you think."

I lined up on the door. I could either kick it or use my shoulder. I didn't like either option, but they both looked like they would work on the old wood-frame door.

I braced myself and got ready to ram my shoulder into the upper part of the door. Then I froze when I heard a noise. Someone moved the curtain on the window beside the door, then the door started to open.

Dell Streeter popped his head out and said, "What's all the commotion about?"

I blurted out, "You didn't answer the door, you moron. That's what the commotion is about."

"Well, excuse me all to hell. But you know it is late at night. I dozed off in the storm cellar. It's always a cool sixty-eight degrees down there. Are you going to knock on the door every time you don't see me for a few minutes?"

Sandy said, "Mickey Bale was shot and killed outside of the Bear and Buffalo Wings sports bar."

"Looks like you might've been protecting the wrong man. Sorry to hear you lost someone on your watch. Not surprised, just sorry."

At that moment, I wished Dell Streeter had been the one who was shot.

CHAPTER 76

I PULLED UP to the scene of the shooting right behind Sandy. We were in the middle of town. Everyone recognized her car as an official police vehicle. My van didn't warrant a second look from anyone.

There were a lot of people on the street for this time of night. This was not a typical evening in a quaint Maine town. This was a police crime scene involving a shooting, and it looked just like every other shooting scene I had ever been to. It could've been a street in the Bronx, except the buildings were smaller and there wasn't quite the diversity you saw in the city.

Official vehicles were pulled in at odd angles, and a crowd of bystanders was being held back by a young officer. They were looking at nothing. Like bystanders everywhere.

A medical examiner's investigator was photographing the body.

The dead man was a slightly overweight guy in his late thirties with a scruffy beard. His flannel shirt had two giant bloodstains on the front where the bullets had struck him directly in the chest.

I stepped up behind Sandy and said, "Where are the privacy blinds to block the media's view?"

Sandy said, "We don't have any. We've never *needed* any. This isn't Chicago. This is Linewiler, Maine."

"That doesn't change the fact that a body is lying on the street."

She nodded, irritated at my insistence. Sandy looked at a stocky city worker who wasn't a cop. She said, "Chuck, can you get into city hall and bring me three cubicle dividers?"

The tall middle-aged man jumped right to it and grabbed two others as he raced into the city hall. In New York, a city worker would've told me it wasn't his job or that I couldn't tell him what to do. This was impressive.

Sandy had complete command of the scene. She explained to some of the officers why they were doing the tasks assigned to them, such as keeping a list of everyone who entered the crime scene and finding out if any of the nearby buildings had a security camera running.

Sandy turned to one young officer who looked like he had been in the military. He was lanky, with a flattop, and he held himself perfectly straight.

She said, "I need you to talk to everyone in the bar and find out if anyone saw anything."

The young officer said, "Do you want me to talk to them one at a time or as a group all at once?"

Sandy muttered, "God, give me strength."

I chuckled at the frustration that universally afflicts experienced police officers dealing with rookies. I volunteered. "I can handle that, Sandy."

Her smile was all I needed in the way of thanks.

Inside the Bear and Buffalo Wings sports bar, most of the TVs were already turned off. A bored bartender watched a rebroadcast of a Red Sox game on the TV over the bar.

A group of around ten people huddled around someone at a table in the corner of the room. As I walked closer, I realized they were all part of the group Sandy and I had talked to at the fire station.

Then I noticed they were all listening to one person. He looked up at me with sharp brown eyes above a ruddy nose.

It was Tom Bacon. Great.

CHAPTER 77

TOM BACON DIDN'T waste any time when he looked at me and said, "What the hell are you doing here?"

"Helping Sandy figure out who shot your friend out there. But looking at this group, and knowing what you're all riled up about, I have to ask one question."

"What would that be?"

"I think I know the answer, but did you announce this meeting to the public?"

Tom Bacon looked at me, his face flushed an angry red. "Yeah—on Facebook. Why?"

"So if someone wanted to send a message, he knew exactly where and when all of you would be together. That was very thoughtful of you to inform him."

"So Dell Streeter *is* behind this."

"No, he wasn't. I was at his house during the shooting, and he answered the door right afterward."

"But he had someone shoot Mickey, right?"

I had already said too much. It was never a good idea for a cop to reinforce a conspiracy theory. Especially when the people putting the theory together were a bunch of well-armed crackpots who were already pissed off.

Bacon said, "Well, what do you think? Is Dell Streeter behind this?"

"The shooting is being investigated. The local police are doing everything they can."

"Just like they did when they were looking for my son? Just like they're doing investigating his death? Remind me, Bennett. How far did you get on that case?"

"I'm sorry, Mr. Bacon. We really are doing everything we can." What I wanted to say was, *Hey, I don't even work here.* But I didn't want to cause Sandy any grief.

Then the big guy, Anthony, who'd accused Sandy and me of being crooked, stepped up and said, "Dell Streeter didn't pay you enough to keep him safe at his own house."

Again, I bit my tongue.

Anthony said, "We're going to make you earn every penny of it. A good man like Mickey Bale is gunned down, and you won't do a thing about it."

I said, "What do you think we're doing right now?"

"By talking to us? No one in this room shot Mickey."

"I'm trying to find out if anyone *saw* anything that could help us. Unless you have a better idea of what I should do."

The burly man said, "Go arrest Dell Streeter. That would solve everyone's problem."

I didn't want to tell Anthony that I was dreaming about the time when I could finally arrest Dell Streeter.

CHAPTER 78

NO ONE INSIDE the bar saw anything. No one inside the bar really wanted to talk to me, either. Another common experience among cops everywhere. All the witnesses had basically the same story. They heard a couple of shots, but when they made it out the door, there was no one in sight, and Mickey Bale was lying on the sidewalk bleeding to death.

Everyone talked about what a great guy he was. That he was a good father to three kids. That he worked hard for Tom Bacon as a carpenter. Now he was dead.

Tom Bacon told the crowd that I was at Dell Streeter's house protecting him when poor Mickey Bale was gunned down.

So much for private conversations.

It was the middle of the night when I stepped out of the bar and found Sandy still directing the crime scene. At least the body had been removed.

She laughed when she saw me and said, "Mike, I forgot you were still here."

"Story of my life."

"We're getting a pretty good handle on this. Why don't you go home to that family of yours? Maybe you can enjoy your vacation for a while." She gave me a sly smile, and I had to chuckle.

While we were standing there chatting, Tom Bacon and his friend Anthony came out of the bar and walked directly over to us.

Bacon said, "Detective Coles, I know you're a relative new-comer to our community, but—"

She interrupted him. "Eight years. I've lived here eight damn years."

"But somehow you still don't understand how things work. You're a city employee. You need to start listening to what some of the city residents have to say and what they want you to do."

"Such as?"

It was Anthony who answered. "Butt out of this Dell Streeter business. He's an outsider. We know how to deal with outsiders. We also know how to protect our own."

Sandy kept her cool. But I still realized I wouldn't want to be on the other side of her gaze. She said, "You're right. I am a city employee. More important, I am a sworn law-enforcement officer. Part of my oath was that I would faithfully enforce the law. It didn't say anything about enforcing it only when it was convenient."

I watched with interest as the two men just stared at her.

Sandy continued, "I'm going to break that vow right now. I'm not going to arrest you for saying that you intend to assault or possibly murder a local resident. Dell Streeter has not been convicted of jack shit. And frankly, neither of you two assholes knows jack shit about the law. So I'm going to keep on doing my job and pray to God that you're smart enough to stay out of my way."

I was afraid her speech impressed me a lot more than it impressed either of those two dullards. But it still gave me a thrill to hear it. She was as eloquent and tough as any cop I had ever known.

CHAPTER 79

I WAS BEAT. Beat like an old rug. I could feel our family van swerve several times on my way home from the scene of the shooting. All I wanted to do was reach the Ghost House in one piece and fall into bed. I was going to sleep through the day and night again. At this point, I didn't care how many kids were in the bed. I just needed a few feet of soft mattress.

There was no way I would ever complain about the NYPD and its lack of resources again. Every cop deals with shortages of manpower, money, and equipment. But compared to most, the NYPD had plenty.

In a little town like Linewiler, having more than two things to do at once could be devastating. Trying to keep an eye on a shithead like Dell Streeter and investigate a shooting at a sports bar pushed their resources to the absolute limit.

I found it hard to believe it was a coincidence that the man shot outside the sports bar was one of the vocal vigilantes who wanted to lynch Dell Streeter as soon as he had the chance. But there were no witnesses, there was no video, and there was nothing to go on. Just a local man shot twice in the chest as he was coming out of one of the town's most popular bars.

Sandy told me it was the first drive-by shooting Linewiler had ever experienced. One of the reasons she'd been brought in as the assistant chief and detective was to stay ahead of the curve on crimes like this. She admitted she'd become complacent in the years since she left New York.

Now she was not only investigating the crime, she was also trying to teach others what to do in the future. I wanted to help, but at some point your body just shuts down. I couldn't imagine anything getting me to move once I made it home.

The sun was up, but there was an ominous line of thunderstorms creeping toward me from the other side of Lake Nim.

I was a little surprised to see all the kids awake when I came through the front door. Chrissy and Shawna greeted me with their usual extravagant hugs, and the teenagers gave me a wave or a nod. About as much as I could expect.

I made my way to the kitchen, where Ricky was flipping a pancake into the air from a frying pan.

Mary Catherine came in from the outside door. Instantly, from the look on her face, I knew something was wrong. My first thought was Seamus. But the old man followed right behind her.

She rushed across the kitchen and gave me a hug.

Mary Catherine said, "I was so worried about you."

I sighed with relief. "From your expression, I was afraid something was wrong here."

"It is. Sadie is missing. Near as I can tell she left sometime in the middle of the night. Seamus and I have searched around the house and in the woods. If the kids know something, they're not telling me."

Suddenly sleep didn't seem that important anymore. I pictured the poor girl out on the street again. But why? She had to feel welcome here. We really *did* want her here.

I started asking the kids. On something like this I knew to talk to them one-on-one. Just in case there was some sort of teenage honor involved and they didn't want to rat on a friend.

Ricky shook his head and said, "I haven't seen her since last night. She wasn't here for breakfast. I didn't notice until just now."

I moved on, asking each kid. The order depended on location. As soon as I found someone, I pulled him or her off to the side and asked if he or she had seen Sadie or if she had said anything. They couldn't know the danger she was in. All they knew was that this lonely young woman had slid into our family and now she was gone.

Finally it was Chrissy who told me what had happened. She said, "I heard Sadie moving around in the middle of the night. She was on the cot in my bedroom. I followed her downstairs, and she told me I couldn't come with her."

I held the little girl by the shoulders and looked into her eyes. "Did Sadie say anything about where she was going?"

"She said she had business. Serious business. She said the cops would never be able to do anything about Bill Sweeper."

"About what?"

"I think she said the man's name was Bill Sweeper."

Then it clicked in my head. I felt sick to my stomach. She meant to say Dell Streeter.

CHAPTER 80

JUST AS I stepped out the front door, a lightning bolt struck near the lake, and the rain started to fall. The drops were so heavy they hurt my head as I rushed to the van. I wasn't exactly sure where to look for Sadie, but I knew I couldn't stay at home. I also had an idea she might be headed for Dell Streeter's house. It was a crazy idea, but that would be my first stop.

I didn't know what Sadie thought she could accomplish by confronting the drug dealer at his own compound. But I couldn't risk the possibility of a bad outcome.

The downpour became torrential once I was on the highway, but there was no way I was going to stop. I could only see a few feet in front of the van. I pushed it anyway. A gust of wind shoved the van to the right. A clap of thunder made me jump in the seat.

Brian flashed into my head. No matter where I went, there was still a drug problem that was affecting my life. It affected everyone's lives, whether people realized it or not. And drugs were ruining too many lives. At least drug *dealers* were. They were a scourge on society. But the courts weren't helping much.

I called Sandy just to let her know what was happening but got no answer. God knows how busy she was this morning with the shooting and a crowd of vigilantes.

I felt sorry for the little town. It was like the people here had put their heads in the sand so that they could ignore the world around them. Even Tom Bacon knew his son and others were using serious drugs. He dismissed it. It was easier to ignore the issue than have an uncomfortable conversation and take the risk that the boy would want to move back with his mother.

Then there was the issue of that Texas jackass Dell Streeter. He played by a different set of rules. Whereas the people of Maine tended to be polite and considerate, Streeter had shown what being brash and bold could do. He saw a gap in the drug distribution network, a possible new market, and made the best of it.

Drugs weren't a problem in society, they were a symptom. A symptom of something wrong. I wished I was smart enough to figure out what that problem was and offer some solutions. All I was used for was to clean up the mess drugs often caused.

It was hard to explain why Saint Louis had the most murders per capita of any city in the United States. Or why Baltimore came in second. But drugs played a huge role in that. So did gangs and a number of other issues. But drugs and money could always be found at the root of those issues. I saw it every day. Almost 70 percent of the homicides I investigated had something to do with the sale of drugs.

We used to joke in Homicide that if a woman disappeared, all we had to do was arrest her boyfriend or husband and we'd have the right suspect 80 percent of the time. I was starting to feel the same way about drug dealers. If we got them off the streets, I wondered what the streets would look like.

I hoped Linewiler could still be cleaned up. Right now, the only thing I hoped for was to find Sadie safe and bring her back home.

CHAPTER 81

AS I PULLED through the open gate at Dell Streeter's compound, the first thing I noticed was that there were no police cars on-site. I figured the shooting in town had drawn off everyone. But it still seemed like a risk not to leave someone at the house, what with so many people in town screaming for Dell Streeter's head.

I stepped out of the van and surveyed the front yard. One of the cars that was usually there was gone. There were no bodyguards in sight. In fact, *no one* was in sight.

The house looked quiet. There were no lights on. The rain had eased, and I crossed the yard slowly and took each step up to the porch carefully.

Something told me to keep my pistol in my hand. I drew it from the holster on my hip and kept my hand slightly behind my leg. I listened for any sign that someone was moving around the house. Nothing.

I had an uneasy feeling. The problem with being a cop for so long is that you get a lot of uneasy feelings. The issue is figuring out which ones to pay attention to. Some people call it being jumpy. It was an insult to call a cop jumpy. But that's what I was at this moment.

A sound at the edge of the property made me crouch and aim my pistol. It was a feral cat scurrying away from something.

I paused on the porch and took a deep breath.

I wasn't in the mood for any of Dell Streeter's bullshit. If he had seen Sadie, I was going to find out. If he had hurt her, he was going to pay. This was the simple plan that would keep me motivated.

I leaned in and looked through one of the dirty windows. I saw no movement in the house.

Then I heard it. Plain as day. A single gunshot from inside the house.

I rushed to the front door. It was locked. I threw my shoulder into it quickly, then realized it was reinforced. It looked like it was flimsy, but it wasn't.

Frantically, I searched the porch for options. I grabbed one of the heavy rocking chairs sitting there and spun like Hercules throwing a discus. I threw the chair through one of the main front windows, then jumped into the house with my pistol up.

I was surprised how dark it was inside. I crouched low and moved to a wall so I could scan the area in front of me without worrying about being attacked from behind.

I moved through the house with my gun up. There were three bedrooms. All empty. I had already been through the main room. I paused and glanced into the kitchen as I moved past it.

I found one more door. It was locked. Unlike the front door, it wasn't reinforced. When I threw my body into it, it buckled and broke into pieces. I stumbled into the dark room. I scanned it quickly and stepped back to flick on the light. It was an office of some kind, with a couple of computers. But there was no one there.

Where had the gunshot come from? I had searched the whole house. Maybe it had come from outside. I started back through the house, fearing the worst.

The idea of Sadie with a bullet in her forced me to move quickly. I had to search the house. I had to find her.

I had to deal with Dell Streeter.

CHAPTER 82

AS I PASSED the kitchen, I heard something. I froze and listened intently. The rain was down to a light drizzle. It was a steady drone on the tin roof, but I was still certain I had heard something.

I stepped into the kitchen. It was empty. I had seen everything during my dash through the house. Lots of cabinets and the usual appliances. The kitchen was made to serve a lot of people.

Then I saw it. Blood. On the linoleum near the sink. I dropped to my knee and touched it with my left index finger. It was fresh. It was wet. And I was worried.

I scanned the kitchen quickly. In the corner, on the counter near the door, was a butcher knife. The last inch of the blade had blood on it. Someone had been stabbed, but not hard enough to send the blade deep into the body.

That didn't make me feel any better. The thought of Sadie with an injury from a knife like this made me shudder.

Then I heard the noise again. It was a voice. I listened. It was two voices. A chill went down my spine. Maybe this was the real Ghost House.

Then I heard the voice more clearly. I recognized it. It was Dell Streeter. He was talking to someone. I could even discern the twang in his speech. It was tense, and he was upset.

I wondered if he was speaking with Sadie. That would be a disaster. But how did she make it all the way over here? How did she get past the bodyguards? How did she get into a locked house?

I stepped toward the living room and listened. I could hear the voice in the living room, too. I stepped carefully, conscious of the possibility of creaking boards below my feet.

I realized where the sound was coming from. I got down on my knees and lowered my head toward the floor. This house had a cellar.

I heard the other voice. It was softer and harder to understand.

There was some kind of question-and-answer exchange going on between the two people. Streeter was much louder. He was under stress, I could tell.

Then I heard the other voice again. It was female. And she had an edge of anger in her voice.

It was Sadie.

Where was the goddamn entrance to the cellar? Now I started to scramble around, looking for it. I'd seen too much heartache recently and couldn't deal with the idea of another dead kid. It was as close to panic as anything I had ever experienced.

I headed into the kitchen to cut across the house. Then I saw it.

It could have been mistaken for a tall cabinet door. Wedged between the refrigerator and pantry, it was easy to overlook.

It was the entrance to the cellar.

CHAPTER 83

I HAD TO play this just right. I didn't want to startle Dell Streeter into doing something drastic. I didn't want Sadie to be caught in a shoot-out between me and the Texas drug dealer.

There was no way to disguise the light from upstairs as I took the stairs into the cellar.

I went down the steps carefully, with the gun out in front of me. I ducked so I wouldn't be such an easy target, but I was still headed down the stairs no matter what happened. Dell Streeter could be standing there with a shotgun, and I would've pushed past him to get to Sadie.

It wasn't completely black at the bottom of the stairs. There was a short, twisting corridor, and I could see light coming from the end.

Now I could hear them clearly. Sadie sounded angry.

I came around the corner with my pistol raised so I could fire immediately.

Then I froze.

I lowered the gun slightly and blinked. I wasn't sure I was seeing the scene before me correctly.

Dell Streeter was in the far corner of the room, holding himself up on a table built into the wall. Blood was seeping out of a gunshot wound on his upper left leg. I could also see where Sadie had jabbed him with the knife on his shoulder. Streeter's Emmitt Smith jersey was ripped, and blood dripped down his arm.

Streeter said, "Never thought I'd be glad to see a cop."

When he saw how shocked I was, he yelled, "Do something!"

In another corner, on the opposite side of the room, Sadie stood with a pistol in her hand. A blued 9mm semiautomatic. It looked like a Beretta. And she was holding it pretty well.

I was very careful when I said, "Sadie, are you all right?"

She didn't take her eyes off her target. Good girl. Then she said in a very calm voice, "I'm doing great. The best I've done in a couple of years. But you probably don't want to see what's about to happen."

Then Dell Streeter screamed at me, "Are you crazy? Get that gun away from that bitch!"

Sadie still didn't look at me but said, "Will you please lower your gun? It makes me nervous."

I was still so shocked and, frankly, confused that I lowered the gun without thinking.

Now Streeter yelled, "No! Don't do what she says. Shoot that bitch."

Sadie said, "This is long overdue. I've lived my life in fear. I have nightmares about waking up with dirt over my face. Whenever a kid disappears from high school, I feel like I'm the only one who knows what happened. He's ruining this town, and I can do something about it."

Streeter was shrill. "Are you kidding me? You're listening to this bullshit? She broke in my house. Snuck up on me and stabbed me with a damn knife."

He continued, "When I was all confused and in shock she shoved me down the stairs. Then she shot me in the leg. Now you're worried that *she's* okay. Give me a break."

Sadie said, "I've got to do something. He's a disease, and he's spreading."

I said, "This isn't the answer."

"What is? Arresting him and taking him to jail, where they'll release him the same day? Or is the answer to protect him from people in the town? Because so far everything I've seen anyone do fails."

She didn't seem to be the least bit afraid. And that made me afraid. If she truly believed she had nothing to lose, then she was desperate. And desperate people are rarely open to negotiation.

Sadie said, "Mike, you've been good to me. But I know how seriously you take your job. And when this is all over, I want you to be able to say you did your duty."

I turned from Dell Streeter back to her and said, "What are you talking about?"

"I want you to toss your gun onto the ground. You know I'm not going to hurt you. But I don't want you to try to interfere."

I hesitated.

Sadie said, "Mike, put your gun on the ground right now."

I had heard that tone before. Many times. It was the tone used by people who weren't bluffing. I bent my knees, then tossed the gun a few feet away onto the raw concrete floor. I had given up my gun in tough situations before. It always gave me a sick feeling in my stomach.

This was no exception.

CHAPTER 84

I IMMEDIATELY WENT into my negotiator mode. I said, "We can work this out, Sadie. It's not too late."

"Too late for what? This is exactly what I should be doing. There's nothing that can happen to me that's worse than what I've already been through."

I thought about that, and it made me sad. She was right. Life had dealt her a bad hand. But she was bright, determined, and so very, very young. She probably didn't believe it at that moment, but she had a lot of life in front of her. I couldn't let her give it up. Especially because of a shitbag like Dell Streeter.

My heart broke at the thought of Sadie getting in trouble for this. I tried not to sound like I was pleading, but it was hard to do anything else.

"Sadie, sweetheart, please don't use that gun."

She stared straight ahead over the barrel of the pistol pointed at Dell Streeter.

"Think about the consequences. You're smart. Really smart. You can do anything in this world. But not if you're rotting in some jail."

"Who says I plan to go to jail? And if I don't do anything to him, it's only a matter of time before he kills me. You know that. I'm a witness against him. It's bad business to let someone like me live."

I was at a loss. And I was desperate. I felt like I was falling down a hole and couldn't get my footing. How could I stop her from doing something crazy? She was too far away for me to try to make a grab for the gun. I also wasn't sure I wouldn't hurt her if I threw my whole body against her.

I looked over at Streeter. He was still on his feet, but blood was pouring out of the bullet wound in his leg now. He was sweating, and his hair was pasted to his forehead.

Sadie said, "You don't have to be here. I'm fine. Really. It would be better for both of us if you just left."

"I can't do that, Sadie. I couldn't walk away from anyone in as much pain as you."

Now Dell Streeter sounded outraged. "She's in pain? Are you kidding me? Look at me. The gimpy bitch stabbed me and put a bullet in me."

Sadie was very calm when she said, "Please believe me. I'm okay. I'm fine. I know what I have to do."

I said, "What do you think you *need* to do?"

"I need to make this guy admit everything he's done. If you're here, I might as well make him tell you where he hides his heroin. That way, no matter what, you'll at least have something on him."

Streeter said, "C'mon, Bennett. I'm not much for gun control, but you need to disarm her. Right now."

Sadie directed her comments to Streeter. She said, "I'm going to make you talk. You're going to tell us about all the shit you've done around here."

"I'm not saying nothing. You can't make me talk. I don't even have to invoke my Fifth Amendment rights. You're not a judge, and I don't have to say shit."

That's when Sadie pulled the trigger again.

CHAPTER 85

I FLINCHED AT the sound of the gun going off. Inside the cellar, with the tight walls and good insulation, it sounded like a bomb. The acrid smell of gunpowder made me queasy when I thought about the consequences.

The croak that came out of Dell Streeter when the bullet struck him made me realize there was no turning back. He let out a strangled cry. No real words, just some whimpering.

And Sadie kept her steady stance, with the pistol still up in front of her. She was cool and calm. And that was frightening.

I looked over at Dell Streeter, who had fallen back onto a box. The second bullet had struck his other leg almost at his hip. He squirmed in pain as blood pumped out of the wound.

Now it was important to keep Sadie engaged with me. I had

to keep her mind off what she had just done. I didn't want it to be a stepping-stone for something worse. Although at this point, it couldn't get much worse.

I said, "Sadie, look at me, sweetheart."

She kept her focus on the wounded Dell Streeter.

"You have to believe me when I tell you this will all work out. Just give me the gun, and we'll walk out of this house together. No one will hurt you. I swear to God." I meant that more than anything else I had ever said. I would kill anyone who tried to harm this girl. This girl who, despite everything else, was still just a child. Vulnerable and desperate. I had to help her.

Sadie said, "You've been good to me. You're a good father. Living back in the Ghost House with your family showed me what life could be like. What I missed out on. And it's all because of men like this. And nothing ever happens to them. Bad things only seem to happen to people around them."

I thought about the drug dealer who had used Brian. How Brian's life was ruined because he met that man. Maybe Sadie was right. This was the only way to deal with scum like this.

Sadie took a step forward.

I could see a change in Dell Streeter's attitude as she crept closer to him with the gun still in her hand.

Sadie said to Streeter, "Tell us about all the evil that went on around here. Tell us where you hide your drugs. Tell me how you're going to explain yourself when you meet God."

Streeter started to jabber at me. "Bennett, stop fooling around. Do something. You're a cop. You can't let this happen."

Damn it. He was right. But I couldn't hurt Sadie, either.

Now she was standing directly in front of the drug dealer. He still hadn't admitted to anything. He hadn't done anything other than plead for his life. It made me wonder how many people had pleaded for their lives in front of him. Had he ever listened?

Then Sadie touched the barrel of the pistol to his chest.

CHAPTER 86

I WATCHED, FROZEN in time and space, with Sadie holding the gun to Dell Streeter's chest. I calculated the distance across the room and realized Sadie would have plenty of time to pull the trigger before I made it halfway there.

Dell Streeter's face reflected the light from the single bulb hanging in the middle of the room. Sweat poured off his nose and chin as he tried to maintain some sense of composure. But his body betrayed him. He was shaking uncontrollably. The blood from the bullet wounds in his legs had now stained his pants past his knees.

And the girl he had tried to bury alive was holding a gun to his heart.

I felt helpless as I watched the scene unfold.

Sadie didn't look nervous or frightened. This was something she had considered doing for a long time. Then I realized that part of her motivation was to protect my family. She didn't want anyone from the town, or Dell Streeter himself, to do anything that might hurt one of the kids. She was trying to help.

Quickly I said, "Sadie, I can protect the family. I can protect you. The kids, Mary Catherine, and Seamus are all safe. We'll be headed back to New York soon. You don't have to do this."

Sadie kept staring at Dell Streeter, not moving the gun an inch. She said, "What about protecting the kids he keeps selling this shit to? What about the next time he gets away with some terrible crime? What happens if he just runs away and I have to worry about him coming back to kill me someday?"

"I can protect you."

"I can protect myself." She pushed the gun against Dell Streeter's chest even harder. For the first time she raised her voice. "Talk. Tell us where the drugs are." She meant business, and I knew it.

Streeter stared straight ahead like he was imagining he was someplace else. A place where someone wasn't holding a gun to his body. He didn't make a sound.

Sadie said, "Tell us where the drugs are or you'll hear this gun go off again, and you won't like it. I've already shot both legs. I'll need a new target."

Streeter cut his eyes to the gun but remained silent.

That's when Sadie took a step back, looked down the barrel of the pistol, lowered it slightly, and pulled the trigger.

Again the sound erupted in the small room like a lion's roar. I was a little more prepared for it, but it was still shocking. The muzzle flash blinded me for a second. As soon as my hearing came back I heard a wild wailing.

My eyes focused, and I realized that Sadie had shot Streeter in the hand. She had blown off a couple of his fingers, and blood was gushing out of the stumps.

Streeter's eyes bulged at the sight of his mangled hand.

Now Sadie stuck the warm barrel of the gun to Streeter's temple.

That did it. I don't know if it was the sight of his destroyed hand or the feeling of the gun mashed against his skull. Dell Streeter started to talk.

"Okay, okay, okay. The stash is in my office. The room with the computers. At the top of the closet, there's a hole in the ceiling that's hidden. We keep everything there. I swear. Just lower the gun."

Sadie said, "That's all I needed to hear." She looked at me. "That would be enough to send him to jail, right?"

I just nodded. I didn't care what it took—I wanted her to step away from him while he was still alive.

Sadie said, "Good." Then she took half a step away from Streeter and aimed the gun at his head.

Now I rushed forward and shouted, "No!"

Once again, the sound of the gunshot in the enclosed cellar was deafening. The smell of the gunpowder was sickening. And the idea that this young girl had been pushed to murder was devastating.

Then I looked across the room. Sadie was starting to cry as she dropped the pistol.

Dell Streeter just stared at me. Terrified.

Sadie had fired over his head intentionally. And now everything had caught up with her. She leaned against the shelves on the wall of the cellar and started to weep.

I crossed the room to hug her.

CHAPTER 87

THE LAST THING I wanted was Sadie facing some
kind of attempted murder charge. I left her sitting on the
bottom step of the cellar stairs. I grabbed some rags off a work-
bench and did my best to stem the blood pouring out of Dell
Streeter's legs. He whined the whole time.

His hand was the ugliest injury. The fingers were gone.
There was nothing I could do about that. He flinched and
grunted as I wrapped a towel around his bloody stumps.

I said, "Hold that in place with your other hand."

All he had the strength to do was nod.

The wound on his shoulder was superficial, but I could see
where it would've startled the shit out of him. I'm sure he
never expected a teenage girl like Sadie to sneak up behind
him and stab him with a butcher knife. It didn't matter what

the knife did to him: the shock was what allowed Sadie to get control of him.

As I was tying a rag around the wound on his right leg, Streeter seemed to focus and looked at me.

He said, "Is it going to be hard to arrest her for attempted murder?"

"What the hell are you talking about?"

"That crazy little bitch tried to kill me."

"That's how it may look from your perspective. I saw a girl acting in self-defense. I suspect just about any jury would view it the same way. I don't see any story line in which a drug dealer under investigation for murder isn't considered a threat to a helpless girl."

"That girl is anything but helpless."

I had to smile. "You're right. I meant *helpless-looking* girl."

"So all that talk about justice is just bullshit?"

"Justice comes in many forms. Some might say you're escaping justice by being arrested and not giving the people of this town a chance to deal with you."

"I'm not worried about any charges you try to file against me for information I gave up while being tortured. This is still America. No judge will allow anything you find in this house in court. Nothing I said will ever be repeated in front of a jury."

He wasn't quite as stupid as he looked. He had a point, and I'd already considered it. I heard someone shout from upstairs.

"Police. Is anyone down there?"

I shouted, "Yeah, we're down here. We need some paramedics."

A few minutes later, after professionals were tending to

Dell Streeter, Sadie and I were safely upstairs. Police cars from the state and county were starting to pull into the compound along with a fire engine. I guess the fire department didn't get enough calls and wanted to be in on anything that might happen. Firemen are like that. They like to be involved. It makes them feel better about getting paid to sleep and work out.

I sat in the living room with Sadie. She was quiet, and I wanted to make sure she was okay. She'd been careful to wipe the tears from her eyes and make sure no one would realize she had been crying.

I just sat next to her on the couch quietly. We both watched as the paramedics came through and the state police started to secure the house. I hadn't told them anything yet. They knew who I was and suspected that I had quite a tale to tell.

First I needed to talk to Sadie about a few things.

"Sadie, sweetheart, I need you to listen to me very carefully."

She turned those big, intelligent eyes to me but didn't say a word.

"Someone is going to ask you questions about what happened down there. I don't know who it will be or when, but it's going to happen."

She nodded.

"You need to tell them how scared you were and that you were just protecting yourself."

"I wasn't really scared. I knew what I was doing."

"And that's exactly what I don't want you to tell anyone."

She gave me a sly smile. "Doesn't giving me advice like that violate your oath as a police officer?"

"I can't watch another kid go to jail. I can't bear to see you sent away for something like this. That's why I'm asking you to do it as a favor to me."

"You want me to lie?"

"Did you think Dell Streeter was going to come after you at some point?"

"Yes."

"Then you won't be lying. It was self-defense. You had to do it to save yourself. Be very vague on everything else. Tell them you'll only talk to Detective Coles from the Linewiler PD. They won't realize you already know her."

I could see her considering it. Finally she said, "I'll do it for you. But you've got to make sure Dell goes to jail."

I was already working on that in my head. There were a few problems. Streeter himself had already mentioned the biggest problem. Anything he said and anything we found could be suppressed by a judge.

I had to figure a way around that.

CHAPTER 88

AS THE HOUSE became crowded with paramedics and cops, Sadie and I moved out to the front porch to wait for Sandy Coles to arrive. I'd already made Sadie run through her story a couple of times and was starting to feel confident that we would at least be able to walk away from the scene.

That still left the problem of finding a way to use the information Streeter provided while under duress. Legal procedure dictates that cops shy away from torture when questioning suspects. We needed another source of the information.

Sadie and I both suppressed smiles as they brought Streeter out of the house on a stretcher. He was already yapping like a little dog. His twang made his tirade even more comical.

When the wheels of the stretcher scuffed the hard wood, he barked, "Easy on the floor, asshole. I paid a lot of money to have that floor laid down just right. You ruin it with this stretcher, and the county will be hearing from my attorney."

As they brought him down the stairs on the porch he was jostled pretty hard, and one of the wheels of the stretcher bounced off the second step. I knew it was probably done on purpose.

Streeter yelled, "Great! Now I'll have spinal issues along with everything else. Have you guys ever been able to rescue someone alive?"

Then, when they turned him around to load him into the ambulance, he saw the two of us sitting outside on the porch swing. That really agitated him.

He pointed with his left hand—the only one that still had fingers available to point—and said, "She did this to me. Someone needs to arrest that girl. I mean right damn now."

As they closed the ambulance door, we could still hear him shouting for someone to do something about Sadie.

I looked at her and said, "See? He was threatening you again. Anything you did was in self-defense."

Sandy pulled up and parked outside the fence of the compound. The property was already filled with rescue vehicles and police cars. She made her way around them and headed for the porch.

As soon as she saw Sadie sitting safely next to me, she started to cry. I had never seen Sandy Coles cry in my entire life. She bounded up the steps and embraced the girl. When she squeezed her tight, Sadie started to cry as well.

I was about to explain to Sandy exactly what had happened and what I'd told Sadie to say. I was also going to tell her about the drugs in the closet. Then fate stepped in. That's the only way I can describe it. I suddenly saw a chance to fix the biggest problem with our case.

A Dodge Charger drove past the compound slowly. I stared through the open window at the passenger and driver.

Next to me, Sadie said, "That's D.T. and Billy Ray."

"Those are Streeter's bodyguards, right?"

Sadie said, "They're the other two who live here full-time. I don't know what their exact job is. They came from Texas with him."

I said to Sandy, "Let me borrow your keys."

She said, "What are you going to do, Bennett?"

"Fix this case's biggest problem. But I've got to do it right now, and I've got to do it alone."

CHAPTER 89

I KNEW THE road went on for more than a mile before it petered out into an unpaved trail. Eventually it just stopped in the woods. Either I would catch up to the bodyguards or they would have to come back the same way. There were no other options.

I can honestly say that while working for the NYPD, I had never chased anyone named Billy Ray before. Still, this wasn't actually a chase. They weren't running from me. I wasn't even sure what was going to happen if I caught them.

I passed a few houses similar to Dell Streeter's on the way up the winding road. One house looked out of place because it was spectacularly well maintained and had a stable behind it with two horses loitering in front of the building.

But I still didn't see the Dodge.

Finally, just as the paved road turned into the trail, I saw the car turning around and preparing to head back down the road. This was the moment of truth. How much force could I use to stop them? How could I explain the force I used? Were they suspects? Were they witnesses? I had to play this smart.

I pulled Sandy's car at an angle across the road. There was no mistaking it was a police car, and I didn't want them to drive past me. I stepped out of the driver's-side door and kept the car between me and the two associates of Dell Streeter.

The driver—I didn't know if it was Billy Ray or D.T.— revved the engine. The powerful Hemi motor sounded like a jet preparing for takeoff.

I pulled my pistol from its holster but kept it out of sight. I was starting to question my judgment in chasing down these two by myself. But I had a plan and intended to stick to it.

The tires of the car squealed and kicked up gravel as it started down the road directly toward me. I judged the distance, figuring out whether I needed to spring off to the side or fire a couple of rounds into the windshield.

Then the driver hit the brakes, and the wheels skidded along the road, causing smoke to come off them. The Dodge slid to a stop inches away from the car I'd borrowed from Sandy.

I kept my cool and walked around the police vehicle's trunk. I kept my eyes on the Dodge and noted that neither of the occupants moved a muscle. They were both staring at me. That's when I noticed how young they were. Probably not even thirty. That worked into my plan very well.

I stayed at the trunk and used my left hand to motion both of them to come over and talk to me. It was a casual movement, not an order from an angry cop.

They both showed some decent judgment as they eased out of the car slowly and made sure I could see their hands clearly as they approached.

The taller one, who had a scraggly beard, said, "Is there something we can do for you, Officer?"

I gave him a quick smile and said, "Let's cut through the bullshit. You're Billy Ray, right?"

The lanky young man looked a little surprised and nodded.

I kept my eyes on both of them to make sure no one did anything stupid. My pistol was still in my right hand, hidden from sight below the trunk of the car.

I said, "You saw we had the entire cavalry at your house. I know you've got to be curious about what's going on."

They both stared at me silently. Then the shorter one, D.T., shrugged. "I wondered what could attract so much attention."

Good—I had them hooked. The first step in my plan.

I said, "Your boss, Dell, is in custody. He's already told us quite a bit. He told me that you hid the heroin in a compartment at the top of the closet in his office."

That got their attention. Just the way I wanted it to.

Now I took a little risk. "He told us about the bodies, too." I let that sink in. "But I know you two work for him, and I want to give you a chance to save yourselves some serious prison time. Prison time up here, in a place where you have no family and no friends and where no one really likes Texans."

Streeter was right all along. If I went into court and said he told us where the drugs were hidden while he was being threatened with a pistol, he'd be out in less than an hour. But if these guys volunteered the information, if I used their statements, then we had a much better chance in court. But I had to sell it. This is what cops did all the time. They sold their ideas to peers and superiors.

I said, "Boys, you better make a business decision real quick. You can be on the train as it leaves the station or under it. It doesn't make much difference to me. I just want to make a better case against your boss. He's already implicated you guys. I was just curious if you wanted to act tough or go home and see your families."

It was Billy Ray who cracked. He realized I wouldn't know about the drugs in the closet unless Dell really had said something. He had no idea how much or how little his boss had said, but he had definitely talked. That's all it took.

The lanky young man said, "What do you need from us?"

I smiled. I knew Sandy had a voice recorder in the car. This was going to work out just fine.

CHAPTER 90

I SHOWED UP back at the house and met Sandy on the porch. I had a well-deserved smug smile on my face. She looked over my shoulder at her car and saw D.T. and Billy Ray sitting in the backseat.

She said, "What's this? Do you have probable cause on these two?"

"They're on our team now. They're not even cuffed." I held up her voice recorder, which I had used to take statements from both young men.

I hit Play, and Billy Ray's voice said, "There's a hidden compartment at the top of the closet in the office. We always keep as much as ten ounces of heroin in that compartment, plus whatever else we're selling."

Sandy just stared at me. It was exactly the kind of reaction I was hoping for. I like to surprise people once in a while.

I said, "They both have lived here in the house for more than two years, and I had them write out their consent for us to search the entire premises."

Sandy was still speechless.

I liked it more as each second passed. I said, "Now no cheesy lawyer can attack the search warrant we were going to get. And it doesn't matter what Dell Streeter babbled about before they took him to the hospital."

Sandy said, "So you're saying there are drugs hidden at the top of the closet in the office?"

Two state cops overheard it and raced into the house. Someone would claim a great stat and possibly a cash seizure. It wasn't in Sandy's jurisdiction anyway.

Sandy said, "All I've gotten out of Sadie is that she was in fear for her life and defending herself. She keeps repeating it like a mantra. If I were the suspicious type, I would think she was coached by a professional."

"Is that something you want to look into?"

"Not a chance."

I smiled as I sighed with relief. I said, "My two new partners have some other interesting information for us. I just got a few details, but it's pretty good stuff. I thought you might want to invite one of your state friends in for a longer interview."

"What did they say?"

"That the Canadian mob has been trying to corner the market on synthetic drugs. They've made a big push into meth, ecstasy, and anything else that can be cooked up in a half-assed lab."

"Interesting, but will it help with our case at all?"

"It seems that a couple of Quebecers with an attitude came to explain the market to Mr. Streeter around five months ago. During the course of the explanation, Mr. Streeter lost control and shot both of them. For one reason or another he and D.T. and Billy Ray buried the bodies behind the barn. That should be pretty easy to check out. That would also give us a murder rap on good old Dell."

Sandy let out a little laugh and shook her head. "Could you be any more satisfied with yourself?"

"Not as it relates to this investigation. Neither of these two admitted to shooting Mickey Bale. I didn't want to scare them off by mentioning something they could be charged with. Maybe during the longer interview, you and one of the state cops can get them to talk about it."

"I'd say you did all right. At least for a rookie Linewiler cop. Maybe you've got a future in this business."

"It's funny you say that. I've been looking at all my options recently. I'm going to leave it up to other people. I've missed out on too many things with my family not to include them in any decision I make about my career."

"Good for you." She looked over her shoulder at Sadie, who was swinging gently in the little porch swing.

I said, "Do you think she's going to be okay?"

"I'll keep a close eye on her. I think she might have exorcised some of her demons today. But she's got a lot of healing to do."

Then Sandy looked me in the eye and said, "Now what? You've only got a couple more days of vacation. What's your plan for that family? You've solved all the world's problems here. Now you've got to focus on them."

"I've got big plans for them. Right now I'm going to go home, grab a few hours' sleep, then run into town for a couple of errands. By this time tomorrow, everyone will have a clear idea of how serious I am about my family's future."

CHAPTER 91

IT WAS LATE in the afternoon by the time I drove into town. Linewiler was abuzz with rumors and comments about what happened at Dell Streeter's compound. The best one I heard was that he was running a cult that involved human sacrifice. I hoped that one would keep spreading. I made no comment when I heard a woman in one of the stores I visited say it.

It was big news, and two different TV stations had sent teams to cover it. The fact that there were so many police at the house meant that something big had happened. I watched one quick news report designed as a promo for the evening news. All it said was that a man was being treated for gunshot wounds as a murder investigation was unfolding at a residence outside the city limits. Close enough.

It was only a matter of time before stations up and down the East Coast cruised in for the story. There was too much to ignore. Drugs, guns, bodies. The media would have a field day with this. CNN would give the story its own theme music.

I'd already been through two stores when I found exactly what I was looking for. The man behind the counter agreed with my choice and happily accepted my American Express card.

When I stepped out onto the sidewalk in the quaint little downtown area, I almost ran into a large man in a red-and-black plaid shirt. It took me a moment to realize it was one of the vigilantes from the other night. The guy with a big mouth. Anthony.

It turned out he was obnoxious even without his friends behind him.

He immediately said, "I figured you'd be in here, spending someone's money. Did you find a stash of cash at Dell Streeter's house?"

"Look, I don't know what you want, friend. Dell Streeter is in custody. We told you it would happen."

"All you New Yorkers are the same. You think you're so much smarter than everyone else around the country. You look at me and just see a country boy who's not sophisticated enough to know how the world works. I got news for you, Bennett. I went to the University of New Hampshire. I've been around. I know how things work."

I avoided any cracks about a university not named New York or Columbia. It wasn't easy, but I ignored my smart-ass instincts. "I'm sorry you feel that way. Now, if you'll excuse me, I've got things to do."

The beefy man didn't move. He just stared at me with his brown eyes set under bushy black eyebrows.

He said, "What are you charging Streeter with?"

"Not that I need to explain the criminal justice system to you, but I believe they have a decent narcotics charge on him for a start. They're looking into some kind of homicide charges for the bodies that were buried at the house. I'm not involved in that part of the investigation."

"Sounds like we'll never get an answer about who shot poor Mickey Bale. He was a great guy who lived right. He was gunned down in our own little town, and the cops aren't going to do shit about it."

Somehow I managed to keep my cool. I don't even know why I continued to engage this moron. He sounded like the people who spouted off about officer-involved shootings but didn't have any more facts than a newscaster did and had no experience in police work.

I counted to five silently, then said, "I think the drive-by shooting will fall into place once they get clear statements from everyone. Just show a little patience and calm down. I think you'll be surprised by how satisfied everyone will be with the efforts of the police." It was a subtle little dig to tell people to calm down when they were agitated. Usually it only served to upset them further. Maybe I wanted to take this argument to the next level. But it wasn't worth worrying about anymore.

Anthony said, "I ought to call the FBI and ask them to look at how the police department is run here. We never should've brought in an NYPD detective to run operations. And she never should've brought you in on anything they were doing. The whole thing stinks."

Then I let my instincts run wild. I leaned in a little closer to him and said, "No offense, but if I were you, I would never mention the word *stinks*. There's nothing like a fat guy in an old shirt during the summer to remind me why people should shower every day."

That didn't sit well with the big man, and he balled his right fist.

It was like a neon sign saying, "Watch out—this guy is about to swing at you." Then he did. A wild, looping haymaker.

I ducked easily and brought my right hand hard into his solar plexus, then twisted and hooked my left elbow into his chin. He spun, bounced off a wall, then tumbled off the sidewalk onto the muddy street.

He landed so perfectly, with just the right amount of mud on his face, that I took a quick picture with my phone.

He was slowly working his way to his feet by the time I pulled away in our big passenger van.

CHAPTER 92

IT WAS OUR final full day at the Ghost House. With the sun shining, the house looked anything but haunted. A breeze from the east was blowing, and the storm felt like it had washed away a year's worth of crime. Everything seemed fresh. Including me. I felt renewed somehow. Sadie was safe, and Dell Streeter was secure in jail.

Mary Catherine and I sat on the edge of the porch with our feet dangling down as we watched the kids play on the dock and in the water. Parents understand how special days like these are. I was just glad I realized it, too, before the days ran out. The kids seemed like they were growing up awfully fast.

We watched as Ricky ran down the dock and launched himself over the side. He was now able to perform a fairly spectacular atomic cannonball. He may not have carried as big a payload as I did, but he still splashed Jane and Juliana as they attempted to act sophisticated. They had been lying on blankets, away from the other kids. Slowly but surely they were distancing themselves from childish activities.

After the wall of water fell on top of them, I was worried about a spurt of acrimony. But these were my girls. They exacted revenge by jumping into the water on top of Ricky. Everyone appreciated their spirit.

Seamus felt well enough to stand on the shore and watch. He still wouldn't wear shorts. Instead his pants were rolled up almost to his knees. That exposed his white Irish legs, which almost glowed in the sun.

The entire picture showed all I could ever want out of life. Almost.

It was time.

I turned to Mary Catherine and said, "Let's go for a walk."

"Who'll watch the kids?"

"Seamus and Juliana. It'll be fine."

We took the path that wandered away from the lake a little. There was more shade there, and it was cooler. The heat and my nerves had made me start to perspire. I needed a little shade and a slight breeze. I looked around us as we walked. It was beautiful. The deep green of the trees, the sound of the birds.

It's rare in life when everything you want lines up just right. This was perfection.

Mary Catherine held my hand and chatted as we strolled along slowly. It was always easy to talk to Mary Catherine.

She said, "What a fine vacation."

I turned to see if she was being sarcastic. As usual, she had no bitterness or alternative meaning in her words. She really had seen the best of the trip.

She looked out over a meadow and said, "Our last full day in Maine."

"Paradise, for a while."

She laughed. "A short while."

I faced her and took her hands in mine. "Look. We need to talk."

Mary Catherine said, "Michael, I understand why you helped Sandy. I'm proud of you."

"That's not what I want to talk about." We had taken another path and were winding back toward the lake.

She started to ask me more questions, so I just stopped. She stopped with me, realizing how serious I was.

I eased down on my left knee, because my right knee was sore—either from kicking in the door or from some other crazy shit I had done. I reached in my pocket. It took longer than I expected. Then I pulled out the small square box I'd bought the previous day. Just before I had to punch that loudmouth Anthony.

I hadn't prepared anything. Typical. But looking up at that beautiful face, I was scared. Terrified is probably more accurate. Why on earth would she say yes? I just stared. Speechless.

She knew what was coming. She had to. It felt like I'd been down there on one knee for two hours.

"Mary Catherine," I began. I was trying to think of the perfect phrase.

Once again she saved me. A smile erupted on her face as she said, "Yes, Michael."

I just stared at her in stunned silence. Finally, I regained my wits and said, "I love you. I love you more than my own life. You mean everything to me, and I can't imagine my life without you. Will you marry me and grow old with me and…"

I had run out of things to say. It didn't matter. She said, "Yes. Yes, Michael. I'll marry you."

I thought, *Whew, am I a lucky man. She gets me.*

Then I was startled by cheering. Loud cheering.

When I looked up, I realized we had walked back along the lake, and the kids had joined us. They'd seen us from the dock and wanted to be part of this incredible event.

Chrissy did a cartwheel.

Fiona looked like a cheerleader as she jumped up and let out a loud whoop.

As I stood I said, "How'd you guys sneak up on us?"

Seamus stepped forward. "Are you kidding? You were focused. Finally. We've been waiting for this for a long time." Seamus stepped over to Mary Catherine and said, "You've always been part of this family. This just makes it legal."

When he hugged her I could see streams of tears running down her cheeks.

Mary Catherine hugged each child. Then she got around to me. It was worth the wait.

We kissed.

Then the kids closed in. We were surrounded. It was the greatest hug ever.

CHAPTER 93

THE VAN WAS packed. That's no small accomplishment with thirteen—sorry—I mean twelve people plus luggage. I took a last look at the Ghost House. Somehow it looked like a comfortable home now instead of a foreboding Victorian spook house.

Mary Catherine stood at the edge of the van and said, "Good memories."

"The best."

Mary Catherine said, "Then why do you still have that guilty look on your face? I hope you're not sorry about working and missing time with the family."

I shrugged. "A little."

She said, "Don't be. You changed the world. At least for this town and certainly for Sadie. That makes this vacation a win all around."

Her smile captivated me. It had such subtleties. Like a diamond. No two were exactly the same, but they were all brilliant.

Our one stop on our way out of town was in a nice residential neighborhood. Some of the houses were older than others, but they had character. There was nothing superficial about the houses. This was genuine Maine.

I pulled the van over in front of a neat one-story home. Before we all filed out of the van, which sometimes took more than ninety seconds, Sandy Coles had opened her front door and met us on the path.

Sandy and Mary Catherine embraced. The first thing Sandy wanted to see was the ring.

Then Sandy took Seamus by the arm and led him into the house.

I noticed his walk was a little more steady. He was still recovering, but I was confident he'd be back to his old self soon.

Inside the bright house, I envied her backyard and view into thick woods.

I said, "This place is perfect."

"We think so." As she said it, Sadie came out of her bedroom.

Chrissy said, "You're living here?"

Sadie said, "For now."

We all had a great little chat in the living room of my former partner's house.

Around ten minutes later, as I stood on the back porch, looking out into the woods, Sadie joined me.

She said, "Thank you for all you did."

I just hugged her.

Sadie said, "Sandy says I can stay with her as long as I want."

"Good."

"She on the level?"

"Levelest person I ever met."

We both laughed.

Sadie said, "She worried someone might try to hurt me one day?"

"Maybe. A little. But she worries about everyone. That's what makes her a good cop. She invited you to stay here because she sees something in you."

"Not much to see in me."

I wrapped an arm around her. "I think you'll see what we all see soon enough. Just be happy and spend some time with Sandy."

"I am. I never had my own room or nice clothes like this before."

"It's a lot to get used to. Maybe you can come visit us in the fall. We can watch the Thanksgiving Day parade."

She hugged me, and I had a flash of worry about whether she would still be here in the fall. Just a little anxiety. You never know what might happen.

CHAPTER 94

ON THE WAY home we made a detour. More of an entirely separate trip. We visited Niagara Falls. Both sides of it. We stayed in a nice hotel that had a Ripley's Believe It or Not museum just outside the front entrance.

And we did all the tourist stuff. Took the Maid of the Mist tour, stood under the Horseshoe Falls, and ate tough prime rib at a rotating restaurant on top of a tower. It was wonderful. The kind of thing we didn't do too often.

The next day we left early for our real destination.

The Gowanda Correctional Facility.

This visit wasn't quite as startling as the first one. We knew to expect bars and barbed wire and guards and guns. We took it in as we drove up along the access road.

Once again we were able to visit Brian and sit across a glass partition from him with a corrections officer standing in the corner of the room.

Brian looked tired. He had a hint of a fading black eye. His hair was buzzed short, like that of most prisoners. It was easier to take care of that way. And it broke my heart.

I sat while everyone filed in two at a time.

Mary Catherine and I shared our good news. Brian tried to be excited. It was clear he had other things on his mind.

The boys kidded with him, as boys do. Ricky asked about sports on the inside.

Brian said, "I play basketball and soccer twice a week."

"What about baseball?"

"No. They don't want us to have bats. We can't even have cleats on our shoes. We play everything in these." He raised his foot to show off a cheap Keds knockoff.

Ricky and Eddie seemed fascinated that someone could play a sport without proper equipment.

Later Fiona listened as Brian explained the crafts projects that were available.

He said, "The idea is to keep us occupied and see if we have a particular talent. Two guys got out and became printers. Another works in Albany as an auto-body mechanic. He writes us to show how well things are going."

As I listened, I recalled thinking a few years ago that Brian would have his choice of colleges. Maybe on scholarship. Now I just wanted him back home. Free. Part of society. It was humbling to have my expectations lowered so drastically.

It also made me think about Diego, the teenage hit man. He'd never have a chance to have any kind of life. And

I still couldn't help but feel like it was my fault. If I had gone by the book, maybe I'd have avoided the gunfight in the library.

On the other hand, Diego might have murdered someone else. Doing the right thing was never easy. Sometimes it wasn't even necessarily clear what the right thing is.

When all the kids were done visiting, Seamus huddled with Brian. They had always been close, and Seamus was clearly passing on advice and wisdom. But it was not something he wanted me to hear. I understood that.

Finally I was alone with Brian for a few minutes. It felt weird. Awkward. Which was different for us. We'd always had an open and easy bond. It hurt to feel like a void had opened between us. I hoped we could rebuild that bond.

Brian asked me about the trip. He'd seen something in the newspaper about the little town in Maine. Bodies, drugs, and kids were something the media couldn't pass up. There were too many elements to sensationalize and too many subjects to explore and fill space with.

I filled him in on what had actually happened. It wasn't as interesting, but at least he knew the truth. After what he'd seen back home and the people he'd dealt with, nothing surprised him. Drug dealers were everywhere, and most people had no idea how ruthless they were.

I didn't know whether they were ruthless because being in the business changed them or whether they were willing to do that kind of thing because they were ruthless in the first place.

Brian looked serious as he leaned in close to the speaker built into the partition. "Dad, I need to tell you something."

I leaned in, too.

He said, "I think there's a big problem coming to New York City."

"What kind of problem?"

"I didn't talk about the people I worked for because I was afraid for the family's safety, but now it seems like someone might get hurt no matter what."

"I'm listening."

"I heard the man I worked for, Caracortada, complaining about some Canadian mob guys trying to work their way into the drug business in the city. They had meth and X and needed distribution. Sounded like Caracortada wanted to do something violent to scare them off. He told me to tell him if they approached me."

I nodded. "That's good to know. I'll keep my eyes open at work."

"That's not all. Since I've been here, I heard about how tough the Canadian mob can be and that they are expanding down into the United States. They mean business and have a lot of cash."

I thought about the two bodies buried behind Dell Streeter's barn. This could get ugly.

Brian continued. "There are a couple of French Canadians here who are having a beef with Mexican cartel members over it. They think there's going to be some kind of gang war. I just want you to be prepared."

I looked at my son. The little boy who lost his way. I knew how hard it was for him to tell me this kind of stuff. I knew no one could ever find out.

"Thanks, Brian. I'll be careful."

I placed my hand on the glass, and he put his hand against the other side.

I'd worry about drug wars when the time came. There was always enough to keep cops busy. No matter what the state of the economy or world politics or religion, there would always be murders. If they happened in Manhattan, I'd be ready.

For now, I was content to spend a few more minutes with my son.

**THE ONE WHO KNOWS
THE SECRETS IS THE ONE
WHO HOLDS THE POWER.**

FOR AN EXCERPT, TURN THE PAGE.

THERE WERE ONLY four words beneath the tattoo of the Grim Reaper on Aubrey Davenport's inner left thigh. But they spoke volumes.

Death is my aphrodisiac

And nowhere in the entire city was her libido more on point than at the Renwick Smallpox Hospital, a crumbling three-story, U-shaped monster on the southern tip of Roosevelt Island.

Once a marvel of neo-Gothic architecture, Renwick was now a rotting stone carcass, the final way station for thirteen thousand men, women, and children who had died a painful death.

For the city fathers, Renwick was a historical landmark. For the urban explorers, it was New York's most haunted house. But for Aubrey Davenport, it was a sexual Mecca, and on a warm evening in early May, she and a willing partner scaled the eight-foot fence, made their way into the bowels of the moldering labyrinth, and spread a thick quilted blanket on the rocky floor.

She kicked off her shoes, removed her shirt and bra, shucked her jeans, and stood there, naked except for a pair of aquamarine bikini panties.

Her nipples responded to the caress of a cool breeze that drifted over her breasts, and she inhaled the earthy scent of the decay around her, mixed with the dank overtones of river water.

She dropped to her knees on the blanket, closed her eyes, and waited for her partner.

She shuddered as he silently slipped the noose around her neck. His fingers were long and slender. *Piano player fingers,* her mother used to call them. *Like your father has.*

As a child, Aubrey wondered why a man blessed with the hands of a concert pianist never played an instrument, never even cared to. But somewhere along the way she came to understand that Cyril Davenport's long, slender fingers made music of another kind: the crescendo of sound that came from her parents' bedroom on a nightly basis.

Aubrey felt the rope pull tighter. Rope was a misnomer. It was a long strand of silk—the belt from a robe, perhaps—and it felt soft and smooth as he cinched it against her carotid arteries.

He took her shoulders and guided her body to the ground until her belly was flat against the cotton blanket below her.

"Comfy?" he asked.

She laughed. *Comfy* was such a dumb word.

"You're laughing," he said. "Life is good, yes?"

4

"Mmmmmm," she responded.

"It's about to get better," he said, tugging at the waistband of her panties and sliding them down to her ankles. His fingers teased as they walked slowly up her leg and came to rest on the patch of ink etched into her thigh. His thumb stroked the shrouded figure and arced along the scythe that was clutched in its bony claw.

"Hello, death," he said, removing his hand.

Crack! The cat-o'-nine-tails lashed across her bare bottom, burning, stinging, each individual knotted-leather strap leaving its mark. She bit down hard and buried a scream into the blanket.

Pain was the appetizer. Pleasure was the main course. Her body tensed as she waited for his next move.

In a single, practiced motion he bent her legs at the knees, tipped them back toward her head, grabbed the tether that was around her neck, and tied the other end to her ankles.

"Hand," he ordered.

Aubrey, her right arm beneath her stomach, reached all the way down until her hand was between her legs.

"Life is good," he repeated. "Make it better."

Her fingers groped, parting the pleats, entering the canal, tantalizing the nerve endings. The effect was dizzying: the man with the whip, the foul-smelling ruins, and the inescapable presence of thirteen thousand dead souls.

He said something, but she couldn't hear over the sound of her own labored breathing. And then—the point of no return. She felt the swell of gratification surging through her body, and with near surgical precision she gently lowered her feet toward the ground.

The silk rope around her neck tightened, compressing her carotid arteries. The sudden loss of oxygen along with the buildup of carbon dioxide made her light-headed, giddy, almost hallucinogenic. The orgasm came in waves. It left her gasping for air, but the euphoria was so powerful, so addictive, that she intensified the pressure around her neck, knowing she could go just a few more seconds.

If erotic asphyxiation were an Olympic event, Aubrey Davenport would have been a world-class contender. Her brain was just on the threshold of losing consciousness when she released the death grip, and brought her feet back toward her buttocks.

But the noose refused to relax. If anything, it felt tighter. Panic seized her. She thrashed, pulled her hands up to her throat, and clawed at the silk, fighting for air and finding none.

She never made mistakes. Something must have snagged. She reached behind her neck, desperately trying to find some slack, when her fingers found his hand. He jerked hard on the silk cord, and her arms flailed.

She slumped, too weak to struggle, all hope gone. Everything went black, and as the reaper stepped out of the darkness to claim her, tears streamed down her cheeks, because in the last seconds of her life, Aubrey Davenport finally realized that she didn't want to die.

THE COTILLION ROOM at The Pierre hotel bubbled over with New York's wealthiest—including a few who were wealthier than some countries.

They were the richest of the rich, the ones who get invited to fifty-thousand-dollars-a-plate dinners when one of their own wants to tap them for a worthy cause. In this case, the charity with its hand out was the Silver Bullet Foundation.

The thirty-foot-long banner at the front of the hall proclaimed its noble mission: FIGHTING FOR THE LESS FORTUNATE.

The man in the black tie and white jacket busing tables in the rear had boiled when he first saw the sign. *They haven't done shit for me, and I'm the least fortunate person in the room.*

They're like swans, he thought as he watched them glide serenely from table to table: *so elegant, so regal, but fiercely territorial and vicious when they feel threatened. And like swans,* he observed, *they are oh so white.*

He counted half a dozen black swans among them, but for the most part, the people of color were there to serve. He fit right in.

With his shoulders slumped, his jaw slack, and a cheap pair of clear-lens nerd glasses to dial down the intensity of his piercing black eyes, he was practically invisible, and definitely forgettable.

The only human contact he'd had in the three hours since donning the uniform was with a besotted old patrician who'd slurred, "Hey fella, where's the men's room?"

Shortly after nine, the lights dimmed, the chatter died down, and the commanding voice of James Earl Jones piped through the sound system.

"Ladies and gentlemen, please welcome the cofounder and chairman of the Silver Bullet Foundation, Mr. Princeton Wells."

The staff had been instructed to stop work during the presentation, and the busboy dutifully stepped into the shadows near a fire exit as Princeton Wells bounded onto the stage.

Wells was his typically charming, still-boyish-at-forty, old-moneyed self. And lest any man in the room suspect that someone that rich and that good-looking wasn't getting laid, Wells kicked off the festivities by introducing his current girlfriend, Kenda Whithouse, to a captive audience.

Ms. Whithouse stood up, waved to the room, and threw her billionaire boyfriend a kiss. She was only twenty-three, an actress who was not quite yet tabloid fodder, but who clearly had the talent to fill out an evening gown. Those who knew Princeton Wells had no doubt that the gown would be lying crumpled on his bedroom floor by morning.

Having trotted out his latest eye candy, Wells got down to the serious business of reminding all the do-gooders in the room how much good they were doing for the city's less fortunate.

"And no one," he decreed, "has been more supportive of Silver Bullet than Her Honor, the mayor of New York, Muriel Sykes."

The city's first female mayor, her approval rating still sky-high after only four months in office, was greeted by enthusiastic applause as she stepped up to the podium.

The busboy did not applaud. He slid his smartphone from his jacket pocket and tapped six digits onto the keypad.

One, two, two, nine, nine, seven.

He stared at it, not seeing a sequence of numbers but a moment in time that had changed his life forever: December 29, 1997. His finger hovered over the Send button as the mayor began to speak.

"I'm not a big fan of giving speeches at rubber chicken dinners," she said, "even when the chicken turns out to be grade A5 Miyazaki Wagyu beef."

Everyone but the busboy found that funny.

"On the second day of my administration, I had a meeting with the four founders of Silver Bullet. They showed me a picture of an abandoned old warehouse in the Bronx, and I said, 'Who owns that eyesore?' And they said, 'You do, Madam Mayor. But if you sell it to us for a dollar, we will raise enough money to convert it into permanent housing for a hundred and twenty-five chronically homeless adults.'

"I accepted their offer, framed the dollar, and am thrilled to announce that next month we will start construction. I'm here tonight to thank you all for your generous contributions and to introduce one of the four men who spearheaded this project. He is the brilliant architect whose vision will turn that dilapidated monstrosity into a beautiful apartment complex for some of our neediest citizens. Ladies and gentlemen, please welcome Del Fairfax."

Fairfax, architect to the one percent, stepped onto the stage to show off what wonders he could create for the indigent. Spot-on handsome and aw-shucks personable, he rested a laptop on the podium, flipped it open, and said, "I know how fond you all are of PowerPoint presentations, so I put one together for you. Only ninety-seven slides."

The half-sloshed crowd warmly gave him his due.

"Just kidding," he said. "Princeton told me if I showed more than five, you'd start asking for your money back. The new facility will be called Tremont Gardens. First, let me show you what it looks like now."

He picked up a wireless remote and pushed a button.

The explosion rocked the Cotillion Room.

Del Fairfax's upper torso hurtled toward the screen behind him, while the bomb's jet spray of ball bearings, nails, and glass shards chewed into his lower half, scattering bits and pieces across the stage like a wood chipper gone rogue.

Thick smoke, flying shrapnel, and abject fear filled the air.

The busboy, standing far from the backblast, slipped through the emergency exit, leaving in his wake sheer pandemonium, as four hundred New Yorkers found themselves caught up in the nightmare they had been dreading since September 11, 2001.

KYLIE AND I had never been attached to Mayor Sykes's security detail before, but once she agreed to speak at the Silver Bullet Foundation fund-raiser, she recruited us for the night.

The word came down from our boss. "The mayor wants to do a little fund-raising of her own," Captain Cates said. "She comes up for reelection in three and a half years, and as long as she's going to spend the evening rubbing elbows with her biggest donors, she wants to assure them that she's not just a champion of the unfortunate poor. She cares deeply about the disgustingly rich. And what better way to demonstrate her concern for their welfare than by trotting out a couple of poster cops from NYPD Red?"

"Thanks, but no thanks," Kylie said. "Doesn't she realize we already spend sixty hours a week overprotecting the overprivileged? Now she's inviting us to suck up to them at some—"

Cates cut her off. "Did I use the word *invite?* Because the last time I read the department manual I didn't see anything about *invitations* being passed down the chain of command. The mayor specifically instructed me to assign Detectives Kylie MacDonald and Zach Jordan to her security detail. Consider yourselves assigned. No RSVP required."

I figured it would be the most boring night of the week. And I was right—until the podium exploded.

It was one of those shock and awe explosions. The blinding flash, the deafening boom, the thick smoke, the chemical stench, and the flying chunks of wood, glass, metal, and Del Fairfax.

Mayor Sykes had just come off the stage and returned to her seat when the bomb went off. Kylie and I were only an arm's length away from her. We yanked her from her chair and, shielding her body with ours, bulled our way through the chaos toward our prearranged exit door.

At least fifty other frenzied people had the same idea.

I keyed my radio and yelled over the din, "Explorer, this is Red One. Vanguard is safe. Egress Alpha is blocked. We're making our way toward Bravo."

We did a one-eighty and shoved the mayor toward the kitchen. The path was clear, and the vast stainless steel hub of the hotel's multimillion-dollar banquet business was almost deserted. Except for a few stragglers, the staff had beaten a quick retreat through a rear fire door and down a stairwell to the employee locker rooms.

At that point, many of them decided that they were out of harm's way, and at least twenty of them were standing in the corridor, almost every one with a cell phone to his or her ear.

"NYPD. Get out of the way! Get out of the fucking way!" Kylie bellowed as we elbowed our way through the logjam.

A hotel security guard saw us coming and pushed open a metal door that led to the outside world. As soon as she felt the cool night air and heard the sounds of her city, the mayor stopped.

"Please," she said. "I'm too old for this shit. Let me catch my breath."

"Sorry, ma'am," Kylie said. "Not here. We only have another hundred feet. Keep going, or Zach and I will carry you to the car."

The mayor gave Kylie an enigmatic stare that could have been anywhere on the spectrum from contempt to gratitude.

"Nobody…" she said, breathing heavily, "carries…Muriel Sykes…anywhere. Lead the way."

We single-filed down a narrow alleyway, past a row of Dumpsters, and I radioed ahead to her team.

The alley came out on East 61st Street between Madison and Fifth Avenues. Just as we got to the far end, the mayor's black SUV drove up onto the sidewalk. Her driver, Charlie, jumped out and swung open the rear door. I offered to help the mayor into the back seat, but she waved me off.

"This is as far as I'm going," she said.

"Ma'am, this is not the place for you to be," Kylie said.

"A maniac just set off a bomb in my city, Detective. This is *my* responsibility."

"Yes, ma'am, but maniacs have a bad habit of setting off secondary bombs targeting people who have just run from the first," Kylie said. "And it's our responsibility to get you to safe ground."

"Madam Mayor," Charlie said, "they're setting up a command center at the Park Avenue Armory. I can have you there in two minutes."

Crisis averted. The mayor got in the car, shut the door, and rolled down her window. "Thank you, Detectives," she said. That was it. Three words, and the window went back up.

Within seconds, the oversize, bulletproof Ford Explorer peeled out and, with lights flashing and sirens wailing, whisked Muriel Sykes away to the longest night of her fledgling administration.

"I hate these boring babysitting jobs," Kylie said. "Let's go do some real police work."

The two of us ran back down the alley and up the stairs toward the smoke-filled ballroom.

KYLIE AND I joined the influx of first responders who raced to help the injured. It was just cops and firefighters at first, but when a bomb explodes in a public place, it sets off a Pavlovian response. Law enforcement agencies everywhere start salivating.

By the ten o'clock news cycle, The Pierre was the most famous crime scene in America, and everyone—Feds, staties, NYPD, FDNY, even the DEA—wanted a piece of the action.

Fortunately, the turf war dust settled long before the acrid gray cloud in the Cotillion Room, and Kylie and I were thrown together with Howard Malley, an FBI bomb tech we'd run into before.

Malley is a hawkeyed post-blast investigator and a pull-no-punches New York ballbuster, but he can also get testy as a cobra when you disagree with him. In short, he was a lot like Kylie. Maybe that's why I liked him.

The two of us suited up—disposable Tyvek coveralls, sock boots, face mask—and we crossed the threshold to ground zero. The rear of the room was remarkably intact. Flower arrangements and wineglasses were still sitting on several tables, waiting to be cleared.

We walked toward the spot where Del Fairfax, Princeton Wells, and Mayor Sykes had stood less than an hour ago, wooing their wealthy benefactors. Windows were shattered, wood-paneled walls were peppered with shrapnel, and the floor was littered with the detritus of the blast: scorched drapery, sparkling chunks of chandelier crystal, overturned chairs, silverware, shoes, purses—thousands of puzzle pieces that had made a picture-perfect evening and now lay in tatters, covered in thick dust and splattered with blood.

At the center of it all was the man who was supposed to make sense of this seemingly senseless act. He was squatting at one end of the forty-foot charred swath that had been the stage. Agent Malley, a bald-headed, gray-bearded FBI lifer, was squinting at a pair of forceps in his right hand through a pocket magnifying glass. He looked up when he heard us coming his way. "Well, if it isn't Jordan and MacDonald," he said. "How's business at NYPD's Fat Cat Squad?"

"Booming," Kylie deadpanned. "You find something down there?"

"Maybe." He stood up. "If you think of this mess as a four-thousand-square-foot haystack, I may have just found a needle. Take a look."

Kylie and I took turns studying the prize dangling from

Malley's stainless steel pincers. It was a piece of wire. Three pieces, actually—one red, one white, one blue—twisted together in pigtail fashion. It was as thin as a strand of angel-hair pasta and no more than two inches long.

"And that's significant?" I asked.

"Again, maybe. These bomb makers—we see them as mass murderers, but they like to think of themselves as artists." He gave the word a French spin so that it came out *arteests*.

"And like artists everywhere, they are compelled to sign their masterpieces. This little red, white, and blue twisty thing isn't something I've come across before, so the thought popped into my head that maybe it's our bomber's signature."

"Red, white, and blue," Kylie said. "So what does that mean—death to America?"

"The bomb says death. I think the wire is about the guy who built it."

"Red, white, and blue," Kylie repeated. "You think he's an American?"

"Or he could be a color-blind Lithuanian. It would be nice to know what it symbolizes, but what would be really helpful is if this is his trademark, and he's in our global database. I'll take it back to the office and see if we get a hit."

"So, what's your take so far?" I asked.

He bagged the tiny fragment of wire, marked it, and put it in an evidence bin. "It wasn't a terrorist attack," he said.

"You sure?"

"Hell, no. I'm just a humble underpaid government employee, not Harry Potter. But you asked what's *my take*, which kind of means my educated guess after snooping around for twenty minutes. It'll never stand up in court, but right now my take is that with only one dead and twenty-two injured, this is not the handiwork of a dyed-in-the-wool, trained-in-Syria jihadi."

"Not a terrorist?" Kylie said. "Howard, this guy took out twenty-three people with a bomb."

"You're not listening, Detective," Malley said, his defense mechanisms going on point. "I didn't say he wasn't a pro. This guy is top-shelf. But he was using a shaped charge aimed at killing one person. Those twenty-two other people were collateral damage, some from the blowback, but mostly from the stampede. I don't know nearly as much about dealing with zillionaires as you do, but I'm guessing this was an every-man-for-himself crowd. They'd have a lot fewer broken bones if they didn't panic. This guy was only after Fairfax. It wasn't terrorism. It was personal."

"If it were personal," Kylie said, "wouldn't it have been easier just to murder him in his bed?"

Malley shrugged. "I'm guessing he wanted to make a public statement. I just have no idea what he was trying to say." He winked. "But then, that's not my problem."

MALLEY WAS RIGHT. Terrorism was Homeland's problem, but homicide—especially an A-list victim like Del Fairfax—was all ours.

Other than being witness to the final seconds of his life, we knew nothing about him. We needed to talk to someone who did. We tracked down Princeton Wells. He was still at the hotel, only he'd relocated to the thirty-ninth floor.

"Anything I can do to help," he said, opening the door to a suite with sweeping views of Central Park.

He'd traded his formal wear for a pair of wrinkled khaki cargo shorts, a faded gray T-shirt, no shoes, no socks.

The mayor had introduced us to Wells earlier in the evening. We'd given him our cards, and he'd joked about hoping he'd never need them. Yet here we were, only hours later, following him into the living room.

19

"Grab a chair," he said, heading for a well-stocked wet bar. "Drink?"

We declined. He tossed some rocks into a glass and added four inches of Grey Goose. Then he uncorked a bottle of white and poured an equally generous amount into a crystal goblet.

He took a hit of vodka, set the wine on the coffee table in front of us, and said, "What have you got so far?"

"We're sorry for the loss of your friend," I said, "but the fact that he was the only one killed points to the possibility that he may have been the primary target."

"That's insane," Wells said. "Who would want to kill Del?"

"That's what Detective MacDonald and I are here to ask you. How well did you know him?"

"We've been best friends since high school. We roomed together in college. Twenty years ago we cofounded Silver Bullet along with Arnie Zimmer and Nathan Hirsch. Del and I were like brothers."

"Did he have any enemies? Anyone who would want to see him dead?"

"This is fucking surreal," he said, tipping the glass to his lips and draining it. "I need another drink." He padded back to the bar.

The last thing Princeton Wells needed was more alcohol, which is something I would have told him if he were an ordinary citizen, and I were an ordinary cop. But he was a billionaire many times over, and I was a detective first grade trained to deal with the privileged class, be they shit-faced or sober. I watched as he ignored the ice and replenished the vodka.

"This is a beautiful place," Kylie said, backing off the raw subject of his murdered best friend.

He smiled. "Thanks. I've had it for three years now. The view is spectacular when it snows. Point the remote at the fireplace, open a bottle of wine…"

"Did someone say *wine?*"

Kenda Whithouse entered the room, her hair wrapped in a towel, her body somewhat covered by a man's tuxedo shirt.

"Already poured," Wells said, pointing to the glass he'd left on the table.

She picked it up, sat on a sofa, and discreetly tucked her legs under her.

"Kenda," Wells said, "these detectives are from NYPD."

"Nice to meet you," she said. "Did you catch them yet?"

"We're working on it," I said.

"It was terrible. Like one of those disaster movies, only it was real. I was lucky I wasn't killed. Bad enough I got covered with all that crap flying through the air. I looked like one of those homeless women Princeton is building housing for. I had to wash my hair three times to get the smell out."

Wells sat down next to her, took another belt of the vodka, and shifted his body so he could square off with the two of us.

"You want to know what I think, Detectives? I think that bomb was meant for the mayor. I mean, she left the podium just a few seconds before it blew. That's the only thing that makes sense. There's always someone with a hard-on for politicians. But Del Fairfax? Everybody loved him. Hell, they love the four of us. We raise hundreds of millions of dollars. We provide food, shelter, and education for these people, but more important, we give them purpose, hope—"

He stopped, looked at the glass in his hand, and set it down. "Sorry. A couple of drinks and I go all humanitarian commando on you. My point is, nobody wants to kill the golden goose. Silver Bullet doesn't have enemies."

"What about Fairfax's personal life?" Kylie asked.

"Del was a player. Never married. And why would he? He was rich, he was good-looking, and the gals loved him."

"Did any of these *gals* have husbands?" Kylie asked.

"God, no. Del would never poach another man's wife. He was a hound, but he wasn't into drama."

My cell rang. It was Cates. I stepped into the foyer to take the call.

"Fill me in," she said.

"The blast investigator flat out said, 'It wasn't a terrorist attack.' He thinks it was a targeted hit at the victim. But Princeton Wells says the vic was a saint, beloved by all, so the bomb must have been meant for the mayor."

"I doubt it," Cates said. "Sykes was a last-minute addition to the program. This attack was planned, prepped—but I'll alert Gracie security. What else?"

"Nothing else, boss. There were four hundred people in the room, yours truly included, and we can't find a single witness who witnessed anything."

"How soon can you and MacDonald tear yourself away from the scene?"

"About twelve seconds. We're coming up dry here."

"Then get your asses out to Roosevelt Island. Chuck Dryden has a body he wants you to meet."

"Another homicide? For *Red?*"

"What can I tell you, Jordan?" Cates said. "It's a bad night for the rich and famous."

"NEVER UNDERESTIMATE THE insanity of people with money," Kylie said.

"Did you just open a fortune cookie, or is this the beginning of a fascinating observation?" I asked.

We were in the car on our way to Roosevelt Island.

"I'm talking about Princeton Wells," she said. "Why in God's name would he buy a three-bedroom suite at The Pierre hotel when he owns a six-story town house on Central Park West less than a mile away? It's crazy."

"Why does Bruce Wayne dress up in a cape and a cowl and fight crime in Gotham City when he could just as easily sit back and have Alfred, the butler, wait on him hand and foot inside the stately Wayne Manor? Kylie, the rich have their own special brand of craziness."

"You'd think I'd have figured that out after working Red for almost a year, but when we called Wells, and he said he was on the thirty-ninth floor of the hotel, I automatically assumed he rented a room for the night."

"Guys like Wells don't rent rooms for the night," I said.

She grinned. "Just women. Poor thing had to wash her hair three times."

"I take it you don't approve of his choice."

"Just the opposite. She's perfect for the man who wants to devote his energy to being of service to the less fortunate."

I could tell by the glint in her eyes that she was just warming up, and she was ready to slice and dice Kenda Whithouse like a late-night comedian skewering the Kardashians. But her cell phone rang.

She checked the caller ID, smiled, and picked up. "Hey, babe, I didn't think you were going to call."

Babe? Personal call, I decided, my keen detective senses kicking in. I checked my watch and the look on Kylie's face: 11:47 p.m. Delighted. Very personal.

I couldn't hear the voice on the other end, but it went on for a solid minute. Finally, Kylie responded with, "Hey, you win some, you lose some."

A pause, and then she said, "I wish I could, but my partner and I just caught our second homicide of the night." A laugh, followed by, "Don't blame me. You're the one who thought it would be fun to date a cop. I'll talk to you tomorrow."

She hung up. "Damn it, Zach, these dead millionaires are killing my social life. I just had to turn down an invitation for drinks at Gansevoort PM."

She was baiting me, waiting for me to ask who she turned down.

24

Keep waiting. I'm not asking.

"I was there last week," she said. "The music is totally badass, but the bottle service prices in the Platinum Room are off the charts."

I refused to bite. I kept my eyes on the road and my mouth shut.

"Have you ever been to the Ganz?" she asked.

"Not yet," I said, "but if a dead body shows up, I'm there in a heartbeat."

That shut her up.

Normally, cops are happy to share the intimate details of their lives with their partners, but my relationship with Kylie was far from normal. We met a dozen years ago at the academy. She had just dumped her drug-addict boyfriend, and I turned out to be just what she needed to fill the void.

For twenty-eight days we couldn't keep our hands off each other. Somewhere along the way I fell in love with her. But on Day 29, the ex-boyfriend, Spence Harrington, came back, fresh out of rehab, begging her for one last chance. She gave it to him, and a year later they were married.

For the next ten years they were the perfect boldface couple. Kylie was a smart, beautiful, decorated NYPD detective, and Spence became one of New York's most prolific and successful TV writer-producers.

And then one day the drugs pulled him back in, and he began to spiral out of control. To her credit, Kylie did everything she could to save him from self-destructing, only to learn the hard way that you can't save an addict from himself.

Two months ago, Spence walked out on her, and when it was

clear he wasn't coming back, Kylie slowly dipped her toe back into the dating pool.

There was a line of boys in blue hoping to get on her dance card, but she turned them all down.

"I'm not hooking up with any cops," she told me. "One was enough."

I didn't ask if that meant I had set the bar impossibly high or I'd ruined it for every other cop in the department.

For weeks she'd been dropping little hints about the new man in her life, egging me on to probe for details. But I was damned if I was going to ask.

All I knew for sure was that whoever this guy was, he could afford bottle service in the Platinum Room at the fucking Ganz.

I have no idea why he'd want to be surrounded by loud people and even louder music, and then spend thousands of dollars on a bottle of booze he could buy for fifty bucks at a liquor store.

But like Kylie said, "Never underestimate the insanity of people with money."

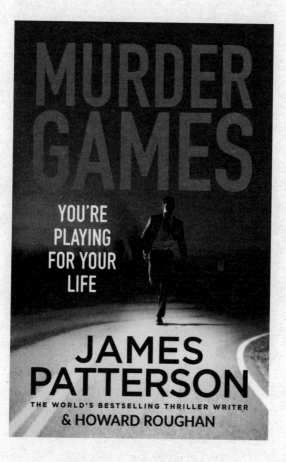

SO YOU want to be a serial killer…

Sure, you can go around just shooting people, bang-bang, but I've found that guns, while sometimes the right tool for the job, often leave me unsatisfied. There's a lack of intimacy involved when all you have to do is pull a trigger. You hear the blast and see the carnage, the way your victim's flesh ruptures and bursts open in an instant, but you don't really feel the same adrenaline as with other, let's say more personal, methods of murdering someone.

Me? I like to mix things up. There are so many wonderful and creative ways to kill people, and I really feel as if I owe it to myself and my cause to make sure that I branch out and keep it interesting. And even when circumstances do call for a gun, I try to add a twist to it, a little something extra. Sundaes always look better with a cherry on top.

Still, you'd be amazed at how much satisfaction can be derived from some of the most rudimentary approaches. Stabbing someone to death, for instance. I can't think of a more personal and intimate experience. The sound that a knife makes when piercing human skin is nothing short of intoxicating. You can't help yourself sometimes. You want to hear it over and over and over.

Of course, repeatedly stabbing someone to death isn't without a downside or two. For instance, it tends to be messy. That's why I like to wear clothes that I can simply throw away afterward. No muss, no fuss. If you want to be a real stickler for hiding evidence, though, burning the clothes would be even better.

But if you're on a budget or partial to a particular outfit— you know, a certain shirt or comfortable pair of pants that you enjoy killing in more than others—remember that you want to treat the bloodstains as soon as possible with a strong prewash stain remover and let it soak in for a good hour or so before throwing the clothes in the Maytag. Also, I highly recommend an extra rinse cycle.

Another downside, or at least a potential one, is that stabbing a person to death requires a tad more preparation. It takes a little longer than simply aiming a gun, and it also puts a premium on the element of surprise. Even then, the first couple of stabs don't always do the trick. Be prepared for some resistance, depending on the size and stubbornness of your victim.

Not all folks, however, will put up a fight. We assume that people have a tremendous will to live, but it's amazing how quickly some of them will resign themselves to their fate, especially when it comes to dying in a massive pool of their own blood.

That about covers it for my first entry. If you have any questions, I'm afraid you're on your own. It's not like I have an 800 number or an e-mail address I can give out. For obvious reasons, too, I can't tell you my real name. But lately people have taken to calling me the Dealer, which I happen to like, so I've taken to it as well. There's a nice ring to it. *The Dealer*. Clean. Authoritative. Quite proprietary, too, given my methods. I'd trademark it if I could.

I mean, the best serial killers, the ones whom people tend to remember, always manage to have a good moniker, the kind of nickname that seems to suit them perfectly. Otherwise, what's the point? The shrinks will tell you that guys like me are first and foremost narcissists, but if that means taking pride in your craft and planning each and every murder with meticulous care, then I suppose there are worse things to be called.

Honestly, I'm just giving you all what you want. A little razzle-dazzle, an escape from your dreary lives. What else are you going to talk about while sipping your four-dollar coffees and acting superior to the rest of the world?

You want me. You *need* me. And in time, you'll all discover that I'm doing you nothing less than a huge favor. Trust me.

Now, if you don't mind, there's someone else I really need to kill.

THE LECTURE hall hushed to a pin-drop silence the moment I walked in, every conversation stopping on a dime, every pair of eyes homing in on me, watching my every move.

For the record, any professor who tells you that he doesn't get off on this bit of catnip for the ego, if only a little, is completely full of crap. We all love it.

Milking the silence a few seconds longer, I took my time unloading my shoulder bag on the table next to the lectern before slowly turning to the class with the same opening speech I've been delivering now for years. The only thing that ever changes is that the faces staring back at me always seem to look just a little bit younger every time I give the speech.

There's nothing like a college campus to make a thirty-four-year-old guy feel over the hill.

And we're off…

"Good morning, my assembled prodigies, all you former class presidents and valedictorians, type A go-getters and relentless overachievers, and hopefully only a tiny smattering of you whose mommies and daddies knew the right people on the Yale admissions committee. Welcome to Abnormal Behavioral Analysis, commonly referred to as Intro to Psychopaths or, better yet, Your Ex-Boyfriend or Girlfriend 101. My name is Professor Dylan Reinhart; that's Dylan with a *y*, and, yes, my mother was a huge Bob Dylan fan. Are there any questions so far?"

Every year, someone takes the bait.

A blonde in the third row raised her hand with an easy confidence that bordered on flirtation. Clearly she hadn't done her homework on me.

"Yes? What's your name?" I asked.

"Heather," she answered. Heather with the come-hither smile.

"Thank you, Heather, but asking if there were any questions was a rhetorical question on my part. I haven't begun teaching you anything yet, so there shouldn't be anything you need to ask about," I said. "And with that we come to the first rule of this class. *Ask only what you don't understand*."

I can be such a hard-ass sometimes.

Although I assure you it's not without a larger purpose in mind for these students. The vast majority of them have been treated like geniuses since the third grade, and the sooner they figure out they're not, the better. As a former patent-office clerk with crazy hair once said, "A true genius admits that he knows nothing." That guy's name was Einstein.

Meanwhile, poor Heather in the third row looked as if she'd just eaten a bad oyster. Don't worry, I'll make it up to her at some point.

I continued. "The textbook for this class is entitled *Permission Theory: Redefining Abnormal Behavior*, and for those of you not familiar with the author, handsome devil that he is, let it be known that he's a bit of a narcissist who enjoys listening to the sound of his own voice almost as much as he does forcing others to listen to it."

Most of the room laughed. Those who didn't had their heads buried in their syllabi to see that, yes, I, Dylan Reinhart, was indeed the author of said textbook.

"This of course brings us to rule number two," I said. "*You will attend every class*. Your only excuse for missing a class will be your own death or someone else's, provided this someone else either breast-fed you, coached your Little League team, or routinely put a five-dollar bill in your childhood birthday card and signed it *Love, Grandma and Grandpa*."

A student in the first row, obviously a freshman, was typing feverishly on his laptop. I remained silent until he finally looked up at me.

"What are you doing?" I asked.

He swallowed hard and glanced at his keyboard, confused. "I was . . . um . . . taking notes," he said meekly.

"*Rule number three,*" I announced with a little added volume. "You will not take notes in this class. I repeat, you will *not* take notes. What you will do is listen. The premise of this course is to challenge the long-standing conventional thinking about abnormal behavior, and as far as I'm concerned there's nothing more abnormal than my lecturing to a roomful of stenographers." I paused, smiling. "Are there any questions?"

This time, no one raised a hand. Geniuses or not, they were all still students at Yale. They didn't get there by learning *slowly*.

"Good," I said. "Now let's get started."

But before I could, a noise in the back of the room had every head turning. It was only the door opening, nothing more.

Still, there was something different about it.

Sometimes you just know the sound of trouble even before she walks into the room.

8

"SHIT!" SHE announced from the top of the aisle as she realized everyone was staring at her. Immediately she slapped her forehead. "Shit, I just said that out loud, didn't I?"

"Yes, you did," I said. "Lucky for you, I don't give two shits about someone cursing in my class." I stepped out in front of the lectern. "Welcome."

Writers can spot their own books a mile away, and she had mine tucked under her arm. "You're Professor Reinhart, right?" she asked.

"Yes," I answered. "And you are?"

"Clearly interrupting," she said.

She was either a student or someone who happened to look young for her age. I couldn't tell.

For sure, though, she was attractive. The proof wasn't so much the way the male students were staring at her but rather the female students. If you don't understand that, then you probably have no clue why women buy expensive shoes. Hint: it has nothing to do with men.

"I'm sorry, I still didn't get your name," I said.

"It's Elizabeth," she answered. "Elizabeth Needham."

"Are you a student here, Ms. Needham?" I asked.

"*At Yale?*" She laughed deeply from her gut. "You're kidding me, right?"

"Apparently I am," I said.

She looked around the room. "I mean, no offense, of course."

"I'm sure I speak for everyone here when I say none taken. But if you're not a student..."

"Then who am I? Yes, that's a good question," she said.

"Will there be a good answer?"

"How about I just sit in on the class and we'll talk afterward?"

She half tiptoed over to an empty chair in the back row. For good measure, she gave me a nod as if to say, "Carry on."

Whoever she was, she had balls.

As if the entire class were sitting midcourt at Wimbledon, they all turned their heads back to me—*whoosh!*—to see what would happen next. The ball was clearly in my court.

"Sixty-eight thousand, two hundred and thirty dollars," I called out.

Whoosh! went everyone's head back to her.

"Excuse me?" she said.

"That's the cost of a year at Yale, Ms. Needham, of which approximately forty-nine thousand dollars is for tuition," I said.

"Are you asking me to leave?"

"No, I'm asking if you have your checkbook."

Whoosh! Whoosh! Whoosh!

With that, she stood with a huff and began walking toward the door. I couldn't help feeling a twinge of guilt. My damn conscience. It's my Achilles' heel.

"I hope I didn't offend you, Ms. Needham," I said.

She stopped, raising a palm. "That's quite all right. For the record, though, it's *Detective* Needham. The reason I'm here is because I'm pretty sure someone wants to kill you."

Then *whoosh!*

She was gone.

"GO AFTER her!" a few students shouted.

I was tempted, but I figured if someone really did want me dead there was no better place to be than in a roomful of potential witnesses.

I stayed put and delivered my lecture as planned. Okay, so maybe it wasn't the best lecture I'd ever given, and maybe I rushed through it just a wee bit. A guy can compartmentalize only so much.

I obviously needed to talk to this woman, and I knew it would take only one call after class to know whether she was still on campus.

"No," said the guy who answered the phone at the New Haven police department. "We don't have a Detective Elizabeth Needham."

I didn't think so. There was something "big city" about her. Or at least a bigger city than New Haven. That meant she traveled a distance to see me. No way she would leave without our talking.

Sure enough, within seconds I felt the vibration of a text message. *She's a detective, she flashes her badge, and the dean or some other keeper of all things confidential coughs up my cell number.*

Meet me @ Jojo's.

No address and none needed. A coffee shop that everyone on campus knows. It was close by, too.

A few minutes later, I was walking toward her at a table in the back. She had my book and some colored folders laid out meticulously, everything perfectly aligned. She was peering at me with her dark brown eyes over an oversize mug.

"Fancy meeting you here," I said, taking a seat.

Of course, the charm of Jojo's, on Chapel Street, is that there's nothing fancy about it. Wooden tables and chairs on a scuffed-up wood floor were scattered about, and some grandma-style curtains were hanging in the windows. Very college.

"How was the rest of class?" she asked. Her flashing of a wry smile would've been redundant:

"A third of the students wanted me to chase after you while another third actually thought you were a plant—you know, someone I hired. The course is about abnormal behavior, after all."

"And the remaining third?" she asked.

"Too busy wondering what grade they'll get if someone does indeed kill me before the term is over," I said.

I waited for her to tell me that she'd been a tad melodramatic; that no one really wanted to kill me. Instead she opened the folder directly in front her. It was green.

"Let's back up a bit," she said.

She reintroduced herself. Elizabeth Needham, NYPD detective second grade. I could call her Elizabeth, though.

Then she basically introduced me to myself.

I sat there listening as she quickly reduced my life to a series of bullet points, reading in a near monotone off a hand-scribbled piece of paper in the folder. At least it wasn't a cocktail napkin.

"Dr. Dylan Reinhart... Yale undergrad... PhD in psychology, also Yale... three-year research fellowship, University of Cambridge... then another PhD, this time from MIT, in statistics with a focus on Bayesian inference." She paused and looked up. "Am I supposed to know what that is? Bayesian inference?"

Maybe if you're dating Nate Silver...

"Bayesian inference is why most women shouldn't have routine mammograms until they're fifty," I said.

"And why's that?"

I nodded at the folder. "You're the one who apparently likes to do her research, Elizabeth."

"This bothers you, doesn't it?" she asked. "My looking into your background?"

"No. What bothers me is that you still haven't explained who wants to kill me. Anytime you're ready."

She closed the folder, resting her hands on top of it. No wedding ring. No jewelry of any kind. "Do you know who Allen Grimes is?"

"Grimes on Crimes?" The guy wrote a daily column for the *New York Gazette*. I'd heard about it—catchy name and all—but never read it.

Elizabeth nodded. "That's him," she said. "Two days ago, Grimes received an anonymous package in the mail. Inside it was your book."

"Is that a crime?" I asked.

I was half joking. Not Elizabeth, though.

"As it turns out, it was a crime," she said.

ELIZABETH REACHED to her left, pulling another folder in front of her. This one was red. *Red's never good.*

"Your book came with a bookmark," she said.

She opened the folder and removed a small evidence bag. It was sealed, labeled, and just big enough for a ham sandwich. That made it the ideal size for what it was actually holding.

I leaned in, staring at it. "A playing card?"

It wasn't a question; that was clearly what it was. A playing card. The king of clubs.

"Does this mean anything to you?" she asked.

"That's silly. Why would it?"

"Yeah, you're right," said Elizabeth, rolling her eyes. "Clearly the reason I drove all the way out here from Manhattan is so I could ask you silly and irrelevant questions."

"You get the word *feisty* a lot, don't you?" I asked.

"I prefer *spirited*," she said. "What do you prefer instead of *smug*?"

"Actually, I'm okay with *smug*."

To her credit, she kept the straight face a good five seconds before she smiled. *Peace begins with a smile,* said Mother Teresa.

"No, the card doesn't register anything with me," I said. "Of course, it is pretty common for people to use playing cards as bookmarks."

"Agreed," she said. "Here's something not so common, though. In fact, it's pretty damn rare."

Elizabeth turned the bag around so I could see the back of the card. There was a dark red blotch on what was a harlequin-patterned blue-and-white background. It was blood.

"I assume you've already had it tested," I said.

"It's type AB negative," she said. "Only around 1 percent of the population has it."

"Yeah, I'd say that's rare, all right. I'd also say it was on purpose."

"You and me both," she said with a nod. "Blood type as bread crumbs."

"So where did it lead you?" I asked.

ELIZABETH REACHED for her red folder again and took out an eight-by-ten photo, black and white. As crime scenes go, this one was particularly grisly. Even the most devout Wes Craven fan would've flinched.

"The victim's name is Jared Louden, ran a large hedge fund," she said. "He was stabbed to death—to put it mildly—six days ago in the entryway of his Upper East Side town house. No witnesses, no leads. Nothing."

I stared at the image of Louden in a pool of his own blood, his dapper-looking suit shredded from seemingly endless entry wounds. Absolutely brutal. "How many days ago did you say?"

"Six," she answered, "and since then there hasn't been another murder victim with AB negative blood in a two-hundred-mile radius."

"What about before this guy?" I asked. "Any other unsolved cases?"

"There's one from more than eight months ago. A prostitute shot to death in Queens." Elizabeth nodded at the back of the playing card. "This blood's not eight months old. The lab put it at no more than a week."

"You said the card, along with my book, was mailed, right? It wasn't delivered by messenger?"

"Yes, definitely mailed. Routed through Farley."

She assumed I knew that was the main post office in Manhattan, the James A. Farley building, a.k.a. the one with the famous inscription. *Neither snow nor rain nor heat nor gloom of night stays these couriers from the swift completion of their appointed rounds.*

"The address wasn't handwritten, was it?" I asked, speaking of inscriptions. I figured there was no chance.

"Actually, it was," she said. "But it was Toys'R'Us."

That reference I didn't know. "Toys'R'Us? As in the toy store?"

"As in writing with your nondominant hand so it's childlike," she explained. "That's what we call it, at least. Nearly impossible to trace."

"And the card itself: what was it again?"

Elizabeth spun the evidence bag around again to show me.

"The king of clubs," she said. "My first thought was a God complex. The killer thinks of himself as a king."

"Does that make me his subject?"

"He obviously identifies with you or your book in some way. But whether he loathes you or reveres you, the chances are pretty good that he wants to kill you."

"I'm sure it's a possibility, but that's a pretty big leap," I said.

"A big leap, huh?"

"Sure. Fixation disorders play out in many ways."

"You're right," she said. "Then again . . ." Her voice trailed off.

"What do you mean?" I asked. *What haven't you shown me?*

Elizabeth picked up the book, turning it around so I could see my author photo.

Damn.

"How's that leap looking now?" she said.

WITH SEVENTY-FIVE miles between New Haven and the Upper West Side of Manhattan I could either suffer through the round-trip journey every week or make the best of it. I chose the latter, with more than a little help from a restored 1961 Triumph TR6 Trophy motorcycle, the same model that Steve McQueen rode like a boss in *The Great Escape*. A few hard twists of the wrist, a rev of the engine, and the world and its worries are always left behind.

Not today, though.

Keeping pace—or, more aptly, tailgating like a son of a bitch—was that picture of me on the back of my book. What was left of me, at least. My eyes had been cut out, and the rest of my face had been slashed to threads with a precision blade. Unfortunately the artist didn't sign his work, but he did manage to clip and paste a short sentence across my forehead, ransom note–style. Two words. *Dead* and *Wrong*. For good measure, *Dead* was underlined in red ink.

Yeah, just in case everything else was too subtle, pal…

Between the countless case studies I've read and the handful of actual murder cases I've been involved with as a forensic witness, I've had both a front-row seat and a backstage pass to the ultimate freak show, the things killers do to announce their horrific intentions. Really sick and depraved stuff.

This guy going to town on my photo, on the other hand, was pretty tame by comparison. Still, for the first time, I wasn't looking at some stranger, a person I didn't know and had never met. I was looking at me.

On this day of all days, too.

"You're late!" Tracy called out from the kitchen before I'd set two feet in our apartment. "Hurry up and shower."

Normally, I would've cracked a joke along the lines of, "My day was good, thanks for asking," but that little touch of sarcasm would've only brought Tracy out of the kitchen to actually ask how my day was, and it just didn't feel like the right moment to announce that there might be some crazed lunatic out there who wants to kill me.

So instead I hurried up and showered.

"What are you going to wear?" asked Tracy, appearing in the doorway of the bathroom minutes later as I was toweling myself dry.

"Let me guess," I said, although I was hardly guessing. "Whatever you just laid out for me on the bed?"

"That depends. Were you about to throw on some old jeans and a T-shirt?"

Guilty as charged. "Yep."

"Then, yeah," said Tracy with a laugh. "What I just laid out for you on the bed."

"You do realize the whole purpose of this visit is so they can see that we'd be normal parents," I said. "How much more normal does it get than jeans and a T-shirt?"

"Do you think the gentleman interviewing us will also be wearing jeans and a T-shirt?" asked Tracy.

Rats, outsmarted again. No wonder we're together...

"Hey, how do you know it's a guy who's coming?" I asked.

"Don't you remember? We briefly met him," said Tracy. "Barbara introduced us."

Barbara was the head of the adoption agency. "Trust the process," she told us during our initial screening meeting. "It will feel like hell sometimes, but it will all be worth it."

Amen. There's nothing on this planet that Tracy and I want more than a child of our own to love. It's just so dangerous to get our hopes up too much, though.

"Oh, yeah, I remember that guy," I said. "He looked like Mr. French."

"That's another thing," said Tracy. "No obscure references during the interview."

"What do you mean? *Family Affair* isn't obscure. Uncle Bill, Buffy, Jody... Mr. French? It's a television classic."

Tracy gave me "the Look." I never fared well against the Look.

"Okay," I said. "No jeans, no T-shirt, and no classic television show references. Anything else?"

Tracy came over with a kiss and a smile. "Don't get me started."

Shortly thereafter, the doorbell rang. I tucked in my button-down and straightened out the pleats on my very respectable-looking khakis before joining Tracy at the door.

Trust the process. Let the home interview begin.

Too bad it was over before it even started.

"OH," SAID the woman. It was one measly little word.

But, oh, the way she said it...

She was standing in the hallway and staring at us, wondering if she had the right apartment. She quickly checked the clipboard in her hand. Once, then twice.

"Dylan and Tracy?" she finally asked.

"Yes, that's right," I said as cheerfully as I could.

Again she checked her clipboard. "Yes, well, then...I'm Ms. Peckler from the Gateway Adoption Agency. Mr. Harrison had a family emergency this afternoon, so I was asked to step in," she said. "You were expecting him, correct?"

"Yes, that's right," said Tracy, albeit far less cheerfully.

Shit. The fuse was lit.

Ninety-nine percent of the time, Tracy was the calm and patient one while I was the loose cannon, the sufferer of no fools. But look out for that damn 1 percent of the time.

For instance when a priggish woman with a clipboard says "Oh" with just the wrong kind of inflection.

To most people it would have all the resonance of a dog whistle, but for those of us who have been on the receiving end of it more times than we'd ever care to remember, it might as well have been screamed through a bullhorn.

Still.

"Please don't," I whispered out of the side of my mouth.

Tracy turned to me. "Don't what?"

"It's the name thing," I said. "She didn't—"

"It's not my name she has a problem with," said Tracy.

"What's going on?" asked Ms. Peckler.

Bad question, lady.

"What's going on is that it doesn't matter how many times you look down at that clipboard of yours, because every time you look up I'm still going to be a dude," said Tracy.

Boom, there it was.

"Excuse me?" said Ms. Peckler.

"I think you heard me," said Tracy.

"I don't think I like what you're insinuating," said Ms. Peckler, placing her nonclipboard hand firmly against her hip.

"Then I'll ask you very clearly," said Tracy, his law school degree kicking in, as it often did when he wanted to cut to the chase. "Do you personally have a problem with two gay men wanting to adopt a baby?"

I so wanted Tracy to be wrong on this one. I wanted Ms. Peckler, all prim and proper with pearls, to set the record straight—that she didn't have time to read our case file and had assumed that Tracy would be a woman, understandably so, and that her "Oh" was nothing more than the surprise of realizing she was mistaken.

This was the Upper West Side of Manhattan, after all, the supposed tolerance capital of the world.

But it was wishful thinking, and I knew it. I heard what Tracy heard. After a few seconds of silence—which also spoke volumes—Ms. Peckler essentially confirmed it.

"What I personally think of the lifestyle choice you two have made is separate from the job I have to do," she said. "I'm a professional, and I'm insulted that you would accuse me of being otherwise."

Lifestyle choice?

Tracy turned to me again. "I don't really know where to begin with that," he said.

Nor did I. But I gave it my best shot. "You know, this reminds me of an episode of *Family Affair*..."

By then Ms. Peckler was already halfway down our hallway, heading to the elevator.

I closed the door. The sound of the latch catching—*snap!*—jolted Tracy out of the moment.

"Oh, Christ, what have I done?" he asked.

We'd been married for four years. We were a couple for three years before that and had first met almost fifteen years ago, in college. By now we could do more than finish each other's sentences; we could start them. We always seemed to know what the other was thinking, and this was no different.

But what got me was the expression on Tracy's face. It was unlike anything I'd ever seen with him. Never, not ever, had he looked so panicked, so consumed by instant regret.

Still, I could've been mad. Furious, even. *The process.* We'd already devoted so much time and energy to it. Stacks of paperwork. Endless phone calls to government offices. On the surface it seemed crazy that Tracy couldn't overlook the ignorance of one person. It was all a dog and pony show anyway, this in-home interview.

Yet I wasn't mad. Far from it. If anything, I was more convinced than ever that Tracy and I were ready to be parents. Good parents.

"What you've done is the same thing we would've taught our child," I said. "Always stand up for yourself."

Also by James Patterson

ALEX CROSS NOVELS

Along Came a Spider • Kiss the Girls • Jack and Jill • Cat and Mouse • Pop Goes the Weasel • Roses are Red • Violets are Blue • Four Blind Mice • The Big Bad Wolf • London Bridges • Mary, Mary • Cross • Double Cross • Cross Country • Alex Cross's Trial (*with Richard DiLallo*) • I, Alex Cross • Cross Fire • Kill Alex Cross • Merry Christmas, Alex Cross • Alex Cross, Run • Cross My Heart • Hope to Die • Cross Justice • Cross the Line • The People vs. Alex Cross

THE WOMEN'S MURDER CLUB SERIES

1st to Die • 2nd Chance (*with Andrew Gross*) • 3rd Degree (*with Andrew Gross*) • 4th of July (*with Maxine Paetro*) • The 5th Horseman (*with Maxine Paetro*) • The 6th Target (*with Maxine Paetro*) • 7th Heaven (*with Maxine Paetro*) • 8th Confession (*with Maxine Paetro*) • 9th Judgement (*with Maxine Paetro*) • 10th Anniversary (*with Maxine Paetro*) • 11th Hour (*with Maxine Paetro*) • 12th of Never (*with Maxine Paetro*) • Unlucky 13 (*with Maxine Paetro*) • 14th Deadly Sin (*with Maxine Paetro*) • 15th Affair (*with Maxine Paetro*) • 16th Seduction (*with Maxine Paetro*) • 17th Suspect (*with Maxine Paetro*)

PRIVATE NOVELS

Private (*with Maxine Paetro*) • Private London (*with Mark Pearson*) • Private Games (*with Mark Sullivan*) • Private: No. 1 Suspect (*with Maxine Paetro*) • Private Berlin (*with Mark Sullivan*) • Private Down Under (*with Michael White*) • Private L.A. (*with Mark Sullivan*) • Private India (*with Ashwin Sanghi*) • Private Vegas (*with Maxine Paetro*) • Private Sydney (*with Kathryn Fox*) • Private Paris (*with Mark Sullivan*) • The Games (*with Mark Sullivan*) • Private Delhi (*with Ashwin Sanghi*) • Private Princess (*with Rees Jones*)

NYPD RED SERIES

NYPD Red (*with Marshall Karp*) • NYPD Red 2
(*with Marshall Karp*) • NYPD Red 3 (*with Marshall Karp*) •
NYPD Red 4 (*with Marshall Karp*) •
NYPD Red 5 (*with Marshall Karp*)

DETECTIVE HARRIET BLUE SERIES

Never Never (*with Candice Fox*) • Fifty Fifty (*with Candice Fox*)

STAND-ALONE THRILLERS

The Thomas Berryman Number • Sail (*with Howard Roughan*)
• Swimsuit (*with Maxine Paetro*) • Don't Blink (*with Howard
Roughan*) • Postcard Killers (*with Liza Marklund*) • Toys (*with
Neil McMahon*) • Now You See Her (*with Michael Ledwidge*) • Kill
Me If You Can (*with Marshall Karp*) • Guilty Wives (*with David
Ellis*) • Zoo (*with Michael Ledwidge*) • Second Honeymoon (*with
Howard Roughan*) • Mistress (*with David Ellis*) • Invisible (*with
David Ellis*) • Truth or Die (*with Howard Roughan*) • Murder
House (*with David Ellis*) • Woman of God (*with Maxine Paetro*) •
Hide and Seek • Humans, Bow Down (*with Emily Raymond*) •
The Black Book (*with David Ellis*) • Murder Games
(*with Howard Roughan*) • Black Market • The Midnight Club •
The Store (*with Richard DiLallo*) • Texas Ranger (*with Andrew Bourelle*)

NON-FICTION

Torn Apart (*with Hal and Cory Friedman*) • The Murder
of King Tut (*with Martin Dugard*) • All-American Murder
(*with Alex Abramovich and Mike Harvkey*)

MURDER IS FOREVER TRUE CRIME

Murder, Interrupted (*with Alex Abramovich and Christopher Charles*) •
Home Sweet Murder (*with Andrew Bourelle and Scott Slaven*) •
Murder Beyond the Grave (*with Andrew Bourelle and Christopher Charles*)

ROMANCE

Sundays at Tiffany's (*with Gabrielle Charbonnet*) •
The Christmas Wedding (*with Richard DiLallo*) •
First Love (*with Emily Raymond*) •
Two from the Heart (*with Frank Costantini,
Emily Raymond and Brian Sitts*)

OTHER TITLES

Miracle at Augusta (*with Peter de Jonge*) •
Penguins of America (*with Jack Patterson*)

FAMILY OF PAGE-TURNERS

MIDDLE SCHOOL BOOKS

The Worst Years of My Life (*with Chris Tebbetts*) • Get Me
Out of Here! (*with Chris Tebbetts*) • My Brother Is a Big, Fat
Liar (*with Lisa Papademetriou*) • How I Survived Bullies,
Broccoli, and Snake Hill (*with Chris Tebbetts*) • Ultimate
Showdown (*with Julia Bergen*) • Save Rafe! (*with Chris
Tebbetts*) • Just My Rotten Luck (*with Chris Tebbetts*) •
Dog's Best Friend (*with Chris Tebbetts*) •
Escape to Australia (*with Martin Chatterton*) •
From Hero to Zero (*with Chris Tebbetts*)

I FUNNY SERIES

I Funny (*with Chris Grabenstein*) • I Even Funnier (*with Chris
Grabenstein*) • I Totally Funniest (*with Chris Grabenstein*) •
I Funny TV (*with Chris Grabenstein*) • School of
Laughs (*with Chris Grabenstein*) • The Nerdiest, Wimpiest,
Dorkiest I Funny Ever (*with Chris Grabenstein*)

TREASURE HUNTERS SERIES

Treasure Hunters (*with Chris Grabenstein*) • Danger Down the Nile (*with Chris Grabenstein*) • Secret of the Forbidden City (*with Chris Grabenstein*) • Peril at the Top of the World (*with Chris Grabenstein*) • Quest for the City of Gold (*with Chris Grabenstein*)

HOUSE OF ROBOTS SERIES

House of Robots (*with Chris Grabenstein*) • Robots Go Wild! (*with Chris Grabenstein*) • Robot Revolution (*with Chris Grabenstein*)

JACKY HA-HA SERIES

Jacky Ha-Ha (*with Chris Grabenstein*) • My Life is a Joke (*with Chris Grabenstein*)

OTHER ILLUSTRATED NOVELS

Kenny Wright: Superhero (*with Chris Tebbetts*) • Homeroom Diaries (*with Lisa Papademetriou*) • Word of Mouse (*with Chris Grabenstein*) • Pottymouth and Stoopid (*with Chris Grabenstein*) • Laugh Out Loud (*with Chris Grabenstein*)

MAXIMUM RIDE SERIES

The Angel Experiment • School's Out Forever • Saving the World and Other Extreme Sports • The Final Warning • Max • Fang • Angel • Nevermore • Forever

CONFESSIONS SERIES

Confessions of a Murder Suspect (*with Maxine Paetro*) • The Private School Murders (*with Maxine Paetro*) • The Paris Mysteries (*with Maxine Paetro*) • The Murder of an Angel (*with Maxine Paetro*)

WITCH & WIZARD SERIES

Witch & Wizard (*with Gabrielle Charbonnet*) • The Gift (*with Ned Rust*) • The Fire (*with Jill Dembowski*) • The Kiss (*with Jill Dembowski*) • The Lost (*with Emily Raymond*)

DANIEL X SERIES

The Dangerous Days of Daniel X (*with Michael Ledwidge*) • Watch the Skies (*with Ned Rust*) • Demons and Druids (*with Adam Sadler*) • Game Over (*with Ned Rust*) • Armageddon (*with Chris Grabenstein*) • Lights Out (*with Chris Grabenstein*)

OTHER TITLES

Cradle and All • Crazy House (*with Gabrielle Charbonnet*) • Expelled (*with Emily Raymond*)

GRAPHIC NOVELS

Daniel X: Alien Hunter (*with Leopoldo Gout*) • Maximum Ride: Manga Vols. 1–9 (*with NaRae Lee*)

PICTURE BOOKS

Give Please a Chance (*with Bill O'Reilly*) • Big Words for Little Geniuses (*with Susan Patterson*) • Give Thank You a Try • The Candies Save Christmas

For more information about James Patterson's novels, visit www.jamespatterson.co.uk